D0340733

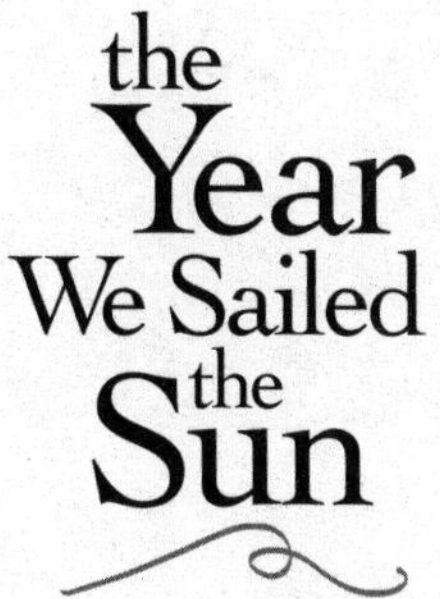
the
Year
We Sailed
the
Sun

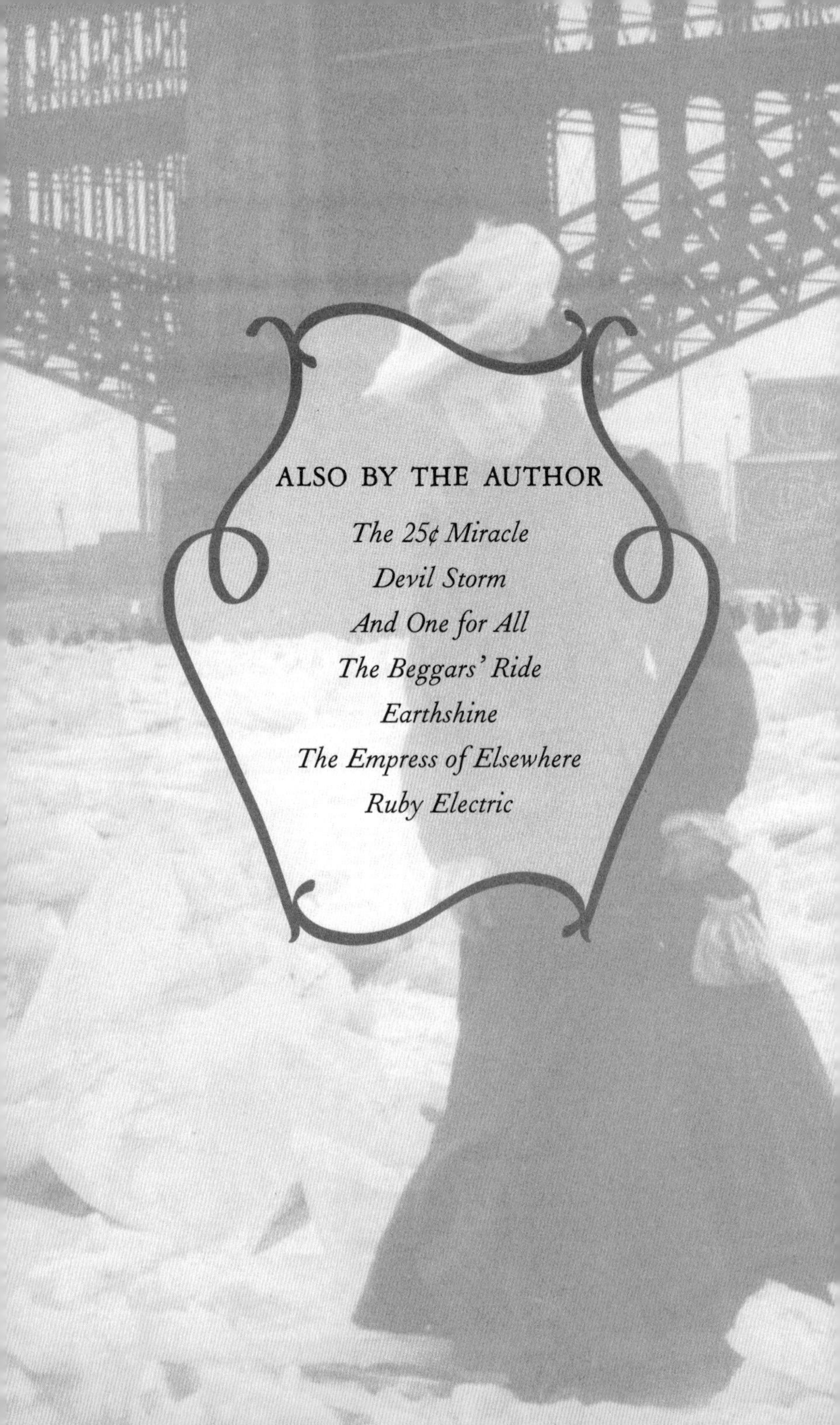

ALSO BY THE AUTHOR

The 25¢ Miracle

Devil Storm

And One for All

The Beggars' Ride

Earthshine

The Empress of Elsewhere

Ruby Electric

the Year We Sailed the Sun

by Theresa Nelson

A Richard Jackson Book

Atheneum Books for Young Readers
New York London Toronto Sydney New Delhi

ATHENEUM BOOKS FOR YOUNG READERS
An imprint of Simon & Schuster Children's Publishing Division
1230 Avenue of the Americas, New York, New York 10020

This book is a work of fiction. Any references to historical events, real people, or real places are used fictitiously. Other names, characters, places, and events are products of the author's imagination, and any resemblance to actual events or places or persons, living or dead, is entirely coincidental.

The hymn "In the Bleak Midwinter" (pp. 270–272) is taken from the poem (of the same name) by Christina Rossetti.

Title page and Part I photos are used with permission of the Missouri History Museum, St. Louis.

Part II photo is a vintage postcard, courtesy of the Missouri State Archives.

Book design by Sonia Chaghatzbanian
The text for this book is set in Fournier MT Std.
Manufactured in the United States of America
0215 FFG
First Edition
2 4 6 8 10 9 7 5 3 1
Library of Congress Cataloging-in-Publication Data
Nelson, Theresa, 1948-
The year we sailed the sun / Theresa Nelson.
pages cm
Summary: In St. Louis, Missouri, in 1911, orphaned eleven-year-old Julia Delaney rails against countless disappointments and the nun's strict rules at the House of Mercy, especially after her sister Mary turns fourteen and must leave, but she, her family, and best friend get tangled up with a gangster and a decade-old mystery.
ISBN 978-0-689-85827-7 (hardcover) — ISBN 978-1-4814-0649-9 (eBook)
[1. Orphanages—Fiction. 2. Orphans—Fiction. 3. Nuns—Fiction. 4. Behavior—Fiction. 5. Brothers and sisters—Fiction. 6. Gangsters—Fiction. 7. St. Louis (Mo.)—History—20th century—Fiction.] I. Title.
PZ7.N4377Ye 2015
[Fic]—dc23 2014034956

For Julia Catherine Kraemer Cooney

and her children, in every generation—

for Bill and Sheila and David and Mary and Joe—

and especially for Julia's youngest son,

my husband, Kevin Michael,

who makes me laugh

and takes me traveling

The bravest are the tenderest,—
The loving are the daring.

—Bayard Taylor, "The Song of the Camp"

CONTENTS

IN JULIA'S WORLD

The Living

DELANEYS

Julia Catherine *herself, age 11**

Mary Patricia, *13–14*

William Joseph (Bill), *15–16*

BOCKLEBRINKS

Aunt Gert

Otto (her son)

DOYLES

Officer Timothy

Mickey (his son, 17)

AT THE HOUSE OF MERCY (INDUSTRIAL SCHOOL AND GIRLS' HOME)

Nuns

Sister Maclovius

Sister Gabriel

Sister Bridget (niece of Officer Doyle, cousin of Mickey Doyle, sister of Harry "Two-Bits" Brickey, and aunt to Betty Brickey)

Sister Sebastian

Sister Genevieve

Girls

Mary Elizabeth (Betty) Brickey, 9 (daughter of "Two-Bits" Brickey and Maggie Meehan, and niece of Sister Bridget)

*While all characters (as portrayed in this story) are fictional, those in boldface type have counterparts in actual history.

Girls *(continued)*

Marcella Duggan

Winifred O'Rourke

Hazel Theedy

Little Hannah Hogan
Agnes Crouse
Geraldine Mulroney
} *with Julia, the Beggars' Brigade*

Hyacinth (horse with a history)

Harriet (a doll, at least 10)

Little Bear "L.B." (a kitten)

Dr. McGill

Dr. Rolla Bracy *(St. Louis County Coroner)*

Henry Tyborowski (Henry the Hired Boy)

AT FATHER DUNNE'S NEWS BOYS HOME

Father Peter Dunne

Jimmy Brannigan

Little Joe Kinsella

ON THE STREETS OF ST. LOUIS, MISSOURI

Thomas Egan

(self-styled "businessman" and boss of the Rats)

Edward "Fat Eddie" Farrell

(Egan's hired thug and bodyguard)

Assorted Rats, Nixie Fighters,

firemen, policemen, strangers in storm

Doc Monaghan of the River Arcade and Pawn Shop

Mr. Patrizi (greengrocer)

Father Timothy Dempsey *(Pastor of Saint Patrick's)*

Jelly Donahoo (the milkman)

OF THE OPTIMA PETAMUS SOCIETY

Cora Downey

Daniel Hanratty-Maguire

Mrs. Horace Merriweather

The Dead

DELANEYS

Cyril (Papa, Pop)

Catherine "Kitty" (Mama)

Gran

Helen

Larry

DOYLES

Mickey's ma, Officer Doyle's wife

BRICKEYS

Harry "Two-Bits" (father of Betty, brother of Sister Bridget)

Ma and Pa Brickey (parents of Sister Bridget and all her brothers)

Dzadzio (Polish grandfather of Sister Bridget and Officer Doyle)

Irish granny (wife of Dzadzio)

Maggie Meehan (chorus girl, wife of "Two-Bits", mother of Betty)

DOWNEYS

Cora's Aunt Lizzie

Cora's mother and father

OTHERS

Cecilia Forney

Saint Hyacinth *(man, not horse),*
patron saint of those in danger of drowning

First . . .

Imagine a door.

Just that, to begin. You could draw it in four straight strokes on a Big Chief tablet.

Not much of a door, really. Just the frame, or what's left of it these days: an empty door frame with busted hinges, standing all alone in an endless sea of prairie grass.

There are some who'd call it gold, that grass, but that's not it exactly. It's too light for gold, not yellow enough for straw. Or for amber, either, never mind what the song says, though the waves are true enough.

My brother Bill would have claimed it was camel-colored. (He'd been to the Cairo Spectacular at the World's Fair. Twice.)

Whatever name you give it, it stretches on for miles, wave after camel-colored wave, stirring ever so softly as the wind breathes through it, and the clouds move over it, casting shadows like dark ships, sailing beneath them.

There's a storm coming. Can you smell it? Look there—you can see the rain falling already. Great purple thunderheads away off at the horizon, weeping across the land. Wyoming, maybe? Hard to say. Where you stand right now—three miles from Alzada, Carter County, Montana—you could spit in the air and have it come down in any of three states, if there's a fair enough breeze. No lines in the earth here to map it out neatly, not even a tree to mark your place or mar the view. Only the land, and the sky, no different than they were a hundred years ago. Only that gently rolling prairie sea, forever and ever . . .

You shiver, just a little. What was it we used to say? *Got a rat runnin' over your grave*.

The wind's blowing colder.

The old cowboys at the Homestead Restaurant & Lounge will be talking snow tonight, shaking their heads over bitter black coffee and coconut pie.

That's all it is, probably: a change in the weather. That's what chilled you just now.

Most likely.

Then again—

That door. The old door.

Take another look.

Do you see a little girl with blue eyes, looking back?

Just a trick of the light, you're thinking. There's no one there.

Is there?

Look again.

Look deeper.

Do you see me now?

Not as I am, but as I was, when we were all a hundred years younger.

My name is Julia.

I've waited such a long time.

I knew you'd come.

PART ONE

The Kerry Patch, St. Louis, Missouri
Fall–Winter, 1911

September

Chapter 1

I suppose I will go to hell for biting the nun.

Mary says it's a mortal sin, for certain.

Never mind. It was worth it. I would bite her again, if I got the chance.

Bill says Pop's down there frying already, so I won't be lonesome.

"JULIA CATHERINE DELANEY!"

It was Aunt Gert who started it, and that's the God's truth. I never planned on biting a soul at the time. I was out by the back stoop, shooting marbles and minding my own business, when the back door opened—*bang!*—and the hollering commenced.

"Oh, for shame, for shame, Julia! Get up out of that

dirt this instant! What do you think you're doing, you bad girl?"

And what did it look like? I knuckled down and closed one eye, taking aim at a fat purple immy. I was winning, that was what, shooting straight as an arrow just the way Bill had taught me, and beating the pants off Snotty Otto, Aunt Gert's scourge of a kid.

"Julia's cheatin' again, Mama!" he went to whining the second he saw her. "She stole my good nickel!" Which was a flat-out lie. And the whole world knew it, too, including his own mother. But you think she'd let on?

"Dirty little guttersnipe!" she hissed, just like a great nasty cobra. So I figured now was the time to run, but I couldn't leave my marbles with Otto, and while I was trying to get 'em gathered up safe in the bag, Aunt Gert came charging down the steps and yanked me by the hair. "Saint Chris on a crutch, will you look at you? Wallowing in the filth in your Sunday best, and your poor grandma not two hours in her grave!"

A lot you care, I wanted to tell her. I tried, but the words stuck in my throat. Aunt Gert didn't give a hang about Gran. She wasn't even our aunt, really, only dead Uncle Somebody's second wife, and the landlady on top of it, and a meddling old sourpuss, to boot.

"Don't you growl at me, you dirty girl! Come along, now; there's someone here to see you." She gave my hair another jerk and started dragging me inside, stopping long enough at the kitchen pump to grab a wet cabbage-smelling rag and rub my face till it burned. "And don't be giving me that evil eye, neither, Miss High-and-Mighty. You got something to say, then say it. You think it's my pleasure, playing nursemaid to the likes of you?"

I craned my neck toward the door that opened on the parlor, trying to catch a glimpse of the visitors. I could halfway hear murmuring, but I couldn't make it out. I'd had the fever when I was little, and now one ear didn't work so well.

Someone to see *me*?

There'd been a pack of freeloaders traipsing through the house for the past two days, crying by the coffin and eating the funeral pies, but so far none of them had looked my way twice. Which suited me fine.

"Who is it—*ow!*—that's here?" I asked.

"Your betters, that's who. Stop your scowling. And mind your manners, or I'll give you something to scowl about."

Old bat.

Bill would show her what's what, soon as he got

back. Bill wouldn't take that kind of guff off nobody.

And what was keeping him all this time, anyhow? He'd been standing right by me at the graveyard—him and Mary both; they let you out half a day from the shoe factory when your kinfolk got buried. But once the praying was over, I saw him going off somewhere with Mickey Doyle and that crowd. "Can't I go with you, Bill?" I ran quick and asked him, but he shook his head and said, "Go home, J." And then he gave me a wink. "You stick with Mary. I'll only be a minute."

Except it wasn't any minute. That was ages ago. They'd been ringing the Angelus bell at Saint Pat's, so it must have been noon. And now the ferry this side of the Eads Bridge was blowing its three o'clock whistle, and Egan's Saloon would have been open for hours and I didn't trust that Mickey and—

"Sorry to keep you waiting," Aunt Gert said to somebody, pulling me after her through the parlor door.

That's when I saw 'em.

Not Bill or Mickey or any of the others neither, but a pair of nuns—a big one with a face like George Washington on a dollar bill, and a little-bitty plump one, like a pigeon with spectacles—sitting up prim on Gran's purple settee, talking to Mary.

"Ah," said the first, when she saw me staring. "Here's

the younger girl now. What's her name again?"

"Julia," said Aunt Gert, sweet as syrup, hauling me closer. "Say hello to the Sisters," she hissed in my good ear, "and stand up straight, for the love of Mike."

I'd have been out of there that minute, except the old bat was pinching my arm so tight, I couldn't exactly move.

"Oh!" The pigeon's eyes lit up. Even her dimples had dimples. "Julia Delaney—like the fiddle tune?"

Aunt Gert sighed. "The father was some sort of a musician." She might just as well have said he was some sort of a toad fryer, for all the feeling she put into it.

"Oh my," said the pigeon. "Julia Delaney . . . isn't that lovely? I danced to it once in Dublin. And what a lovely little girl!"

Where? I wondered, looking over my shoulder. There wasn't any lovely girl behind me. Only that snake Otto, leering at me with his little snake eyes.

Aunt Gert made a sound halfway between a sniff and a snort. "You're too kind, Sister Gabriel. You'll be turning her head. Shake hands with the nice Sister, Julia." She gave my arm a twist. "Don't you know a compliment when you hear one? What do you say?"

But I kept my hands to myself, and I didn't say a word, because there was something fishy going on around here. I looked at Mary for some sort of a signal—she was nearly fourteen and understood these things—but Mary only looked back with her green eyes round as quarters and gave me the tiniest wag of her head, like a warning. And while Aunt Gert was pulling one way and I was pulling the other, and trying to think where I had seen this brand of nun before, George Washington spoke up:

"Never mind, Mrs.—"

"Bocklebrink."

"Mrs. Bocklebrink," the nun repeated. You could hardly say it without laughing, but not a nose hair quivered. "It's perfectly natural, under the circumstances." And then she fixed me with a smile that sent shivers down my spine. "Come here, dear," she said.

I wouldn't. I wasn't budging.

But Mary was still over there, nodding at me like it mattered, so I took one step.

"That's better. Now, then. I'm Sister Maclovius. You're not afraid of me, are you, Julia?"

Afraid? Ha! I stuck out my chin. I wasn't afraid of anybody.

I'd have said it out loud, too, if only my mouth had been working.

"Well, of course you're not. A big girl like you!

Eleven years old already—two weeks ago today, isn't that right?"

And how would this Sister Mac-Whatsit know a thing like that? I wondered. But then nuns were friends with God, who knew everything. A fine birthday it had been, too, with Gran hardly sick at all that evening and Mary's famous dumplings for supper and Bill getting home just in time for the cake and candles. I still had the marble he had given me out of his own bag—his moonstone, no less, with magic in it—not mixed in with my others, but hidden away for emergencies, tucked in the secret pocket of my scratchy woolen undershirt. It would bring me good luck and good looks, he had promised, and a husband with pots of money. Which was more than *this* pair could ever hope for, even if they had a hundred birthdays.

So why were they looking at me like I was the one to be pitied?

"It's a terrible thing to lose a loved one," said Sister Maclovius. "But your granny isn't really lost, now is she? Our Blessed Lord has taken her to heaven with himself and his Blessed Mother—and your own dear mother, too, and all your relatives and the holy angels—where you'll be seeing her by and by, if you're a good girl."

I frowned at my muddy boots. I wasn't any good girl. That was Mary; she was the good one. Just ask Aunt Gert. Mary slept with her rosary under her pillow and knew the Apostles' Creed by heart; they'd let her into heaven for sure. And there'd be Gran, sitting up there waiting by the teakettle, same as always, with her soft lap and tapping foot and crinkled-up twinkly eyes. "Where's Julia? Late again?" she'd ask. "Three guesses," Mary would answer. "Ah, well." Gran would sigh. "God knows she was warned."

I hadn't so much as sniffled this whole day, but now my throat ached all of a sudden. I'd never be good enough, would I? I'd swapped *my* rosary for a ten-cent ticket to the House of Wax.

"You believe that, don't you, Julia Delaney?" the littler Sister asked gently.

"Well, of course she does," said the big one, waving away the silly question. "And in the meantime, he hasn't forgotten you and Mary. Not for a minute. He's sent us here to be your friends. We have his own word for it: 'I will not leave ye orphans.'"

My stomach gave a terrible lurch, like I'd come down hard on the wrong side of a see-saw. Ah, sure, what a thickhead I was! They were orphan nuns, weren't they? From that scurvy neighborhood west of here—the Bad Lands, Bill always called it—*that* was where I'd seen 'em, marching their charges to church on Sunday mornings. Drab-looking girls in brown-and-white uniforms, each one homelier than the last, trudging down Morgan Street with their eyes straight in front of 'em, past the pool halls and the whiskey bars and the ramshackle floozy houses, tramping along in lockstep, two by two.

O bless the orphans of the storm;
Sweet angels send to guide them. . . .

Saint Chris on a crutch. We'd stepped in it now.

"Run!" I hollered to Mary, wrenching free from Aunt Gert with one last desperate wriggle. "They're tryin' to take us to their damn orphanage! Come on, Mary! *Run!*"

But Mary never budged an inch, just stood there gaping like a ninny, while Aunt Gert got all red in the face and came lunging and sputtering after me. "Come back here, you ungrateful . . . Catch her!" she gasped, looking wild-eyed at the startled Sisters. But they were as old and fat as she was, and slower than molasses, and Bill always said I was fast as a fox. I dodged left around the purple couch and right under the table between the wooden lion's paws and was out the other side in half a heartbeat, while the others were still creaking to their feet and reaching for my skirt tail and closing their claws on air. *Ha!* I told myself as I scrambled through the front door. *They'll never catch me. Never!*

And then I was flying down the porch steps and bolting into the sunlight; in another ten seconds I'd be free as any bird. . . .

"Stop that girl!" George Washington shouted. "Get her, Sister Bridget!"

Sister Bridget?

What—another one?

They'd left her outside to mind their horse and buggy. Ah, hell. I should have beaten it out the back. And didn't I know her somehow or other? An interfering freckle-face, that's what she was—wearing white, not black like the old ones. Which meant she was still just a trainee and really only half a nun, though she looked twice as tall as the other two put together.

"Whoa, girlie!" she said, and before I could blink, Sister Bridget had caught me by the collar and would have dragged me into the buggy itself, if I hadn't grabbed hold of the lamppost in the nick of time.

"Let *go*, Julia," they all kept telling me, till it made me sick to hear it, the old ones clomping down to circle like buzzards, while the half-a-nun tugged away. The sleeves of her habit had fallen back, and you could see that her arms were just as pink and freckly and baby-fied as her face, but they had some string in 'em for all that. So I held on tighter, that's what, though it felt as if my own arms were getting yanked right out of their sockets. I wrapped them around that post and gritted my teeth and shook my head no, no, *no!*

"Come on, now, pet, there's no use fighting," said Sister Bridget, just as smooth as apple butter. As if she wasn't squeezing the life out of anybody in particular, only sitting in some meadow, picking daisies. "I've got eight brothers at home, and not a one of 'em's bested me yet. So let's just take it nice and slow, why don't we? Easy does it, now. . . . That's right. . . . That's better. . . . Nobody's going to hurt you, not in a million—*ow!*"

"Merciful heaven!" cried the head nun. "She's bitten Sister Bridget!"

And then everybody was tugging and talking at once, and a crowd was gathering on the sidewalk:

"It's all right; it's nothing. . . ."

"Your hand is bleeding!"

". . . barely broke the skin . . ."

"Come and lie down, Sister. . . ."

"No, really, I'm fine. . . ."

". . . like a mad dog entirely . . ."

"She'll have to be tied. . . ."

"It's *nothing*. . . ."

"You want me to fetch the clothesline, Mama?"

"Oh, for heaven's sake, Julia, *stop* it!" This time it was Mary talking. Looked like she'd got back her powers of speech and movement, finally, and had joined the others at the lamppost. "That's enough, now. Just let *go*."

"No! They ain't takin' me to that place! They'll have to shoot me first!"

"Don't tempt me." Aunt Gert's eyes shrunk up to mean little pinpoints. "Yes, Otto, get the clothesline, please."

"Yes'm. . . ."

"Oh, no, surely not! That won't be necessary, will it, dear?" Was that the pigeon cooing? And who was it trying to peel my fingers from their death grip, one by one? I didn't know for sure; I'd shut my own eyes tight now and was kicking out blind as a bat and shaking my head harder. No, no, *no*. . . .

"Stop that, Julia!" Mary again, no question. "Look at poor Sister limping. Do you want 'em to put you in the loony bin?"

"Now there's an idea. . . ."

"Possibly we should come back tomorrow. . . ."

"Don't just stand there, Otto!"

"I AIN'T GOIN' TO THEIR DAMN ORPHAN-AGE!"

"Julia? Mary—what the devil is this?"

"Bill!"

Thank God.

Chapter 2

And if our great-great-great-grand-something-or-other (Brian Boru himself, High King of the Irish) had come charging down the sidewalk, flags flying, in my eyes he'd have rated a sorry second to my brother Bill. Not that the family armor was exactly shining at the moment. He still had on the good shirt he'd worn to the funeral, but it had lost all its starch, and his collar and tie were stuffed in the pocket of his trousers. And there was dirt on his left cheek and dried blood on his lower lip and a brownish stain—fist-shaped?—on his shirtfront, about heart high. (Which wasn't proof positive he'd been fighting again, necessarily. Could be it was nothing more than a splash of innocent coffee—or a bit of beer, more likely, though God knows he was scarcely fifteen and shouldn't have been drinking at all.) And he wasn't wearing any plumed helmet, neither, but his usual old mud-colored cap, cocked sideways on his raggedy crop of blazing-red hair.

"What the devil?" he asked again now, as I let go of the lamppost finally and threw myself into his arms. So Mary opened her mouth to explain, but Aunt Gert and the old Sisters were talking at the same time, and the half-a-nun was putting in her two cents, and over all the babble I kept saying, "I ain't goin', I won't go, don't let 'em take me, Bill; you won't let 'em take me, will you?"

"Hold on there, J, hush. . . ."

"Don't let 'em take me, Bill!"

"You ain't hurt, are you? If anybody's hurt you . . ." He was nearly twice my size, but he knelt right down on the sidewalk by me and I had him 'round the neck now; I was sobbing into his shoulder. "Tell 'em, Bill. They'll listen to you. Tell 'em to take Mary—she don't mind."

"Well, I like that!" Mary sniffed.

"Take her where?" Bill asked.

"To the orphan girls' home!" Otto piped up cheerfully. "And you've got to go live at the priest's house with the orphan boys!"

"Like hell I will," Bill muttered. I heard it in my good ear, and my heart swelled with pride. But then they were off again—all the voices—with Aunt Gert complaining and Sister Maclovius explaining and Sister Gabriel cooing and Sister Bridget saying, "Ah, come on, love, no use beating a dead horse. . . ."

When all of a sudden a hush fell, and the crowd on the pavement parted, and caps were doffed, and amid respectful mumbles of "Hello, Father; lovely day, Father; God bless you for coming, Father," a tall figure in black came striding our way.

"Father Dunne!" said Sister Maclovius. "Thank heaven you're here."

My stomach sank to the sidewalk. I looked at Bill. His eyebrows had puckered together in one fierce red line.

"No," I began again. "We won't go!"

"Hush, J." A muscle twitched in his jaw. "Let me do the talking."

We both knew Father Dunne, of course. Everybody knew him. He was famous for his goodness to the downtrodden. "A saint on this earth," Gran herself had called him, when he'd taken in Jimmy Brannigan six months earlier. This was after Jimmy's house had burned down, with all his folks in it, and him alone spared but with his right leg shattered due to jumping from the second story. And now Jimmy was one of Father Dunne's boys, like all the rest, the lot of 'em hauled in from every stinking rat's nest in the city: cleaned up and set straight and given three squares a day and a decent set of knickers, then trotted out for the whole world to stare at.

Poor beggars.

They got preached about in pulpits. They won city-wide spelling bees. They put out their own newspaper and then had to stand on street corners, selling copies. (I'd spotted Jimmy only the week before, leaning on his crutch over by Healy's Dry Goods. He'd turned beet-red and pretended not to know me.) And just in case—after all that—you'd somehow still managed to miss 'em, at Christmas time their choir came around to the churches and sang like the bleedin' angels. Last year at Saint Pat's, after the bucktoothed kid hit the high note in "O Holy Night," even Skinflint Gert had handed over a nickel.

"Charity cases" was what they were. Bill wouldn't be caught dead with a gang like that.

"Hello, Bill," said the priest. He put out his hand.

Bill hesitated, then shook it. "Afternoon, Father."

I shot him a look: *Careful, Bill, they're full of traps; watch out for the con. . . .*

His left hand tightened on my right shoulder.

Aunt Gert cleared her throat. "Thank you for coming, Father," she began, pushing her way through the gawking strangers. "As you can see for yourself . . . that is, as I told you in my letter, these unfortunate children have been left in—"

"Look out for the little one!" somebody shouted.

"She's a biter!" yelled somebody else.

"In my care," said Aunt Gert, heaving a sigh. "But of course with my own to tend to, and times being what they are, well, much as I'd like to—"

"Did you bring a muzzle, Father?" called a man in the street behind him, puffing smoke rings from a fat cigar.

The crowd hooted at that. I'd have spit at every last one of 'em if Bill's fingers hadn't been cutting clear through to my collarbone. But Father Dunne held up his hand for quiet, and they shut their traps. He was looking at me and Mary now. "I'm sorry for your loss," he said.

He took off his hat.

He was younger than I'd thought, up this close. Younger and bigger. If it weren't for the priest duds, you might peg him as a dockworker, or a farmhand, maybe. He had jug ears, and a long neck, and a headful of brown hair, kind of bristly looking. His wrist bones stuck out of his cassock sleeves like he'd only just outgrown 'em this morning.

"Thanks," said Bill.

"Thank you, Father," Mary murmured. Ah, crikey. Was she *blushing*, for Pete's sake? I gritted my teeth and waited for him to go on about Gran being up with the angels. But he just stood there looking at us, holding his big black hat in his two big hands.

"We're prepared to take the girls, Father," said Sister Maclovius, squinting severely at me down her great beak of a nose. "*If* they're ready to behave themselves."

"No," I said.

Mary elbowed me in the ribs.

"I can take care of my sisters," Bill said.

"Of course you can," said Father Dunne. "When you're a bit older, why then—"

"I have a job."

The priest smiled. "I know you do, son. But two dollars a week—"

"Three and a quarter."

"Is that right?" Father Dunne looked impressed.

"I'll be top of my shift by January; that's three fifty, guaranteed. I'm the fastest button-fitter on the floor, next to Mickey Doyle."

"Well, that's fine, Bill. Highly commendable. Still, even three fifty—well, it doesn't go as far as it used to, I'm afraid. Rent alone will set you back the better part of it, and then there's food to buy, and fuel for the fire, and of course with winter coming on, the girls will be needing new coats and shoes. . . ."

Bill's eyes followed Father Dunne's to my boots, blast the both of 'em. There was a hole in one, and the sole flapped loose on the other. Not that I cared a lick! Still, I wished I'd wiped off the mud, like Mary. Her boots were no newer than mine but looked clean enough to eat.

She started to say something, but Bill shook his head. "Delaneys don't take charity."

"Charity?" The priest put his hat back on. "And who said anything about charity? I've got a paper to run, sir! This is nothing but a temporary arrangement—isn't that so, Sisters?—a hand till you're ready, that's all. Why, when you're earning a grown man's wages we'll be kicking you out on your ear, won't we, to make room for them that need it. We'll be knocking on your boardroom door, asking you to contribute to our building fund."

I waited for Bill to smash that argument all to blazes, but he took his sweet time, for some reason.

"Go on, tell 'em," I said.

He was studying my boots again. They'd been clean as a whistle when I found 'em sitting under my bed last Christmas. Bill had acted more surprised than anybody, though the writing on the note was in his own hand:

To J. C. Delaney, from S. Claus, Esquire

"*Tell* 'em, Bill!"

He looked at Mary. She touched his arm. "We don't have a choice," she told him.

I tugged on his other arm. "Sure we—"

He didn't let me finish. "Look, J," he began, and then he stopped and pulled me aside, away from all the nosy-noses. One old lady was bent nearly double, trying to catch every word. Bill lowered his voice. "It wouldn't be for as long as they're saying. Only a little while, a week or two, that's all. Just till I can get enough together to—"

"No! I won't go! I won't—"

"Stop that, now. Do you suppose I'd leave you with that bunch? Just a couple of weeks, I promise—no, now, listen to me, Julia—a month, tops. There's ways, all right? We got plans, me and the fellers—"

"What fellers? Not that Mickey!"

"You'll be all right; you'll have Mary looking out for

you. I'll spring you loose from there before you know it. You only have to make 'em *think* you're staying; you can do that much for me, can't you?"

I shook my head again, no, no, no.

"Yes, you can; I know you can. It's the only way, Julia. We can't fight 'em right here with the whole world watching."

"Sure we—"

"Listen to me, J! We'll have a signal, all right? Keep your head down and your eyes wide open. You'll be just like Madame What's-Her-Name in the peep boxes, that lady spy you liked so much—"

"Madame Marvella?"

"That's the one! She fooled 'em all, didn't she?"

It was true. Marvella was a wonder. Hadn't I spent the past four Saturdays in Monaghan's River Arcade and Pawn Shop, watching her death-defying adventures on the story reels? You had to know how to sneak past Doc Monaghan himself, of course, high and mighty in the ticket window, but fortunately he did his own sneaking away every hour or so, to wet his whistle at Egan's Saloon. And once you were in, the moving picture boxes were a cinch to jimmy. So then you peeped in the peephole and cranked the crank, and there would be marvelous Marvella, just like magic, wearing one disguise after another, riding camels and dancing on elephants' backs, slipping secret messages to the Maharaja, swimming down the black waters of the Nile with a knife in her teeth. Like to see 'em keep *her* cooped up in some convent!

Still . . .

"I'll send you a sign—"

"*No*, Bill!"

"And as soon as you see it—first minute they ain't looking—you and Mary come away quick as you can. You got that? You stick together like nothing doing and go straight to our old meeting place, and I'll be there waiting for you, just like always."

"But what if you aren't? What if you *can't*—?"

"You ever know me to go back on my word?"

I stared at my boots.

To J. C. Delaney, from S. Claus, Esquire . . .

"Julia?"

I swallowed hard. "What sort of a sign?"

Chapter 3

"It won't be so bad as all that," Mary whispered, as the swaybacked horse pulled us away, *clop-clop* down Biddle Street and *bump* over the trolley tracks.

I didn't bother answering. My throat ached and my heart hammered and the blood shrieked in my bad ear. Sounded for all the world like a pair of cats fighting over a fishbone.

"Sister says they have bunco in the parlor on game nights."

Dear God in heaven. Bunco with the orphans.

But what was the use talking about it, with us already packed tight as ticks in a buggy full of nuns?

The freckled strong-arm was up front driving,

the reins in her left hand, Father Dunne's big handkerchief tied around her right. The pigeon and the president sat directly across from Mary and me, fingering their rosary beads. Our eight boots rested on the pair of boxes Aunt Gert had wedged in at the very last second. *Tap-tap* . . . went Sister Gabriel's, keeping time: *Mother of God . . . tap-tap . . . pray for us sinners . . . tap-tap . . .*

What was it she'd said when Aunt Gert told her my name? Had she really danced in Dublin once? I wondered. A terrible picture rose up in my head: a whole row of fat little nuns with their black beads jangling and their habits flapping and their veils all askew, hopping and bobbing to the music—*my* music—"Julia Delaney" herself.

The First Joyful Mystery . . . tap-tap. . . the Annunciation . . .

"'Tis your lucky reel, Julia," Gran would say, "and your father's before you." That was how she always started the story. "Wasn't it the selfsame tune he was playing when he first laid eyes on your mother, the night of his very own funeral?"

Our Father . . . tap-tap . . . who art in heaven . . . tap-tap . . .

"But he wasn't dead yet, was he, Gran?" I would ask,

knowing my part, and she'd wipe her eyes and say, "Ah, no, not a bit of it. He was as healthy as a horse, my Cyril was, before the drink got hold of him. But he was leaving for America the very next morning, sailing clear to New Orleans on a cotton steamer, then working his way up the Mississippi to St. Louis, where the boatyards were hiring. Four thousand miles from Edenderry, for a job painting smokestacks! Who could say when we'd ever lay eyes on him again, this side of the grave? So seeing as how it might be our last opportunity, we got his cousin Father John the Jesuit to say him a proper Requiem Mass, casket and all—though without your father in it, of course; that was only a hank of his lovely black hair, tied with a ribbon. And afterward we all went down to the Queen of Heaven Hall and gave him a first-class American wake—new potatoes with butter, Guinness flowing to beat the band, the entire butt end of a roasted ham, to boot. And someone handed Cyril his fiddle, for old times' sake, and Father John called for 'Julia Delaney,' as he always did: 'Our great-grand-seventh cousin's sister-in-law, God bless her!' Which only proved he'd had a pint or two, as usual, since even God couldn't remember that far back, or if the girl in the music had ever existed in the first place."

Blessed art thou amongst women . . . tap-tap . . .

"And our mother was there?"

"She was." . . . *tap-tap* . . . "The beautiful Kitty Jordan. She'd come to the funeral with her brother William, who'd promised her a good feed. 'I've always loved that tune,' she said. 'Then marry me,' said your father. 'And if our daughter's eyes are as blue as yours, we'll call her Julia.'

"And she laughed and said, 'Go on with ye,' and waved him goodbye, but he didn't give up so easy. When he got to St. Louis, he wrote her every day: 'Dear Kitty, lovely Kitty, sweet Kitty, please come. I'm standing on the Eads Bridge, waiting for you.' And a whole year passed, and still he was waiting, till he wore her down, finally. He worked every day and night and saved every penny, and then he bought a silver ring and sent it to her. 'Dear Kitty,' he wrote. 'It's getting cold out here. Oh, my darling girl, won't you come?'"

"And seven weeks later she came sailing up the river."

Glory be to the Father . . . tap-tap . . . and to the son . . .

But I wasn't their first child, after all. That was Bill, named in honor of our good-luck uncle. And the next year there was Mary—Mary Patricia—with her green eyes, exactly like Gran's. Then the twins, Helen and

Larry, born brown-eyed, just eleven months before me, both killed by the fever that muddled my left ear when I was four.

As it was in the beginning . . . tap-tap . . . and ever shall be . . .

And our mother sat on their single grave in the raw black mud and prayed that they would haunt her. "Their ghosts would be better than naught at all," she said. She had a rag doll and a bowl of custard in her lap. "For bait," she kept saying. "They'll be wanting their supper." But the little ghosts stayed put. And two weeks later we were back in the graveyard, burying her beside 'em.

The Second Joyful Mystery . . . tap-tap . . . the Visitation . . .

"Whoa, Hyacinth, there's a good boy," said Sister Bridget, pulling back on the reins with her unbandaged hand.

Hyacinth, for Pete's sake.

Not that the poor old bag of bones gave a fiddler's fig what they called him. He'd had a whole new spring in his step ever since we'd turned on Morgan Street, where the Bad Lands breeze started blowing. Now he left off his *clop-clop*ping, sighed a shuddering sort of horse sigh, and had his head drooping over the hitching post practically before the words were out of the half-a-nun's mouth.

The buggy came to rest with one last rumble and squeak.

"Here we are!" piped the pigeon, fluttering a hand toward the tall brick building that faced us.

THE HOUSE OF MERCY, announced the square black letters over the door. And under the knocker, in smaller print: INDUSTRIAL SCHOOL AND GIRLS' HOME.

My chest felt crowded, as if something was stuck there.

Mary squeezed my clenched fist. "It won't be so bad," she whispered.

Sister Maclovius heaved herself to her feet, her veil flapping in the wind like a crow's wing. She looked down at us and smiled that smile again, fair set my teeth a-chatter. "Even the sparrow hath found a home," she said, "and the swallow a nest for herself."

Directly behind her, a white face flattened itself against a window and crossed its eyes.

Chapter 4

The big door swung to with a whispering sound—*shhhusshhhttt*—though I never saw the hand that opened it. I was half-blind as we walked in out of the daylight, going from sun to gloom. Not a thing to see at first but a glimmer of movement in the corner of my left eye; naught to hear but a kind of low chuckling, close to my good ear.

And then the creak of a floorboard and the soft pad of footsteps, running away.

And the door opened wide, and Beauty entered the great dark castle, and her hat went flyin' off her head, and all about her there was sighin' and stirrin', though she never saw a soul. . . .

"Never mind, it's only Betty Brickey," said Sister Bridget, clumping past us in her big black boots.

"Betty who?" Mary quavered.

The half-a-nun didn't hear. She was busy with our boxes, hauling both at once, like there was nothing to it. Like they were stuffed with feathers—or soap bubbles—which they might have been, for all I knew. Were my marbles in there? Had Aunt Gert thought to pack 'em? Or were they still scattered in the dirt by the back stoop, just waiting for Otto to pounce? Ah, the great slobberin' sneak-thief! He'd cry uncle the next time I saw him. I'd give him a good swift kick in the rear, I would—

If there ever was a next time.

And how was it that the pleasure of *not* seeing him felt like such a cheat, all of a sudden?

"Sister Bridget will get you settled," said the president. "Go with her now, and mind what she says."

"Yes, Sister," said Mary.

But the old nun wasn't looking at Mary. She leaned in close, till her face was an inch from mine. Her breath smelled like mothballs. I found myself staring at a lone white hair sprouting out of her left cheek. "Don't think that I won't be watching you, Julia Delaney. Don't imagine I'll be tolerating your shenanigans. If there's one thing that'll never be tolerated in the House of Mercy, it's shenanigans."

With that she lifted several of her chins and sailed off down a corridor to the right. "Come along, Sister Gabriel!" she hissed as she passed. "Your tea will be cold." And the pigeon nodded and blinked, and patted Mary's head, and would have patted mine if I hadn't jerked away in the nick of time. And then she sighed softly and went trotting off after the boss nun, puffing a little.

My eyes were getting used to the dim now as we followed the freckled giantess down the main hall. Mary was pulling me with her at a fast clip toward a steep, curving staircase, directly ahead. Tall, papered walls loomed over us, speckled with ugly brown roses, climbing up and up like Jack's own beanstalk. A sad-eyed Jesus and his mother stared down from heavy wood frames, pointing fingers to their flaming hearts. On either wall past the pair of 'em was a row of doors—shut tight, for the most part, as dark and serious-looking as doors could be.

But the last on the left was cracked just a smidgeon, and through the crack came a thin wedge of yellow light. It seemed to have a sound, too, this light—a kind of singsong humming. And as we got closer, the humming became a chorus of girls' voices:

Full fathom five thy father lies;
Of his bones are coral made. . . .

"Ah, great gobs, Sister Sebastian," Sister Bridget grumbled to the door, stopping for a moment to get a better grip on the boxes, "not the bones again! Would it kill you entirely to give 'em a nice cheerful poem that wouldn't scare 'em out their wits?"

Those are pearls that were his eyes. . . .

I peeped through the crack and saw yet another nun—about as big as a peanut, this one, hardly taller than I was (and Bill called me the Runt). I couldn't see her students from where I stood, only this tiny teacher, beating time with a ruler on the palm of her own hand. She had a little pointed face and the blackest eyebrows I ever saw, and spectacles resting low down on her sharp little nose, and a pair of squinty black eyes peering through 'em, bright as two hot coals.

Nothing of him that doth fade
But doth suffer a sea change . . .

Sister Bridget looked back at us and shook her head.

"Ah, well. At least it's not *Macbeth*. Winnie O'Rourke woke the whole house after that one, hollering about witches." The half-a-nun craned her neck and peered into the shadows under the stairs, just ahead. "Didn't she, Betty?"

Into something rich and strange. . . .

"Ah, now, Betty, I know you hear me. You don't fool us for a second. Come out from back there and meet the new girls."

It was only her foot we saw at first. Not the whole foot, really—just a bit of shoe: a dirty pink dancing slipper, inching out from the stairwell, dragging its ribbons behind it.

"There she is!" said Sister Bridget. "That's right; come on out, Betty; be a good girl, now. There's not a soul here that would hurt you." She gave us a warning wink, as if the kid was some wild creature, like that old stray cat Bill was always coaxing out of the alley with a scrap of sausage. "That's right. . . . That's the way. . . ."

Sea-nymphs hourly ring his knell. . . .

So we kept quiet and waited, and little by little, the rest of the girl appeared: the corner of an apron, the back of a grubby hand, the tail end of a scraggly brown braid . . .

And the very same moonface that had crossed its eyes in the window, not five minutes before.

"Mary and Julia Delaney," said Sister Bridget, "meet Betty Brickey."

Ding-dong.

Hark! Now I hear them. . . .

As if she'd been under some spell till this moment, and the words of the chant had smashed it all to pieces, Betty grinned a crooked grin and brought out her left hand from behind her back.

She was holding a bell.

Ding-dong, bell.

"No, Betty!" cried Sister Bridget. "School's not over; it's another twenty minutes yet—"

But it was too late. Betty was already ringing the thing, holding it by its long handle and swinging it in great, curving arcs.

"Ah, sweet Mary and Joseph," the half-a-nun muttered, dropping our boxes and trying to grab her.

"How'd you get it this time? Stop that, Betty! Sister Maclovius will have your hide again; you know it!"

But Betty ducked and twirled and ran away, laughing out loud now, swinging that bell so hard, the clamor could have waked the dead. And before the half-a-nun could do a thing about it, all the dark doors had opened wide, and suddenly the hall was teeming with girls—dozens and dozens of 'em—and no two alike, though they all wore the same hideous plaid pinafores. Big girls and little girls, tall and short, fat and skinny, tucked in to their toenails or rumpled as unmade beds; spotless, ink-stained, smooth-haired, frowzy-headed girls, making such a noise even my bad ear could hear it.

Sounded like a crowd of dock birds screaming when the fishermen cleaned their nets.

"Back!" Sister Bridget shouted. "Back to your classrooms or we're done for!"

But nobody paid her the slightest bit of attention.

Chapter 5

Now the sea of brown plaid was dotted with black, as more nuns joined the hubbub in the hall: the peanut with the eyebrows (Sister Sebastian?) and the other teachers, shouting, "Quiet!" and "Order, young ladies!" But still the girls pushed and giggled and shrieked, and covered their ears with their hands, and Betty Brickey's bell rang on and on—

And then it stopped.

Just like that.

A hush traveled through the crowd in a trail of whispers: "*Shhhhhhhhhhhhhhh*," it breathed, till the hall was still as a tomb.

"Who rang that bell?" demanded Sister Maclovius.

I never saw her coming, but there she was. Not a hairsbreadth from my left elbow. Standing there like doom itself, brushing crumbs from her wimple. I swear, you could all but hear 'em hitting the floor.

"I'll ask you once more, ladies. Though you know how I dislike—" Sister broke off and turned her steely gaze on the pigeon, who was just now bustling in breathlessly, still clutching a napkin. "—how I dislike repeating myself." The head nun's voice was deadly quiet. *"Who rang that bell?"*

Every eye went to the stairway—up and up, halfway to the landing—where Betty had perched in midflight. She had her bell-hand behind her back again and was watching the rest of us with interest, the grin still stuck on her moonface in a crooked slash.

"Mary Elizabeth Brickey," said the president, "what's that you're hiding?"

The grin got wider.

"It was my mistake, Sister," the half-a-nun began, all in a rush, stepping over our boxes where she'd dropped them and pushing through the mob. "You know how she loves it; I meant to put it on top of the bookshelf, so she wouldn't be tempted again, but then you called for the buggy and the bell went out of my head entirely; I must have left it on the table by the *door*, of all places, where of course she was bound to—"

"That will do, Sister Bridget." Sister Maclovius held up a hand, and the flood of words stopped cold. Her eyes never left crazy Betty. "I'm waiting, Mary Elizabeth."

Little by little, tooth by tooth, the grin shrank, until it disappeared altogether. Slowly, slowly, Betty brought out the bell. . . .

And gave it one last clang.

"Half-wit," someone muttered, a couple of orphans to my right—a long-necked, hard-eyed girl who sneered when I looked at her.

A smothered titter ran through the crowd.

"Silence!" said Sister Maclovius, and the hall went dead again. She turned back to Betty, calm as cream. "Bring me the bell, Miss Brickey."

Miss Brickey didn't budge.

"Unless you'd rather I came up there for it?"

Terror darted across the moonface.

Run! I wanted to shout. *Just look at the size of her; she couldn't catch you in a million years!*

But it was too late. Betty was coming down the stairs already, dragging her feet in those dirty old dance shoes; she was tripping over the ribbons while the plaid girls smirked. And weren't *they* having themselves a fine time? A little fat kid was crying, but the rest only nudged one another and pushed in closer, jostling for a better view, craning their necks like they were at the circus—like Otto, the big lily-liver, that time he tricked Bill's cat out of the alley with a piece of spinach, and cut off its whiskers, and laughed when it walked so crooked. I hated him then and I hated them now but dear God in heaven if the loon herself wasn't grinning again, grinning *back* at the whole sniggerin' lot of 'em, and handing the bell to the head nun, and the head nun was handing it to the pigeon, and now Sister Maclovius had Betty by the ear; she was saying, "Teachers, take charge of your students," and leading Betty off who knows where, and I couldn't stand it, that's all. Mary was tugging on my arm to keep me still but my heart was pounding and the bile rose up in my throat—*no, no, no, no*—

"NO!"

I didn't realize, at first, that I'd said it out loud.

"No?" Sister Maclovius stopped in her tracks, still holding tight to Betty—stopped so suddenly that the pigeon (hard on their heels) barreled into both of them. "Did someone say *no*, Sister Gabriel?"

All around me there were little gasping noises, like dry leaves rustling in the wind: *Huh huh huh huh huh huh*—

"Now you've done it," Mary muttered.

Sister Gabriel stepped back, flustered, unaware that her headpiece had slipped slightly cattywampus. "Why . . . ah . . . I . . . I don't think so, Sister. . . ." Her little brown bird eyes flickered in my direction, then flickered away again. "My . . . my hearing isn't what it used to be, I'm afraid, but—"

"Never mind, Sister Gabriel." Sister Maclovius held up the hand that wasn't latched on to Betty's ear. "Fortunately my own hearing is still quite sufficient."

She was looking me smack in the face.

"Were you addressing me, Julia Delaney?"

Orphan by orphan, the plaid sea shrank back, leaving Mary and me stranded on our own private island.

"Speak up, Julia. Come, now. You have our undivided attention. Was there or was there not something you wanted to say?"

I tried to open my mouth, but it was no use. That god-awful smile of hers had iced it up solid.

"She didn't mean to say anything, Sister. . . ." Mary took a step forward, dragging me with her. "It was an accident, wasn't it, Julia?" Her hand clamped even tighter on my arm. "Go on," she whispered, giving me a shake. "Tell Sister you're sorry."

I might have done it, if my tongue had thawed in time.

But then I looked at crazy Betty, watching me wide-eyed, her head cocked at an awkward angle under the president's thumb.

Sorry for *what*, exactly?

And why should I say it, when I wasn't?

"Ah, for pity's sake, Julia!" Mary's grip was like a vise now. I could feel her palm sweating clear through my sleeve. "Just *say* it, for once in your life!"

"No." I gritted my teeth.

"Dear God," Mary breathed. "She'll eat us alive."

But aside from a slight tic in the middle of her left eyelid, the old battle-ax smiled on. "No again, is it? Well, now. Will you listen to that, Sister Gabriel? If it isn't the Queen of the Kerry Patch, come to tell us her pleasure!"

"The—the Queen?" asked the pigeon, looking confused.

Sister Maclovius gave Betty's ear a jerk, forcing the moonface bolt-upright again, and tugged her over to where I was standing. The kid's eyes—glued to mine—were big as dinner plates now. "Tell us, Your Majesty, what would *you* suggest I do with this child?"

The nun loomed over me, swaying a little, her beads *click-clack*ing like Aunt Gert's teeth.

"Or did you imagine that I'd let her off scot-free?

Was that it? With bells ringing and pandemonium in the hallway?" And suddenly the smiling was done and she was leaning down, all splotchy-cheeked and sputtering, shaking a gnarly finger in my face. "Shenanigans, Julia Delaney! What did I tell you about shenanigans?"

I just stood there, dumb as a post.

She wiped the spit off her chin. "We'll not be having them; that's the beginning and end of it. Do I make myself clear?"

She straightened her spine then, and got a fresh lock on Betty's ear, and started hauling her off once more. But before she'd taken two steps, she whipped back around, spinning the kid with her. "As for the rest of you gigglers and squealers, there'll be no more recreation until further notice. Report to the refectory with your rosaries at six o'clock sharp."

There was a chorus of groans.

"Silence!" Sister Maclovius thundered yet again, and the hall went still.

Her eyelid twitched. "If you don't like it, take it up with the Queen."

Chapter 6

I could feel all the plaid girls leaning in, glaring, breathing their orphan breath in my face. The little fat kid was still crying great slimy tears, sobbing into her hands. The long-neck pointed a finger at me, then drew it across her throat in a slicing motion.

Two weeks, Bill had promised. *A month, tops*.

If we lived that long.

"I saw that, Marcella Duggan!" said the half-a-nun as she hoisted our boxes once again. "Now, there's a nice how-do-you-do for the new girls. Where are your manners? And what are *you* gawking at, Hazel Theedy? Get back to your sums, the both of you. Don't you roll your eyes at me, or you'll rue the day! Ah, for heaven's sake,

Winnie, don't you *ever* have a handkerchief?"

The crybaby shook her head. She seemed in danger of washing away entirely, in one great ocean of snot.

"Well, never mind, take this one. Now, stop that, Winifred; you're perfectly all right. It won't kill you to say an extra rosary or two! Offer it up for the suffering souls in Purgatory. You'd think it was you in their poor shoes, pining away in the heat."

And all this time Sister Bridget was pushing through the scowling mob—"Go *on,* girls! Are you growing roots?"—and herding pupils back to their classrooms—"Look now, Winnie; here's Sister Sebastian waiting for you. Maybe she'll give you a little more Shakespeare, to calm your nerves. 'We are such stuff as dreams are made on; and our little life is rounded with a sleep. . . .' Don't drumble about, ye lollygaggers; are you holdin' a convention?" And before our new acquaintances could move in for the kill, she was hustling Mary and me up the stairs and down another hall and upstairs yet again, until we came through an unmarked door into a long, dim tunnel of a room.

"Here you are," said Sister Bridget, setting down our boxes and stretching her fingers. Her bandage sagged. There was a *pop-pop-pop*ping as her knuckles cracked. "Last two on the left."

The dregs of the day's sun trickled in through a tall, narrow window, falling on slant gray walls and greenish linoleum and two rows of white beds facing each other. Must have been a good twenty of 'em altogether, at least ten to a side.

"Thank you, Sister," said Mary. She gave me a poke in the ribs and jerked her head toward the half-a-nun so I'd say it too, but I clenched my jaw.

"You're welcome," said Sister Bridget, catching hold of Father's handkerchief before it slid off completely. She unwound it the rest of the way and checked her hand for toothmarks—a satisfying little circle of purplish ridges, plain as day even from where I stood—then folded it calmly and whisked it away in one of her sleeves. "All right, ladies. You can put your things here in this middle bureau. They've cleared a drawer for each of you, you see? Try to save a bit of room; you'll be getting your school clothes in the morning. Now then, what else? Boxes, beds . . . I know I've forgotten something. . . . The lavatory's just out the back door, if you'd like to make a visit before supper. I'll send Winnie to bring you down in a quarter of an hour, how's that?"

"That'll be fine, thank you, Sister. Won't it, Julia?"

Poke, poke!

I clamped down so hard on my bottom lip, I could taste my own blood.

Sister Bridget gave me a considering look. "Put away thy sword, Julia Delaney. No use beating a dead—ah, great gobs, the horse!"

And then she was hurrying off to see to the sway-back, and Mary was shaking me again, asking would it have killed me to say, "Thank you, Sister," and oh, yes—while I was at it—beg pardon for attacking her like a mad dog itself? What if I died in the night with nun-biting on my soul? Had I thought of that? People were always dying in the night; they did it every day, and it would serve me right if I didn't get into heaven. To hell with heaven, I told her. And she slapped my face and I slapped her back and we opened our boxes and my marbles weren't there.

But I couldn't stop and think about it. By the time we'd put away our drawers in the drawers, the cry-baby was behind us, having hiccups in the doorway, saying, "Sister said you're to come down now, Your Majesty." Did she think it was my actual name? Or was she making fun? I wondered. But she looked scared as any rabbit, and when I narrowed my eyes at her she made a little gasping sound and skittered away.

"Now's our chance," I told Mary. "We can still make a run for it." But she only jerked my arm and said, "Come *on*, Julia." And then she was pulling me downstairs and it was no use saying no because suddenly I was tired, so tired, too tired to fight her anymore; my head felt thick and my legs were heavy as hams. So I stumbled after her and we found the refectory from the cabbage smell and squeezed in on a bench at one of the long tables—a couple of orphans hissed, but a skinny girl with a cold in her head made room—and Sister Maclovius led the rosary, three times 'round, and somewhere between the Scourging at the Pillar and the Crowning with Thorns they handed out the supper, but I must have fallen asleep because Mary was shaking me for the thousandth time and my left cheek was mashed flat into my plate; there was corn bread up my nose and some sort of yellowish glop caught in my eyelashes, but I couldn't eat; I couldn't keep my eyes open. The long-neck—Marcella?—was nudging her pal Hazel and sneering at me again, one table over, but I didn't care. I was tired, so tired. . . .

And the next thing I knew, it was dark and I was lying in one of the white beds, though I couldn't remember how I got there. At first I thought this was home, but then the curtains moved at the narrow window and moonlight speckled the slant-walled room, and the day came roaring back. . . .

Oh, for shame, for shame, Julia. . . .

Merciful heaven! She's bitten Sister Bridget!

I ain't goin', I won't go. . . . Tell *'em, Bill!*

You'll have Mary looking out for you. . . .

I sat bolt upright. Mary! Where was Mary?

The bed beside me hadn't been touched.

Oh, dear God, I shouldn't have slapped her. Even if she did deserve it.

But then I turned my head and there she was, in the bed to my left. That was Mary's chin, surely, with the scar down the middle that she got last year from tumbling over Otto's trip wire, and Mary's pointy nose, and her brown hair tangled on the pillow. Her cheeks looked wet, though her eyes were closed, and her breathing came in jerks, all raggedy-sounding.

Had she been crying, then?

But Mary never cried.

What was that in her hand?

She was holding on to something—she was dead to the world, but still her fingers were closed 'round it—a shoelace, maybe? Or a bit of old ribbon?

Sort of bluish.

Quick as that came the picture, floating into my head: our mother's red hair hanging down her back, with a blue ribbon in it. . . .

And her long skirts are sweeping the floor as she walks—*swish, swish*—and I am walking behind her, following the blue, when the door swings open and there's my father—there you stand, Papa, with the fiddle in your hand. *Hello, sweetheart. Hello, little dolly*, you say. *Does my dolly love her daddy?* And you fall down, *clunk!* And one eye's all puffed out, black and bloody for the union. *For standing up*, you say, *like a union man should.* But then you wink it to make me laugh and start playing our lucky tune—you're flat on your back but you're fiddling just the same—and Mama kneels down, and I think she's trying to tickle you, but that's not it. She's looking in your pockets, so it must be payday at the boatyard. I know all about payday at the boatyard. All the other days are a kick in the teeth, painting smokestacks till you drop, but on payday we sing the Julia song, with the words you made for Mama:

Oh, come with me, my love!
Come away, come afar. . . .
We'll sing the moon down from the sky

And sail the morning star,
And when we reach bright heaven's gate,
Why, we've only begun;
We'll build a boat with angel's wings,
And then we'll sail the sun!

But Mama's not listening. She's looking and still looking and there's nothing in your pockets, Papa, nothing but two shiny nickels, and she takes them in her hand and shakes them at you; her fist shakes and her red hair shakes and the blue ribbon bobs up and down, up and down, like a little hopping bird. And now she's crying; I know she's crying (oh, that raggedy sound, do you hear?) though I can't see her face—I can never see her face—and I tug on her sleeve but when she turns around, she's not my mother anymore.

Don't think that I won't be watching you, Julia Delaney. Don't imagine I'll be tolerating your shenanigans. . . .

She'll have to be tied. . . .

Did you bring a muzzle?

Take it up with the Queen. . . .

The door creaked, and my eyes jerked open. It was Sister Bridget, with the bell ringer in tow. She led her past the snoring orphans to the bed on my right, where Mary wasn't.

"Go to sleep now, Betty," the half-a-nun whispered, helping the kid off with her dancing shoes. "Tomorrow's a brand-new day." And then she pulled up the covers and started to turn my way, and I closed my eyes tight, before she saw me watching, but for a while I could still feel her standing there, watching me too. Until finally I heard the sound of her leaving, the rustle and click and *tap-tap-tap*ping across the floor.

And when I looked again, there was the moonface looking back at me, grinning her crooked grin.

I'll send you a sign . . .

What sort of a sign?

And the door opened wide. . . .

Ding-dong . . .

Glory be to the Father. . . .

Let go, *Julia!*

You'll know it when you see it. . . .

Chapter 7

EEEEEEEIIIIIIIIYYYYYYY—what the devil?

"Good morning, Your Majesty," said Marcella, the chortling long-neck, pouring a pitcher of water in my face. "Rise and shine!"

"Stop it! Stop!" I sputtered, trying to fight off the icy flood with my hands. "I'll kill you, I will, I'll—"

"Oooof!" Marcella gasped as Betty Brickey butted her in the stomach with her head.

"Hey!" yelled Hazel, the long-neck's lackey, grabbing Betty by the hair and yanking her backward. And then there was water everywhere and the white pitcher broken on the floor and Winnie the Crybaby wailing and a whole pile of orphans pushing and shoving, and me in the middle of 'em, soggy all over and swinging away, and Mary trying to pin my arms and saying, "Stop it, Julia!"—as if it was *my* fault—

Which was how the half-a-nun found us when she opened the door. "Ah, great gobs . . . Order, ladies! Order, I said! Have you all gone daft? Let go of her leg, Marcella, or you'll not get another minute of recreation till you're in your grave."

"That one s-started it," Marcella lied between gasps, pointing to me. "Her and the h-h-halfwit are in cahoots."

Sister Bridget sniffed. "And the rest of you were just sitting there like the Holy Innocents themselves—polishing your halos, was that it? Go on now, the lot of you. Get dressed and go have your mush." She shifted the basket she was carrying from her right hip to her left, then caught sight of Betty, round-eyed, her fists still clenched. "That goes for you, too, Miss. And what were *you* doing fighting? No, no, I'm not tying your slippers. You'll wear your regular shoes today like everybody else. There's been quite enough dancing about."

Betty didn't say a word. She dropped her chin to her chest.

Ah, for the love of Mike, would *she* be crying next?

But then she tilted her head and slid her eyes my way and grinned a small grin, as if someone had told a joke only the two of us understood.

Sister Bridget wasn't waiting for an answer anyhow. While Betty stayed planted on one side of the drenched bed in her untied slippers, the half-a-nun plopped her basket down on the other. "Here you are, Mary and Julia, your school clothes, fresh from the laundry. All marked on the labels with your own particular numbers, see there?"

Oh Lord, not the putrid plaid pinafores! With nubby cotton underdresses, darned-up stockings, knickers . . . orphan duds clear down to our skins, then?

"Forty-five—that'll be you, Mary. Now, there's a lucky number! Rosie Flannigan was forty-five before you—your size to a T. And didn't we just have a letter from Rosie's new family, singing her praises? 'Satisfactory in all departments.' Those were their exact words. You can't go wrong with forty-five."

"Thank you, Sister," said Mary.

"Don't mention it."

I tried not to gag.

"And what have they sent up for you, Julia? Fifty-seven? Let me think. . . . Who was our last fifty-seven?"

The long-neck and her toady—almost to the doorway—whipped back around and chimed in together: "Cecilia Forney!"

The color under Sister Bridget's freckles went from pale to deep pink. "Oh, yes. Of course. Cecilia." She cleared her throat. "Well, she was certainly . . . certainly . . . a fine girl, too."

Dead, Marcella mouthed at me, raising a witchy eyebrow.

Hazel followed her out the door, smirking.

They let it bang behind them.

"It doesn't matter," Mary said, once Sister Bridget had left the room, her basket loaded with wet sheets and pitcher pieces. "Look here—" Mary picked up dead Cecilia's pinafore and shook it out, as if it wasn't making her flesh crawl in the least. "There's not a thing wrong with it. It's been washed a thousand times. I'd trade with you in a minute, if only it fit me." And she said it with her face straight, too, though we both knew she'd sooner eat slugs. In her heart she was all but lighting candles to Saint Rose the Satisfactory.

Still, if *she* could touch the foul thing . . . I gritted my teeth and took it from her. What was I afraid of? A scrap of patched-together plaid?

Hadn't Madame Marvella once spent a whole night

in the sultan's tomb, wearing a shroud itself?

You only have to make 'em think *you're staying. . . .*

Keep your head down and your eyes wide open. . . .

But how on God's green earth could you keep your head down, if Betty Brickey was your friend?

She followed me everywhere, like a moonfaced shadow. Morning till night, there was Betty. She was worse than Bill's cat, who'd catch you throwing out the chicken feet in June and still be hanging around at Christmas. Sleeping, waking, eating, praying—and we were forever praying, till the angels themselves must have stopped their ears—through it all she was never more than two steps behind me, watching my every move.

"Can she speak English, do you think?" I asked Mary on the fifth day, saying it under my breath so Betty couldn't hear me. We'd just come from a solid hour in the chapel, where Sister Maclovius was teaching us the Seven Deadly Sins. I'd nodded off at Gluttony and was dreaming about Gran's pancakes, only to wake with a start and find Betty playing Do-As-I-Do, letting her own eyelids droop and jerk, droop and jerk, till I thought I'd die of shame.

"I don't think you'd call it English," Mary whispered back, as the plaid tide swelled again, filling the hall. The sounds coming out of Betty at the moment weren't any brand of language I'd ever heard—on our block, there'd been near as many Germans as Irish, and the Doyles were part Polish, and Mr. Patrizi the greengrocer spoke Italian—but Betty's noises weren't like any of theirs, not words at all, really, only an odd sort of humming-clicking-whistling like a bird itself.

"Betty Babble, that's all she talks," said Hazel, poking her nose in, though it was no prize of a nose to be poking anywhere, with its dime-size pockmarks. "Babbling Betty from the Land of Babble-Loney."

"Shhh!" said Mary. "She'll hear you!"

"And what if she does? She don't care a whit. Do you, Betty? She can't understand a word we're saying. Ooga-mooga chilly-dilly—"

"Stop it," I growled.

"Ah, dry up," said Hazel. "She likes it, see there? Hinky-plinky waggy-shaggy—you see? She thinks it's funny!"

Sure enough, Betty was grinning again, pausing midstream in her own gibberish to cock a curious eyebrow at Hazel and chuckle softly, more to humor her, it seemed to me, than because Hazel was anywhere near the wit she thought she was. I would have gladly smacked her one anyhow—Hazel, that is, who God knows deserved it—but Marcella was at her elbow, looking daggers at me, as usual, and Sister Maclovius was still standing at the chapel door with her hawk eyes peeled. So Mary held me back.

But by the noon meal, Hazel was pushing her luck again.

"You know what's wrong with her, don't you?" she went on cheerfully from across the table. She jerked her head toward Betty, who sat beside me, rolling her bread into pea-size lumps.

I shrugged and concentrated on chewing the same bite I'd been chewing for several minutes: a wad of stringy grayish stuff, tough as a boot.

"Her pa was a gangster and her ma was a lunatic."

I cut my eyes at Mary, on my left.

"It's the truth," Hazel insisted. "Ask anybody. Ask Sister Bridget. She's her aunt; she's kin to the whole clan. Tell her, Marcella!"

The long-neck, right next to her, waved a fly off her turnips. "Ever hear of Egan's Rats, Your Majesty?"

I shrugged again and devoted myself to my boot leather. But I could feel the blood rising all the way to my eyeballs.

Marcella's thin lips curled at the corners. "That's right. *Those* Rats. Betty's pa was Two-Bits Brickey. Ah, sure, that's ringin' a bell, now, ain't it? Look at their faces, Hazel. I guess their daddy taught 'em how to read the paper after all, when he wasn't knockin' 'em back at Egan's Saloon."

I squeezed my fork. Mary squeezed my elbow. "It's not worth it," she muttered.

"And that ain't the half of it," said Hazel. "Tell about the mother and the chorus line and the shotgun wedding. Tell about—"

Marcella gave her a squashing look, and Hazel shut her mouth. Sister Sebastian was standing directly behind her.

Even the fly stopped buzzing.

"Enjoying your dinner, girls?" the nun asked quietly. (She was always the quietest of any 'em, which only made our hearts hammer all the louder.)

"Yes, Sister." "Yes, Sister." "Yes, Sister," we murmured, nodding and chewing up a storm.

"Well, then. *Bon appétit.*" And she left us half-scorched with her burning eyes, and moved on to the next table.

We started breathing again.

"The mother," Hazel whispered.

"No better than he was," said Marcella. Every girl at the table—even Betty herself—leaned in. "She used to dance in the line at the Standard Theatre, till Two-Bits got her in trouble. So he took her down to Saint Pat's and got the priest to marry 'em, but another Rat followed 'em to the wedding. A much bigger Rat, who had a bone to pick with Two-Bits. He shot the groom dead, right there on the church steps, and the bride saw it all and went loony, and her kid was born too soon—in the nuthouse itself—before her brain was finished cooking."

"And how do *you* know so much?" I hissed at her, though I had a sick feeling she was telling the truth. Every Patch kid had heard of Two-Bits Brickey. Mickey Doyle even claimed to be his cousin. He was forever showing pretty girls the plugged-up bullet holes in the church door.

"You don't believe me?" Marcella snapped her fingers with one hand and caught the fly in her fist with the other. "Show her the mark, Betty."

Without so much as a blink, Betty popped a bread ball into her mouth and tugged down her collar.

"Do you see?" said Marcella, pointing to the small purple birthmark—a backward *L*, tipped over—at the base of Betty's neck. "If it was a dog that had scared her ma, that would look like a bite or a paw print. If it was thunder, she'd have a little thundercloud, black as night. But that right there? It'll never come clean, no matter how hard you wash it. That's the mark of the Rat Man's gun, just as sure as you're sittin' here."

Winnie O'Rourke burst into tears.

"Stop that," Marcella ordered. "*Now,*" she added, handing Winnie her napkin as Sister Sebastian's eyebrows lifted, two tables over.

Winnie nodded and hiccupped and buried her face in the grease-stained cloth, smothering her sobs as best she could.

Marcella shook her head. "Tender as a chicken," she muttered.

"Not *this* chicken," said Hazel, pointing at her plate.

I gave up trying to swallow. "This is chicken?" I asked Mary.

Betty clucked softly and beamed on us all.

"Any more questions?" Marcella opened her fist. The fly fell out, dead as a brick. "We don't have secrets in the House of Mercy, do we, girls?"

"I never asked—" I began, but she barreled right on, ticking off names on her fingers as she went along:

"Little Hannah Hogan there, her pa's in jail for slugging the landlord, and her ma couldn't feed seven children and gave 'em all away. Agnes Crouse's mother died of the galloping consumption—ain't that right, Aggie?—and the dad's a drunk. They all had typhus at the Mulroneys, except for Geraldine, and Lindy Buckley's pa was kicked in the head by a horse. Do you get the picture, Your Worship? That side of the table is for charity cases, like the two of you."

I dropped my fork and tried to lunge at her, but Mary pulled me back down. "She's only teasing, Julia. We're *all* charity cases."

"Speak for yourself," said Marcella. "There are three types of girls in this godforsaken place, as anyone with half a brain can tell you. Ain't that so, Hazel?"

I choked on a laugh.

"Shut up," said the half-a-brain.

The long-neck ignored us. She was counting on her fingers again. "Number one: lace curtains. Day students, like Miss Namby and Miss Pamby there." She pointed at a couple of girls with neat collars and rosy cheeks, whispering and giggling at the next table. Marcella sniffed. "They think they can walk on water. They learn their sums with the rest of us and go home to their stuck-up mothers and sit in their laps sipping tea from china cups with their pinkies in the air."

"We hate 'em," said Hazel.

"Even their *mothers* hate 'em," said Marcella. She

held up another finger. "Number two: salt of the earth. Paying boarders, like Hazel and me." Winnie peeped out—soggy-faced—from behind her napkin. "And Winnie," Marcella added, lifting her eyes to heaven.

"Who is it that pays?" Mary asked.

"What do *you* care?"

"I was only asking—"

"None of your business, that's who. Friends and relations. Who do you think? The whole world ain't in the Beggars' Brigade, for your information."

Mary held me fast. "Steady," she muttered.

"Number three," said the long-neck. "Like I said. Charity cases." She took in the lot of us with a sweep of the hand.

"And the laundry girls," Hazel added. "Ain't that four types, Marcella?"

"Ah, no, they only work here. You can't count the laundry girls. The Sisters don't even bother 'em with lessons."

"Why not?" Mary asked.

"Well, what would be the point? They teach you your two-plus-twos till you're fourteen; then it's straight downstairs to the scrub boards. Unless you get picked to go mind some rich lady's brats, like the famous Rosie Flannigan."

I looked at Mary. *Bloody hell . . .*

Marcella smiled serenely. "What's the matter, Your Majesty? Don't care for the turnips?"

Mary's hand was gripping my arm so tight, I could feel the bruises coming already.

Today was—what?—the eighth of September?

She'd be fourteen in a month.

October

Chapter 8

It didn't matter, I kept telling myself, as September ticked away. We'd be miles from here by October the eighth. Bill's sign would be coming any minute now.

Just a couple of weeks . . . a month, tops . . .

Still, the days were growing shorter—though the shorter they got, the longer they seemed—and dead leaves clogged the gutters, and our breath turned to smoke when they marched us to Mass on Sundays, two by two. And if the wind was out of the east, we could smell the bonfires burning, away across the river, where the hoboes camped.

Had I missed something somehow?

Look deeper, Julia.

Was there a sign of a sign?

"Never mind," Mary insisted, the morning before her birthday. "I'm sick of books anyhow. Gran read us all the good ones already, and she never went to school a day in her life."

But I saw her chin tremble—we were making our beds at the time—and though she turned away quickly, intent on her hospital corners, the early sun caught in the tear that rolled to the tip of her nose and hung there, shimmering.

Betty Brickey saw it, too. She reached over and lifted the drop onto her little finger (Mary brushed her away, but Betty ignored her), then carried it carefully to me and held it up like an offering.

Or a question?

I was no better at understanding Betty Babble than I was when I first heard it, but her eye-talk was clear as glass to me now: *Why is she crying?* That was what she was saying. And clearer still: *Make her stop*.

So I left, was what I did. I went to find Bill. Mary wouldn't have agreed to it in a million years, so I didn't bother telling her. He hadn't forgotten us; well, of course he hadn't. He didn't know we were out of time, that was the trouble. He wouldn't want me sitting around waiting for him while they turned our sister into some class of drudge.

I looked for my chance all morning, but it never came till half past one, when we were marching from the refectory to our afternoon meditation. And then there was nothing to it, really. I just dropped back to the end of the line, pretending to tie a bootlace, waited for the hall to clear, slipped around under the stairs, opened the back door—

And very nearly banged smack into Sister Gabriel, coming in.

"Julia? Goodness gracious! Oh my, you gave me a start. Slow down now, dear. Did you ask for permission to visit the lavatory?"

Thank God it was only the pigeon. "Yes, Sister," I lied.

She gave me a sharper look. "You're not feeling ill, are you?" She touched my cheek. "Your face is hot as fire."

"No, Sister, it's just—I need to go, is all." I danced a little to make my point. (Lucky for me I had a touch of bladder trouble and had wet the bed twice last week—mortifying at the time, but a great convincer now.)

"Well, well, go on, then. . . . And you too, Betty?"

Betty? I swung back around. Now where had *she* come from? I thought I'd made a clean getaway, but of course she was only a hop and a skip behind me.

"She doesn't need to go, Sister. Do you, Betty?"

Betty shook her head.

"You're only following me, ain't you?"

Betty grinned and nodded.

Sister Gabriel smiled. "I see. Well, isn't it lovely to have such a loyal friend? But even friends need their privacy every now and again, Betty. You come with me, like a good girl, and we'll just pop into the kitchen, shall we? Let's see if Sister Genevieve needs a bit of help cutting out the biscuits."

And as simple as that (not wishing to look a gift horse in the mouth, and knowing a miracle when I saw one), I was free and clear and out the back door and running right past the privy; I was ducking under clotheslines full of white sheets and orphan bloomers; I was hustling around the tumbledown buggy barn, where Hyacinth chewed his hay, and climbing over the rickety back fence—

Then climbing back over again, on second thought, and visiting the lavatory after all, making one less lie I'd have to be telling in my next confession.

I didn't know the address of Father Dunne's News Boys Home, but as soon as my boots hit Twenty-Second I spotted a scissors-grinder on the corner, so I hurried toward him and asked politely if he could point me in the right direction. He was a wrinkled old man, all in black, stooping over his pushcart, with a stovepipe hat and a stringy gray beard. He looked up—not at all surprised, as if he'd been expecting me. And then he winked.

"I'll tell you for a nickel."

"I don't have a nickel," I told him, and started to walk away.

"Never mind," said the man, smiling a broad smile. The sunlight danced in his eyes, so they looked all sparkly. "Father Dunne's News Boys Home, was that it?" He put his head to one side, sizing up my plaid. "Would you be looking for your brother, then, young lady?"

I said that I was—though I wondered how he knew—and he said, "Well, well, then, nothing could be simpler. Just keep going south, the way you're going, then turn right on Washington Avenue. Too bad you don't have a nickel; you could catch the trolley and save yourself a walk. You'll cross Jefferson and Beaumont and Leffingwell and so forth, before you get to Garrison. And there you are—the big brick building, right there on the corner. Just keep your eyes wide open and you can't miss it."

"Thank you," I said, and I turned to go.

But he cut me off. "Well, will you look at that? What

do we have here?" He reached behind my ear and pulled out a coin. "I thought you said you didn't have a nickel!"

He held it out to me.

I blushed red-hot—I wasn't a beggar!—and muttered, "No, thank you, all the same," and ran down Twenty-Second Street as fast as my legs would carry me.

Did I *look* like a beggar?

Anyhow, I'd never in my entire life paid a nickel for the streetcar. Bill had showed me how to hop rides when I was no bigger than a flea. We'd ridden all over St. Louis that way, crouching low on the rear platform so the motorman couldn't see us, and never had a minute's trouble, except for the odd policeman, shaking his stick. But the cops didn't bother themselves chasing trolleys, as a general rule, being mostly meat-and-potatoes men with the bellies to show for it, and not a soul gave me a second glance today. So I caught the first car that came clattering west on Washington.

Wait, now, not yet. . . . All right, J, get ready. . . . One, two, three—JUMP! That's the ticket!

And there I was, quick as that, zipping along to beat the band, past the plodders and the trotters and Cavanaugh's Quality Coal wagon and a glowering cigar-chomper in a fine yellow automobile, blowing his horn. And feeling like me again for the first time in weeks—Julia Delaney, her own true self, with not a nun in sight—and the wheels racketing under me and the trolley bell clanging away and the blue sparks flashing on the wire above, where the car sucked its power, and the sun on my face and the wind in my hair and the heart in my chest, pounding like thunder, and Bill waiting for me just ahead—

I'm coming, Bill! I'm on my way!

Even if he didn't know it.

The old man was right; you couldn't miss the place. Father Dunne's News Boys Home was an even bigger pile of bricks than the House of Mercy. It was newer-looking, too, and crisper around the edges, with dozens of tall windows and white paint on the trim that hadn't gone grimy yet.

There were a couple of boys in caps coming out the front door, with newspapers sticking out of the slings they wore over their shoulders, and three more going in, all with their slings empty. Bill wasn't one of 'em. Another boy—a scrawny little kid with his back to me—was tending a makeshift garden in a big box just beside the front step.

Though "tending" wasn't the right word, really. Whatever the flowers in it might have been to start with, they were stone-dead now, and he was making a terrible mess of his pruning job, hacking away at the lot of 'em with a pair of shears nearly as big as he was.

I was halfway past him (intending to go around back and see if there was any way to slip inside unnoticed and look for Bill), when I saw his crutch leaning up against the wall.

"Jimmy? Is that you?"

"Who else would it be?" he growled. He never lifted his chin but just kept slashing away, as if he was chopping the heads off his worst enemies.

"Jimmy *Brannigan*?"

He looked up now and blinked hard. I wondered if he needed spectacles.

"Don't you know me?" I asked.

"Sure, I know you. You're—"

He broke off there and turned his head quickly to the right, then the left. Then he stuck the shears back in the flower box, grabbed the crutch with one hand and my arm with the other, and pulled me around to an alley at the side of the building—not the busy side on Garrison, but a skinny patch of shade over the opposite way.

When he stopped to face me again, his eyes were shining.

"You're Bill Delaney's kid sister, that's who you are. Hot dog! So he changed his mind? I knew he would!"

"Changed his—"

"I told him I could help. I kept tellin' him and tellin' him. Even Mickey said I'd come in handy! But Bill said no, no, no, I was still too little. Can you beat that?"

"Mickey? Mickey Doyle?"

"I ain't little; I'm just short."

Bill was still hanging around with Mickey Doyle?

"I ain't any littler than you, that's for sure."

"Who are you callin' little?" I stood up straighter. "What are you, eight?"

"Who are you callin' eight? I ain't been eight for months!" He grabbed my arm again and started tugging me down the alley. "Come on, come on, we're late; the game started half an hour ago. We can still make the middle innings if we leave right now."

"Leave where? Leave here?"

"Well, what's the use of staying *here*? We're no good to 'em *here* when they're *there* already!"

My head was starting to swim. It was like that muddle of a story Gran used to read us—the one that always gave me nightmares—about that girl, Alice, falling down the rabbit hole. And everybody at the bottom kept thinking she was someone else, so they figured she knew what they were talking about, only she wasn't, and she didn't, and neither did I.

But Jimmy was in too much of a hurry to explain, and at least he seemed to know where Bill was, so I let him tug me after him as he hustled down the alley, hopping along on his crutch. You'd think it would have slowed him down, but it didn't; he was quick as any White Rabbit. He put a finger to his lips as we crept past the kitchen window (I could see the cook inside, polishing a pan), but nobody paid us a bit of mind. And then we were on our way again, going up streets and down streets and back around to Lucas, so that anyone who tried to follow would be as dizzy as I was, ending up on Grand Avenue, finally, where we caught the northbound trolley by the skin of our teeth. I tried to tell Jimmy he'd never make it with his bad leg, but he wasn't listening to a word I said. Just came flying, crutch and all—

One, two, three, JUMP!—

And when I pried my eyes open again, he was hunkered down right beside me, looking happy as Christmas.

Chapter 9

There was no use trying to talk over the clatter of the wheels, but at least now I knew where we were going. To the Browns game—well, sure! Hadn't I taken this same trip dozens of times with Bill himself? And with Papa, too, in the old days, but on the *inside* of the trolley back then, full up with fans and me so small he'd ride me on his shoulders, so I wouldn't be stepped on. We'd always rooted for the Browns, even when the Cardinals had a better record. The whole world had a better record, last I checked. But us Delaneys were American Leaguers, so we were regulars at the park on Grand, and I knew the routine as well as I knew my own name: Off at Dodier and a quickstep down the block to the big gate, then under the turnstiles when the crowd roared and the ticket man left his post to catch the score. . . .

Only before we ever even got to the gate, Jimmy pulled me over behind the flagpole.

"There it is," he muttered out the side of his mouth, tough-guy style.

"There *what* is?"

"Well, what do you think? The Chalmers, that's what!" He jerked his head toward an automobile parked directly in front of the entrance—a bright yellow automobile, at that—either the very one I'd passed earlier, with its horn blasting, or its identical twin.

"You mean the car?"

"Well, sure I mean the car! Mr. Egan's car, what else?"

My stomach clenched. *Curiouser and curiouser* . . . "You don't mean *that* Mr. Egan—"

Jimmy regarded me with pity. "And who else would I be meaning? Mr. Thomas Egan. The head Rat himself."

I looked again. There was a mountain of a man with a squashed-in nose leaning up against the auto's door, picking his teeth. Hadn't I seen him before somewhere? A long time ago, maybe . . .

But I shook my head. "That ain't Tom Egan."

Jimmy rolled his eyes. "Well, of course it ain't. That's just—ah, for thunder's sake, don't *stare* at him! Do you want to get us both kilt? I never said *he* was Tom Egan. Mr. Egan's inside, watching the game. That's just Fat Eddie, standing lookout."

Fat Eddie—that was it! "Fat Eddie Farrell?"

"Just like in the papers." Jimmy couldn't have looked any prouder if Fat Eddie had been his uncle the mayor. "He'll have you on his toast for breakfast if you look at him crooked. You see the scar over his left eye?"

I said I saw it, so what?

"That's from backing up Red Kane in the shootout at the Four Courts."

"Ah, you're full of it. It ain't, either."

"Is too. Mickey Doyle's old man saw the whole thing with his own eyes. There was people yellin' bloody murder and bullets flyin' everywhere and one of 'em ricocheted off the spittoon and—"

The words died in his throat. Fat Eddie Farrell was glaring our way, pointing his toothpick at us. "What are you kids jabberin' about? You think I don't hear you jabberin'? You're givin' me a headache, do you see what I'm sayin'? Go on, get outta here."

He didn't have to say it twice.

"And don't you come fiddlin' around this fine automobile with your sticky fingers," he yelled after us. "If I catch you so much as breathin' on it—"

But we were gone already, so we never heard what would happen if he did.

"It's a beauty, though, ain't it?" Jimmy said breathlessly as we ducked under the turnstiles. (It was clear he knew the routine just as well as I did.)

"What? The car?" I shrugged. "It's all right, I guess." Bill was the one who was crazy about cars. He could have named you every knob and dial and thingamabob. But I didn't have time for any of that now; it was Bill himself I wanted.

"Well, I should say it's all right!" Jimmy upended his crutch, snagged a bag of peanuts from a passing cart, and popped it in his pocket. "Mickey says a car like that costs two thousand dollars."

"Mickey Doyle don't know everything."

Jimmy shrugged. "He knows it if it's *worth* knowing."

"And you believe that? If he's so smart—"

But Jimmy wasn't listening. He was already dodging through the crowd ahead of me and slipping into the grandstand, slick as butter—and not the cheap seats, neither, but the one-dollar boxes, where the stuffed-shirts were sitting, as usual, watching the game through their fancy binoculars and booing the Browns' shortstop, who'd just lost an easy pop-up and was stumbling over his own feet, chasing it down.

"If Mickey's so smart—"

"Go suck an egg, Hallinan!" Jimmy's holler could have reached the moon. "Is that a mitt on your hand or your ma's old skillet?"

A lady in a feathered hat raised an eyebrow at us, then caught sight of Jimmy's crutch and blushed deep red. He saw her looking and beamed her a smile as innocent as an angel's—if angels had snub noses and gaps in their teeth—and the next thing I knew, she was poking the tall man next to her and he was nudging the stubby guy next to *him* and the whole row was whispering and poking and moving over to make room for the two of us—

And there we sat with the hoity-toities, pretty as you please.

And they were good seats, too, you couldn't deny that, just behind the dugout on the third-base side. Kind of took my breath away altogether, for a second there. We could see the wind bending the infield clover, the wad of tobacco in the pitcher's right cheek, the scrape on the Detroit batter's knuckles as he clutched the bat. Why, even Bill himself had never finagled us seats like these! *Just wait till I tell him*—

And then I came back to my senses. "If Mickey Doyle's such a genius—"

"Just *catch* the ball, boys!"

"How come he got himself arrested by his own father?"

Jimmy never took his eyes off the field. "Oh, that. That was nothin'." He took a peanut out of his pocket, put it on the floorboards under his seat, and cracked it with the tip of his crutch. "His pop was breakin' up the fight, that's all."

"You call that nothin'?"

"Well, nobody got convicted."

"You think that was *nothin'*?" Even my ears felt hot, remembering. They'd rounded up Bill right along with the rest of 'em and locked up the whole crowd till morning, and poor Gran had cried and cried. . . .

"Anyhow," said Jimmy, "it wasn't us that was askin' for it. It was some of them loudmouth Learys from the Bad Lands, with the cousin in the Nixie Fighters. You shoulda heard what they said about *Mickey's* cousin. And then they started in on the D and Ds! We couldn't just stand there."

"The D and Ds?"

"Come on, ump! That was right down the middle!"

"Who are the D and Ds?" I had to yell to make myself heard over the noise of the crowd, who didn't like the call any more than Jimmy did.

"Well, who do you think?" Jimmy pushed back his cap and stared at me. "D and D—for Doyle and Delaney."

I knitted my brow.

"Our *gang*, for thunder's sake. Don't you know anything?"

"Ah, go on. You ain't a gang."

"Who says we ain't?" Jimmy shouted. He cracked another peanut. "We're just as good as any of 'em. You don't see all them other fellers takin' on Mr. Thomas Egan!"

Unfortunately just as the words came out of his mouth, the crowd—who by this time had hollered themselves hoarse—got quiet as church mice, so the name "Thomas Egan" rang out for the whole world to hear.

Every last head in the one-dollar boxes turned around and stared.

Jimmy's eyes grew to twice their regular size.

But he was a quick thinker; you had to hand it to him. My stomach was seizing up again so I couldn't say a word, but he smiled and punched me on the arm like an old buddy and said, "Gotcha, Myrtle May! Ha-ha, ain't I a card? Takin' on Mr. Thomas Egan—now, there's a laugh!" And though it was the last thing *I'd* have done, he looked back up at the feathered-hat lady, who was still on his left, smiled her that homely angel's smile again, and said, "Excuse me, miss, but my sister here is afflicted with my-opey of the eyesight, and she's desperate to get a gander at the outfielders. She's got it bad for Bash Compton; you know how girls are"—I kicked him in his good leg but he went right on—"and I couldn't help noticing that those are very fine field glasses you've got there. . . ."

"They are indeed," said the lady, nodding gravely.

"And since they're so fine and all, I was just wonderin' if you wouldn't mind if she took a short look-see?"

"Oh, no, thank you," I began. "I don't really—you don't have to—"

Jimmy cut me off with an elbow to the ribs.

"Why, certainly," said the lady, still not smiling, exactly, but with a sort of upward crinkle to the left corner of her mouth that was at least first cousin to a smile. She started to lift off the strap from around her neck, where she had the glasses hanging, but it was caught in the back some way in a curl that had slipped out from under her hat, and while she was trying to get it untangled, a big, handsome black-haired man on her other side put his hand on her arm.

"Don't be silly, Cora. Can't you see they're a pair of con men? Her eyes look fine to me."

My ears got even hotter. "I never said—" I began, but Jimmy glared at me, so I closed my mouth.

The handsome man sniffed. "I doubt he needs that crutch, either."

"Not so much now," Jimmy agreed. "I'll likely chuck it in a month or two. The smashed leg's a bit shorter than the other one, but I think it's catchin' up." He stuck it out in front of him, hiked his knickers above his bad knee, and inspected the poor twisted limb with interest, the way Fat Eddie might size up a flat tire.

"Oh," said the handsome man. He'd gone gray in the face. "Well, in that case, of course . . ." He took out a spotless handkerchief from his shirt pocket and dabbed at the sweat on his moustache. "What I mean to say, that is . . ."

"What he means to say," said the lady, who had finally gotten her hair separated from her viewing equipment, "is that he's very sorry for the misunderstanding. Isn't that so, Daniel?"

"Hmm?" The handsome man was busy refolding his handkerchief in a perfect square. "Well, certainly if I had . . . that is . . . under the circumstances . . ." He cleared his throat.

She handed me the glasses.

At first I couldn't make head nor tail of the outlook through the eyeholes—just a blur of shapes and colors and then the sun itself, so bright it made me blink.

"Not up *there*," said Jimmy. "What are you pointin' at the sky for?" And he started to jerk 'em away, but the lady gave him a glance that shut him up good, and then she reached right across him and steadied my uncertain fingers with her gloved ones.

"You have to turn this little wheel on top," she explained, "until the picture comes clear. That's it. . . . Keep turning. . . . Do you have it now?"

"Yes, miss," I mumbled. "I've got it."

Sweet Mary and Joseph. Did you ever see the like? Our man Hawk had the ball again, setting up for his next pitch, and it looked just as big as the moon itself in his two huge hands, and his whiskers needed trimming and the wad of tobacco in his cheek was the size of a watermelon now and it bobbed up and down, up and down, when he chewed and—

"All right, all right, my turn," said Jimmy.

I held on tight. "But where's *Bill*?"

"Well, you won't find him on the field, will you? Slide over to your right—your *right*, I said—that's it, a little more now. Do you see home plate?"

I nodded.

"And the boxes just over it?"

"I see 'em."

"You're a hair too far, then. Go back toward first a little. That's it, right *there*—don't act surprised," he added in a piercing whisper, well nigh shattering my one good eardrum. "That's where he always sits when he comes to the games."

"What are you talking about? That ain't Bill."

"Well, of course it ain't; it's Mr. Egan. Ah, just give me the glasses, will ya? Look there, plain as day, between the senator and the two priests. The one with the cigar—do you see him now? The feller blowin' smoke rings."

I grabbed the glasses back. Ah, sure, I could see him now. My stomach went sour at the sight. But why should I give two straws about Thomas Egan? He was no friend of mine, or my brother's neither.

And then I took another look. There was Egan's pal the senator, all right; you couldn't miss him. If this was a parade, he'd be up front, marching. And nearer the aisle—why, that was Father Dempsey, wasn't it? Our pastor at Saint Pat's. And on *his* left—the other priest—the tall one with the jug ears—

"Ain't that Father Dunne?"

I was so startled to see him, I must have said it out loud.

"Father Dunne?" the hat lady repeated. "Is he here today?" She smiled for sure this time, both corners of her mouth at once. "Did you hear that, Daniel? These children are acquainted with Father Dunne!"

Jimmy gave me another warning look, so I kept my own mouth closed now, though I didn't see what he was so touchy about. The archbishop himself could be a Browns fan, for all I cared, as long as I found Bill. But I still hadn't spotted him. So I glued my eyes to the glasses and searched high and low, and meanwhile Detroit kept shooing St. Louis boys off the bases, and our side fumbled the ball like a hot potato straight from the stove, and the crowd was booing every Brown that ever drew breath and Jimmy was louder than any of 'em, when all of a sudden he jerked the glasses out of my hands again and trained 'em on Egan's box and said, "Ah, nuts, they were supposed to wait till the *bottom* of the eighth!"

"Who? Wait for what?"

I'd been so busy looking for Bill, I'd forgotten all about Egan and his buddies. But now Jimmy was peering that way again, muttering cusses, and even with bare eyeballs I could see some brand of commotion brewing. Something to do with that big feller there, galumphing down the aisle—

What was Fat Eddie doing inside the ballpark?

But it was old Ton o' Fun himself, no question, with a pack of policemen trotting just behind him, and Egan and the priests and the senator were standing up to see what the trouble was. And heads were turning and people were staring and no one was looking at the game anymore, and while everybody was talking at once and waving their arms and pointing up behind the stands, Jimmy gave me a nudge and whispered, "Let's go."

"Go *where*?" I wanted to know, but it was too late; we were already going there; we were on our feet and tearing out of the one-dollar boxes. Running like the wind, if the wind had hiccups, hop-hop-running, hopping, running—

We were halfway to the main gate before I saw the field glasses still clutched in Jimmy's freckled fist.

"Ah, for cryin' out loud, Jimmy, the binoculars!" I

yelled after him. "They'll think we stole 'em on purpose! Come on, we have to take 'em back!"

But he never stopped for a second. "Take 'em back yourself!" he hollered.

And then he slung 'em at me, and kept right on going.

Chapter 10

Hell's bells. *Now* what?

I stared at the glasses in my hands.

But there wasn't any choosing to it, really. If I didn't stick with Jimmy, I'd never find Bill. Who cared what the hat lady thought? So I slipped the strap around my neck and kept running, running, running, matching Jimmy's hop-step stride for stride, and pretty soon we were busting back out through the main gate into the slanting sun on Dodier Street—

—where we all but slam-banged into the crowd that had gathered there before us.

The backside of the crowd, that is. A solid wall of backsides—fed-up Browns fans leaving early, I figured—only they'd stopped short, for some reason, just past the exit, and were jammed together now, hemming us in. I craned my neck to get a glimpse of whatever the slowdown was, but I couldn't see a thing, though I could hear little snatches of talk:

"Did they get the whole gang?"

"Just the one. . . ."

"Pack of hooligans . . ."

"Wait till Egan . . ."

"Not *Tom* Egan . . ."

"I pity their mothers. . . ."

Oh Lord. *Whose* mothers were they pitying? I grabbed Jimmy's shoulder. "They don't mean—they couldn't—" I got it out finally: "They ain't talkin' about *Bill*, are they?"

"Well, what do you think? Leggo' me." Jimmy's eyes were so bright, they looked feverish. "They were supposed to wait till the *bottom* of the eighth."

I gave him a shake. "Stop saying that. You said that already."

But he shrugged me off—"I *told* you we're a gang!"—and started squeezing past the tall man in front of us. "S'cuse me, mister, s'cuse me, s'cuse me . . ." and the crutch worked its magic again; the crowd opened up just enough to let us slip through the cracks. And then we were standing on the curb, where more police were messing about, blue coats by the bushel trying to keep the peep-sighters back, and still more across the street, down the block a little, with a whole knot of 'em gathered around—

What?

I had to stand on my tiptoes to see. . . .

Oh no.

It was the Chalmers, wasn't it? The fine yellow automobile—Mr. Egan's two-thousand-dollar car—only now it was lying on its side like a dead bug, smashed all to smithereens, piled up in a heap against the lamppost on the other side of Dodier.

Oh no, no, no . . .

A couple of the cops bent over the wreck with crowbars, wrenching the steering wheel loose. The driver was still inside, then?

Oh dear God in heaven . . .

But it couldn't be him, it wasn't him, not him, I knew it wasn't—I couldn't say his name even in my head or out loud, neither, because I couldn't breathe, my lungs didn't have any air left in 'em—

Maybe it's Mickey, it might be Mickey, please, God, let it be Mickey—

But then they lifted him clear, and his cap went

tumbling, and there was his old curly head, red as ever. "Bill!" I shouted, finding my voice again, but he never heard, he never moved a muscle; his eyes were shut tight as coffin lids and his right arm just hung there, bent and bloody, dangling like a slab of bacon at Murray the Meat Man's.

I started to run. "Bill, it's me! Wake up, Bill—it's Julia—"

But before I'd taken two steps, a pair of burly hands caught me 'round the middle, and I was lifted clear off my feet, kicking and squirming. "Easy, missy; hold your horses. The boy ain't dead. Just knocked himself silly is all. And you there, Jimmy Brannigan, where do you think *you're* going? Get him, Greene—but mind the crutch! He'll be taking your head off with that swing of his. That's enough, now, Jim. Who do you think you are, Ty Cobb?"

Officer Doyle?

I kicked even harder. It was him again, wasn't it? Mickey's pop, the cop. And where was his great gutless wonder of a son this time, while they were carting my brother off like cold cuts?

"Bill!" I kept trying to yell, but it was only a kind of croak now; they were loading him in a wagon, and my throat was closing up worse than ever. *I'm here, I'm right here, oh please wake up! Where are they taking you? Oh dear God, Bill, what were you thinking? Open your eyes!*

And still Bill didn't budge, and the cop hands held me fast and the other hands held Jimmy, and while we struggled and sputtered, the crowd began to part and the chattering died away, and here came Egan and Fat Eddie and their pals, walking out through the gap: crooks first, and then priests and Senator What's-his-name.

But it was Egan everybody was staring at. The famous Mr. Thomas Egan. The Rat of all Rats himself, squinting at me in the sunshine, so close I could smell the smoke from his last cigar.

He just stood there for a minute, surveying the situation.

A halfhearted boo floated out of the ballpark.

A gust of wind knocked over a tin can and sent it clattering down the gutter.

Egan looked from me to Jimmy . . . to the mashed-in Chalmers . . . to Fat Eddie Farrell and his toothpick. And then he did the last thing I ever expected him to do.

He busted out laughing.

"Ah, no. Now, ain't this rich? Ah, Eddie, you big lug. We've been robbed by a gang of *midgets*?"

If I hadn't hated him already for half my life, that would have done the trick.

"We ain't midgets!" Jimmy hollered, but it came out in a high-up squeak, which only caused Egan to break out in fresh guffaws.

"Jimmy Brannigan?" Father Dunne stepped forward. "What in the name of . . . That's one of my boys, Officer; surely there's been some mistake."

"A mistake, is it?" Egan wheezed with laughter. "More like a miracle, Father. Will you look at the size of 'em?" He took out a rumpled handkerchief and wiped the tears from his eyes, then sighed and put it away. "A mistake, he says. Did you hear that, Eddie?" And then without warning he snatched Eddie's derby right off his huge head and started whacking him in the chest with it. "How'd they get past you, you great galoot? Did the little people tie you down? I leave you for—what? A few miserable innings? And before I can finish me popcorn, you're off waterin' the water closet and handin' out car-smashin' badges to a band of half-pint circus midg—"

"We ain't midgets!" Jimmy yelled again. "We're the D and Ds—that's for Doyle and Delaney—and it ain't your car in the first place 'cause you're a crook and a rat; you're all a bunch of rats!"

Thomas Egan turned around.

The wind was picking up.

It swirled the dust on Dodier Street and climbed the pole and set the flag to flapping.

Father Dunne took hold of Jimmy's shoulder. "Close your mouth, Jim," he said quietly. Then he looked at Egan. "The boy's nine years old, Tom. He doesn't know what he's saying."

But that was a lie. Jimmy knew exactly what he was saying, and the whole world knew he knew it. And anyhow, it was too late to take it back. At the word "rat," Egan's head had snapped to attention. Now he narrowed his blue eyes at Jimmy. "My, my. Ain't it a cryin' shame to be so misinformed?"

There were dogs in the Kerry Patch who'd smile at you like that, just before they sunk their teeth in your lip.

"Rat," Jimmy quavered.

Egan lifted his trigger finger and aimed it at him. "Father's right, sonny. Best watch that mouth. You wouldn't want me to lose my temper, now would you?"

Then he chucked Jimmy under the chin. "And all of us having such a grand time on this fine fall day."

And before Jimmy could work up a good spit (though I could see him trying), Egan turned back to Fat Eddie. "Midgets," he muttered, giving him another thump.

"We ain't—" Jimmy began, but Officer Doyle interrupted him. "These children aren't your ringleaders, Mr. Egan," he said, dragging me a step closer with his great steely mitts. "It was all the older boys' doing. They'll pay for their foolishness, I promise you that." He nodded toward the police wagon, already rumbling down the block toward Spring. "There's one on his way to the hospital right now."

"Is that a fact?" Egan reached in his pocket and took out another cigar. "Well, good riddance to bad rubbish. He had it comin'. That car's worth ten of his sorry—"

But I never heard the rest because of the roaring in my ears. My eyes went blurry and the world went red. And with one sharp elbow to Pop the Cop's ribs, I broke loose and flung myself at Thomas Egan; I lowered my head and charged with all my might into his flabby stomach. "Take it back!" I yelled, as best I could with my throat so thick and my nose running and the hot tears starting to spurt. "Take it back, ya big rat face! Bill's worth ten of *you*—"

"Oh dear God, it's his sister. . . ."

"Whose sister?"

"Can you breathe, Mr. Egan?"

"Well of course I can breathe; get off me, ya stupid—"

"Father Dunne?"

"Miss Downey!"

"*Whose* sister?"

"Oh, hello, Daniel. . . ."

"Stop that girl! She's stolen my binoculars!"

Chapter 11

Purgatory, the orphans called it. The Sin Room, where you paid and prayed. Just four square walls and a locked door—too big for a broom closet, too small for much else—in the cellar, below the kitchen, at the bottom of a narrow stairwell, directly across the laundry from the coal hole.

Marcella had told me weeks ago I'd end up here.

"Ah, you'll love it, Your Majesty. The old S. M. and C. The Sorrowful Mysteries and Corn bread. Hail Marys till you're blue in the face and no supper till you swear you've said 'em."

But then I wasn't really hungry.

I sat on the only chair, rubbing my arms. You'd

think it would be warmer in Purgatory. No doubt the laundry girls all roasted down here in July, but now the wind was kicking up again, creeping through the cracks in the plaster above the chamber pot in the corner, rattling the frame around the nailed-shut window. I'd stood on the chair and checked, first thing, but I couldn't budge it, or see through it, neither. Its panes were so thick with street dirt, I might as well have been looking through ashes.

If a person was walking past, up there on the sidewalk, one good kick of his boot might shatter it in a million pieces.

Was Bill awake yet?

There was still a glimmer of daylight pushing its feeble way in—unless it was the moon, or lamplight maybe, spilling down from the nearest pole. Surely it was hours since they'd hauled him off in the wagon and turned Jimmy and me over to Father Dunne. The priest had cadged us a buggy ride with the couple from the dollar box—Miss Cora Downey and Mr. Daniel Hanratty-Maguire—who appeared to know the whole crowd, somehow or other. We'd taken Jimmy back home to the newsboys' first, left him with the scowling cook, then come directly to the House of Mercy.

"She did *what*?" Sister Maclovius had thundered.

She was sitting in the wing chair in her office when we found her, reading the newspaper with a magnifying glass. Her left foot was propped on a stool, wrapped up like a fat cocoon. "She *stole*, Mister Han—" she began, half-rising. And then she winced, and clenched her jaw, and eased herself back in her seat. "You say she stole from you, Mr. Hanratty-Maguire?"

"She did," said the handsome man, standing beside me on the purple rug, chin in air, derby in hand, moustache all aquiver.

"Not on purpose," I muttered. "I never wanted the damn—"

"Wait your turn, Julia," Father Dunne warned me in a low voice. He was on my other side, his big right hand firm on my shoulder.

But now the hat lady was pushing forward, all in a rush. "Pardon me, Sister, but surely this is only a misunderstanding. I don't believe there was any theft intended. They're actually *my* binoculars—you gave them to me, Daniel; don't you remember?—and I had loaned them to—to Julia"—she nodded my way—"and her friend with the—that is, the little crippled boy. And then when all the commotion began—well, as she said, it was never her idea in the first place; if I'm not mistaken, it was the boy who was holding the glasses at the time. So you see, it wasn't really—"

"Say no more, Miss—?"

"Downey. Cora Downey."

"Say no more, Miss Downey." Sister's hands on the chair arms were gripping so tight now, her knuckles were white as chalk. "Don't be taken in by her excuses."

"Oh, but I'm not! That is to say, I'm only trying to explain—"

"Don't trouble yourself, Miss Downey. Excuses and explanations—they're one and the same. We don't hold with 'em here at the House of Mercy."

"But you don't understand—"

"I understand you perfectly. It's your kindness that clouds your judgment. A tender heart is the cross of the well-intentioned. But a girl of this type—a girl with a vicious streak—did they tell you she bites, Miss Downey? Well, suffice it to say, she wouldn't think twice about stealing your binoculars. She may look like a lamb, I'll grant you, but don't let yourself be fooled. There's a wolf under that sheepskin, with teeth to match."

"Oh, now, Sister," Father Dunne began. "I wouldn't say—"

"Well of course you wouldn't, Father. We all know you're the first to turn a blind eye. There's not a soul in

St. Louis who's unaware of your fine reputation in the blind-eye department. And far be it from me to say a word against your methods when it comes to your boys and *their* affairs. But here at the House, you see, Father, we find it's more perspicacious to look the devil in the face and cut off his horns. Isn't that so, Julia Delaney? We don't shilly-shally about with excuses and explanations. If we began saying this one has a temper because her grandmother slapped her, or that one steals because she learned it in the cradle—well, now, where would it all end?"

"Exactly," said the handsome man.

Father Dunne cleared his throat. "I see your point, Sister, as a general rule, but surely in this case—"

"In this *particular* case—" The hat lady's face was bright pink. "I scarcely think—oh, for heaven's sake, Daniel—"

"Say no more, Miss Downey," said Sister Maclovius. "Thinking will get you nowhere. I myself was a Mercy girl once. And if my betters hadn't taken me firmly in hand before my character was hopelessly misshapen and malformed by all manner of excuses and explanations—well, I *shudder* to think, that's what. I tremble at the thought, Miss Downey. There but for the grace of God . . ." She looked at me and smiled.

Even my bones felt cold.

I wasn't entirely alone in the Sin Room. All around me in the half-light, I could see 'em: saints and martyrs in their robes and halos, watching me from the walls. Saint Michael brandishing his flaming sword, Saint Francis blessing the birds, Saint Lucy with her eyes on a plate.

Gran had told us about those eyes.

The ancient Romans had poked out the pair of 'em, for spite, when Lucy wouldn't pray to their gods, but then the real God gave her a new pair, better than the first. So now all of her eyes—all four—were staring down at me, as if two weren't bad enough. No matter where I moved my head, the whole gang followed.

There's no use looking at me like that. You know I never meant to steal those glasses. Go look at Jimmy, that dope, or Mickey Doyle, if you can find him. Go look at Bill—he's the one needs watching. City Hospital—you can't miss him—the tall boy with the red hair. I have his lucky marble right here in my pocket—

The eyes didn't say a word.

I took out the moonstone and squeezed it in my fist. Ah, crikey, why'd I ever let him give it to me? Maybe if he'd had it with him today—if he'd only had a little luck for himself—

But he didn't, did he? Ah, Bill. Ah, crikey. . . .

I brushed away the tears with my knuckles. I should have given the damn marble to Father Dunne. He could have taken it to Bill at the hospital; he said he was going there from here. "I'll be back," he'd promised. "I'll stop by tomorrow to tell you how he is."

But tomorrow was a long time coming in the Sin Room, and four-eyed saints weren't the worst of it, neither.

The devil was the worst of it.

He'd been there all along, though I'd tried not to look at him, sprawled on his belly at the bottom of Saint Michael's picture—the dark angel himself getting stomped on by the bright one, kicked all the way from heaven to hellfire.

But not beat.

Not yet.

Only biding his time till his time came, with that sneer on his puss and his bat wings flapping.

Glaring up from the flames like he knew me.

I knew *him* all right.

I've looked you in your ugly mug before, remember? I saw you at the great World's Fair. You and your Rat friend Tom Egan. But I was too little to cut your horns off then, and Saint Michael wasn't there to do the kicking.

Another gust shook the window. Were those raindrops I was hearing now, drumming on the sidewalk, pattering like a million tiny feet?

Meet me in St. Lou-ee, Lou-ee . . .

"You don't remember the fair," Mary always said. "You were too young. That was ages ago."

But she couldn't see inside my head, now could she?

And somewhere in there I'm wearing a white dress, with lace on the sleeves like snowflakes. The Sin Room is gone, and behind my eyes it's summer back home. And here's Papa at the table and Gran by the stove; she's come four thousand miles to boss us; she's saying, *Ah, no, Cyril, the child should wear black for her poor mother. And who gave her those silly shoes? They're two sizes too small.*

No they ain't, I say, *they're grand shoes; the church lady brought 'em in the basket,* and Papa says, *Hush, for God's sake, Kitty, will ye all ever hush?* But Kitty is Mama and Mama is dead. *She's dead like the twins*, I tell him, and still he won't listen, he never listens anymore. He only looks at me all bleary-eyed and sits there, playing his fiddle—playing it and playing it and playing it—"Julia Delaney" and "Haste to the Wedding" and the one with the peculiar words he sings over and over: *"Ó's a Thomáis Bháin Mhic Aogáin, sé mo léan thú dhul i gcill"*—bowing and plucking till his strings break and his fingers bleed.

"You must have dreamed it," Mary would say whenever I tried to tell her. "You were four. You've only heard us talking, that's all. You just *think* you remember."

But four or no, there I am in the dress and the shoes, and our kitchen door's busting open, and here's Bill coming through it, fresh from sneaking into the Fairgrounds with Mickey Doyle. The pair of 'em chattering up a storm, bounding in to the table all lit-up-looking, like they've swallowed the moon. They've been to heaven and hell and the Streets of Cairo and ridden a two-humped camel; they've gone from the Galveston Flood to the North Pole and back again, and watched a horse poaching an egg. And after sights such as these they feel sorry, they do, for the poor misfortunates whose idea of a good time is stickball with the Murphy brothers. And that ain't even telling the half of it, they say. You have to see it to believe it, that's all.

"Then we'll see it, by God!" Papa lurches to his feet and lifts me out of my chair so suddenly, he knocks over the teapot.

And the next thing I know, there it is, rising up before us, like some great glittering city in a fairy tale, with towers and turrets and a huge wheel turning and turning in the sky over our heads. (Bill's head and Mary's head and Papa's and mine, that is; Gran wouldn't leave the kitchen, and Mickey Doyle had to go home when his ma hollered, and I was glad.) And there are lights twinkling, and music playing, and crowds of people jabbering away, and fountain after fountain shooting up sprays of water all the way to the stars.

"Is this heaven?" I ask Papa, but he doesn't understand, and Bill says, "No, no, this is just the dull stuff; heaven's over on the Pike."

And now my grand shoes are squeaking along the red bricks of the Ten Million Dollar Pike (and pinching my toes till the blisters come, but I never say a word), and here are the camels, just like Bill promised, chewing their cuds and braying like humpbacked donkeys, and a snake in a basket that flicks his tongue at us when a man toots a flute, and a bowlegged zebra, and elephants dancing—sweet Mary and Joseph, how the elephants do stink!—and a monkey in a cap who steals a rattle right out of a baby's hand, and runs away chittering.

Still they ain't what I'm looking for.

And then all at once I spy it—the head of an angel looming over a gigantic door—an odd sort of angel, with no arms or legs, neither, but a pair of wings so wide, they stretch clear across the sky. And in the shadow of those wings there's a man in a striped coat shouting at us: "This way to Paradise, ladies and gentlemen! See it now before you see it later! Don't miss the world-famous River of Death in the Great Here-After!"

"There it is, Papa! *There's* heaven!"

But he's looking in the wrong direction.

"Please, Papa, can we go?"

"Five minutes," he says. "Wait here."

And then he's gone, and we wait and wait and watch a clown play an accordion and listen to the shouting man shout till our ears are aching, and still no Papa. We can't sneak in the front gate, because there's a giant in a white hood guarding it, and the back door's locked tight, so we wait some more. And finally a sausage man walks by pushing a hokey-pokey full of sausages, and our stomachs growl so loud even he can hear 'em, and there's no use just sitting here, so Bill stands up and asks him if he knows where a person might be having a pint or two.

"In the Alps," says the sausage man.

"The Alps?" says Mary.

When he smiles, there's a seed in his teeth. "Do you see the mountains?" He points down the Pike. "There's a beer garden there."

So Bill and Mary take my hands and haul me to the Alps between 'em, though both my feet are throbbing like thunder, and sure enough, there's the beer garden smack in the middle, and there's our father in it.

We hear him playing and singing even before we see him: *"Ó's a Thomáis Bháin Mhic Aogáin"* again. But where'd he get the fiddle? This couldn't be his; he must have borrowed it from the bandstand there. He's playing up a storm on another man's fiddle and changing the words now, to boot, so they're different this time, without the peculiar sound to 'em:

Oh! Fair Thomas Egan, too bad you're going to hang,
Though no one but your mother dear will mourn ye;
If you were only sick in bed, she'd never mind at all,
But a noose around the neck will soon adorn ye.

And he's in fine voice, and it's a fine song, though why would they be hanging Mr. Egan? And *how* could they be hanging him, when he's sitting right there in the corner, smoking a fat cigar? I know it's him; the whole world knows it. Pop used to play his fiddle at Egan's Saloon. Sometimes he took me with him, and I'd dance on the bar for pennies, and if I did the jig proper, Mr. Egan would laugh and give me a silver dime.

Only he ain't laughing now, or hauling out his change purse, neither, and when Pop stops to draw breath there's a hush in the room. And then a huge man with a crooked nose grabs the fiddle away and grabs our father by the front of his shirt and says, "Go on with you, ye drunken fool. Do you want to get yourself kilt? What're you doing singing a song like that with Mr. Egan right there looking at you, for the love of God, and hearing every word?"

And I'm afraid he's about to slug Papa, so I latch on to the large man's leg and Mary gets him 'round the waist and Bill tugs on his arm and says, "Please, mister, let him alone, it's our pop, he didn't mean it; our mother died and he's out of his head; please let him go, mister."

But Papa's looking at Thomas Egan. "I meant every word," he roars. And he's struggling to get loose, but the man only tightens his grip. He's looking at his boss now, too—

Who raises an eyebrow . . .

And taps his cigar ash onto his plate . . .

And shakes his head just a little.

And then the big feller shakes his own big head—as if he finds this disappointing—and shakes the three of us off like flies, and says, "You're one lucky son of a duck, Cyril Delaney, with children such as these. And if you know what's good for all of you—the whole family, if you see what I'm sayin'—you'll count your blessin's and mind your tongue." And he turns our father loose.

Papa dusts off his coat sleeves and straightens his tie, though his fingers seem all stiff now for some reason. Not sure of themselves, like they were just a minute ago on the fiddle strings. So he gives it up finally, and looks at the three of us looking at him, and puts his hand on my hair. "Every word," he mutters. And Bill takes his arm—ever so gentle—and says, "Come on, Pop, let's go home."

But I start pulling him the other way. "Not yet, Papa! Don't you remember? You said we'd go to heaven. You promised."

"Hush, Julia," says Mary. "You don't know the first thing about it. It's only a boat ride, for pity's sake." And she yanks me toward her, trying to shut me up, while Bill keeps saying, "Please, Pop, let's go home."

But our father won't listen to either of 'em. "A

promise is a promise," he says. And he takes my hand and leads me out of the Alps, stumbling a little, and we retrace our steps down the brick street, all the way back to the door with the legless angel, where the Shouting Man is still shouting: "See the secrets beyond the tomb! Enter here if you dare, ye mortals! Ride with Charon the Boatman and have yourself the time of your afterlife!"

So we go to the ticket booth and wait for Papa some more, while he pulls the insides out of his pockets, hunting for nickels. His legs are all wobbly and he keeps dropping things, so Bill has to help him. And I can hardly breathe, thinking of heaven, so close now, and how Mama will smile when she sees us, and once we find her and the twins, we'll put 'em in the boat with us, and then we can take 'em home.

But when we go to climb aboard, it's the giant in the hood who's rowing, and he turns the wrong way and takes us straight to hell instead, with ghosts moaning and chains clanking and fire leaping and sinners shrieking and skeletons jumping out of nowhere and scaring us out of our wits. And wouldn't you know? When I pry my eyes open again, there's the devil himself, horns and all. He's pokin' a scrawny little feller with his pitchfork, over and over. He's roasting him on a red-hot spit and pokin' him till the sparks fly; I swear you can hear 'em sizzle. "Ye big bully," Papa growls. "Pick on someone your own size. And wipe that grin off your mug, or I'll wipe it off for you." But the devil just keeps grinnin' and pokin', pokin' and grinnin', and the next thing you know, Papa's jumped out of the boat; he's knee-deep in the River of Death. He's splashing through the black water till he's standing in the middle of hell itself, shaking his fist at Satan. "Where's Two-Bits, Thomas Egan? Where's the poor dead lad who trusted you? Why don't you kill me too, ye bloodsucker?"

So now Bill's clambering over the rest of us and out of the boat, and the giant in the hood's right behind him; they're both going after Papa, trying to drag him back. "Stop it, Pop!" Bill begs. "He ain't real; it's only a wind-up man!" But Papa never hears him. He punches the devil in the stomach, and the devil topples backward and falls into the flaming pit.

And while the Great Here-After is crashing and burning, Mary holds me so tight, I can't move, and all around us ladies in other boats are screaming like banshees, and more men in hoods come running and try to lay their hands on Papa, and he's punching right and left. "Kitty!" he's shouting now. "Dear God, where's

Kitty?" But no one will give him an answer. And finally they wrestle him to the floor and kick us out altogether, and that's the last thing I remember about the Fair: Papa smashing up hell, and never getting to heaven at all.

Chapter 12

"Pssst! Julia! Can you hear me?"

The straight wooden chair wasn't built for sleeping in, but I must have been sleeping in it anyhow. There was a sour taste in my mouth and a line of drool starting at the corner, when the voice at the Sin Room door made my head jerk up.

"Mary? Oh, Mary!" I was on my feet in a flash. "I'm here! I'm right here! Open the door; they've locked it from the outside—can you open it from there?"

"Shh! You'll wake the whole house!"

"Just open it, Mary! Try harder; maybe it's only stuck or—"

"I'm trying—I tried—it won't budge. It's not just

a latch; there's a keyhole, see there? Is there a key, Betty? There must be a key."

"Betty? Betty's with you?"

"Shh! She brought me here. The key, Betty—do you know where they keep it?"

A faint chuckling, rustling like the wind itself . . .

"Is she nodding?"

"She's nodding."

I could hear my heart beating—

And then the soft pad of footsteps, running away.

"Dear God," I whispered. "If they catch her—"

But they didn't catch her. And unless she had wings I didn't know about, she couldn't have gone far, because she was back in no time, and then the key was clicking in the lock and the knob was turning and the door was opening—oh thank heaven, it was open—and I'd have been out of there like a shot, but now Betty had me around the waist; she was hugging me so hard I couldn't move a muscle, and Mary was no better; she was pushing her way in and pushing us back and closing the door behind her.

"Ah, no, what are you *closing* it for? Let's *go*, Mary—"

"Will you hush for once in your life?" She gave me a shake. "Do you *want* 'em to hear you?"

"But we've got to go!"

"And where would we be going? It's the middle of the night, Julia! And raining fit to float the ark, in case you didn't notice."

"Ah, but—"

"They'll let you out tomorrow; Marcella says they always do. You only have to say you're sorry—"

"Ha!"

"And promise not to do it again. You can stand it till tomorrow, can't you?"

"No!"

"Sure you can. What's a few more hours? It'll be morning before you know it."

I lunged for the door, Betty and all, but Mary was still blocking it. "There's nowhere to go, Julia! You'll catch your death out there in the wet. Do you want to end up in the hospital with Bill? Is that what you want?"

I stepped back. She knew about Bill? "What did you hear? Did he wake up? Is he all right?"

Mary shook her head. "His arm's broken, for sure, and maybe a rib or two. But they say it could have been worse."

"*Who* says?"

"Everybody says. The whole House was talking. Sister Bridget heard it from Sister Gabriel, and—well, what are you asking *me* for? You should know; you were there, remember? Just like old times, the two of you, out gallivanting to ball games, and me wondering if you're dead in a ditch."

She was trembling all over.

"I'm sorry," I muttered. "I had to find him. I thought—"

"You didn't think. You never think."

Betty looked anxiously from me to Mary, from Mary back to me. Then she pointed to Mary's apron pocket.

Mary brushed at her eyes. "Well, eat something, anyway." She took out a lumpy parcel wrapped in a handkerchief: two rolls and a bit of sausage. A half an apple. A piece of cheese.

The smell of it made my stomach curl.

"Not hungry."

"Sure you are. You never had your supper."

"I don't want supper. I just want out of here, please, Mary; they'll put you in the laundry! We can go home; who cares if we get a little wet? We can stay in the tool-shed, remember? Aunt Gert never goes back there. She won't even notice. Just till Bill gets better—"

Betty pointed to the door.

Tap, thump . . .

Someone was coming.

Tap, thump . . .

Down the stairs.

Tap, thump . . . tap, thump . . . tap, thump . . .

And then it stopped.

Dead still.

Not a sound but the rain on the sidewalk.

Whoever it was, was listening.

Ten seconds. Twenty seconds. My chest nearly busting for want of a breath. Then—

Tap, thump . . . tap, thump . . .

Back up the stairs . . .

Tap, thump . . .

The kitchen door creaked above us . . .

And shut with a click.

"You see?" Mary whispered. "I told you they'd hear!"

"All right. I'll be quiet. Can we *go* now?"

"Go where? Go home? For pity's sake, Julia, you know we can't live in the toolshed!"

I opened my mouth to say yes we could, but before I could say it, Betty was tugging at me, her brown eyes big as bird's eggs. She was pulling me toward the door, then going back for Mary and grabbing *her* arm and tugging her, too.

"No, Betty, we can't—don't you understand?" Mary began, but it was no use. She couldn't stop two of us at once. No sooner had she got her arm loose than Betty had the door open and I was through it in a heartbeat, and there was nothing Mary could do but follow us into the great looming cave of a room on the other side. And the dark was even darker here, by the dim red glow of the furnace, and smelled of starch and sweat and soap cakes, and now we were running through the shadows past sheet presses and folding tables and flat-irons standing on the stove near their ironing boards and washtubs waiting on metal stilts, like four-legged spiders.

"What's that sound?" Mary whispered, taking hold of my elbow again.

"What sound?" I whispered back. But I stopped just long enough to cock my good ear and there it was, all right, a low sort of burring, buzzing, thrumming in the air around us, as if the walls themselves were breathing. *Saint Chris on a crutch . . .*

Then I saw Betty pointing to an alcove at the far end of the cellar, filled with narrow iron bedsteads, side by side. It wasn't the walls that were breathing. It was only the laundry girls, sighing and snoring in their sleep.

I looked at Mary looking at 'em. The sun would be coming up soon. "Happy birthday," I whispered.

"Thanks," she whispered back.

And then we were running again, chasing after Betty, who was already in the coal hole, waiting for us, waving us over under the window with the built-in coal chute, where the wagons dumped their loads. The bottom of the contraption was a good four feet over her head, but she'd pulled a stepladder out of the shadows, like magic—as if she'd done it all a thousand times before—and now she was humming a little tune while she propped it on the pile of coal beneath her.

"The *coal chute?*" said Mary, trying to drag me back again. "Ah, for the love of Mike, Julia—"

But I was up the ladder before she could stop me, and squeezing into the chute behind Betty, who was at the top in no time, shoving its lid open. The rain came blowing in and beating on our faces, but we didn't care a lick. And now we were scrambling up through the rusty porthole to the alley outside, and Mary was following, though it was a tighter fit for her; she had to push off from the ladder so hard that it went crashing down behind her. But she made it. We'd all made it. We were covered in dirt and coal dust, and the rain was streaking the whole mess down our cheeks and necks, but we were *out*, we were free, we were breathing the sweet, wet air, and Betty was laughing out loud and lifting her arms to the pouring sky and spinning around and around, until I couldn't help it, I had to spin with her; the puddles sloshed in my boots and froze my toes and set my teeth chattering, but I didn't care. We were out, we were free—

"Julia," said Mary. Just "Julia." That was all. She wasn't fighting us anymore, only standing there, watching us. But there was something in her voice that stopped our spinning. And I guess the string must have gone out of her legs then, or her bones had turned to butter; whatever it was, she seemed to just give way. She had her back pressed against the house like it was holding her up, but now she started sliding down slowly, down and down and down until she was sitting in the mud itself. And there was water in her eyes and streaming down her face, but of course it was raining, that was all; it was only the rain. Still—

"Mary? What's the matter? What are you doing, for Pete's sake?" I knelt down beside her and tried to pull her up. "Come on, now, let's go; they'll find us! We can't *stay* here, Mary—"

But I couldn't budge her.

"I don't feel so good," she said.

Chapter 13

"Ah, now, Julia," said Sister Bridget, "cheer up. It's not the end of the world. The doctor says it's only a mild case. Half the girls in the House had the chicken pox last month, and not a one of 'em died." She rolled up her habit sleeves, lifted a bucket of oats from the barn floor, poured it into Hyacinth's feed bag. And then she tipped me a wink. "I hear Sister Gabriel spoils 'em rotten in the infirmary. She'll have Mary feasting on pheasant and cream cake."

I didn't bother answering. I was too busy shoveling horse manure.

Sister reached for the currycomb and started working it over Hyacinth's hide. "So what do you say, Miss

Delaney, shall we make a bargain? No more running off every five minutes. The Strayaway Queen, the girls are calling you. Great gobs, the racket when that ladder fell! They say they heard it clear to the attic. Of course Marcella's dead jealous. You broke her record, did you know that? Even *she* never got out twice in twenty-four hours. And down in the cellar, Julia—sweet mercy!—we thought it was Armageddon!"

Which was why Sister Bridget's face had scared the wits out of *us*, appearing like an astonished ghost from the top of the coal chute. I never knew she slept in the cellar with the laundry girls! But lucky for us she did. If it had been Sister Maclovius who'd found us first, we'd be dead ducks.

"Not *intentional*?" she'd roared.

Betty and I had been all the way in the kitchen with Sister Genevieve, getting the soot scrubbed off, but even then we'd heard every word:

"Let me see if I'm understanding you correctly, Sister Bridget. You say they stole the key, broke out of the Sin—that is, the reparation room—confiscated the stepladder, and then climbed out of the coal chute . . . *unintentionally*?"

"Yes, Sister," said Sister Bridget. "That's it exactly. In a manner of speaking. Mary had taken ill, you see, and Betty only wanted to help, but—well, you know Betty—sometimes she gets things a bit muddled. . . ."

And by the time the half-a-nun was done explaining it all, the muddle had grown so massive and Sister Maclovius's gout was giving her such misery that she'd washed her hands of the lot of us and gone to soak her foot in salt water.

Leaving our punishment to Sister Bridget.

"I've got just the cure for the both of you," she'd told us when she'd brought us out to the buggy barn. "There's nothing like working with a good honest horse to clear a girl's head."

She was half-right, at least. Betty loved it out here. She had an arm 'round Hyacinth's patchy old neck now and was nuzzling his face and feeding him an apple, babbling soft Betty sounds to him while he chomped away. I didn't see Sister Bridget handing *her* a shovel.

Though I didn't mind, really. I hadn't forgot so soon who it was opened the Sin Room door.

But all of that was last night, when we were a hundred years younger. And today—well, we were stuck again, weren't we? Every one of us, like flies in molasses—Bill and Mary in their sickbeds and me and Betty in this smelly old barn and even the horse and the half-a-nun. (They just *thought* they were happy.)

And the rain was still raining and the wind had a whining sound to it, and the moonstone in my pocket was only a rock.

"That's fine now, Julia. That's lovely. Clean as a whistle. Just push your wheelbarrow over by the barn door, will you? We'll take it out when we're done, once this rain eases up. I imagine Betty's friend here will be wanting a stroll in the clover. Won't you, boy? All right, now, ladies, come and help me with his new hay. Try to spread it around the stall nice and even. That's it. That's the way. Careful, Betty, don't be getting under his feet there. And mind his tail end, the two of you! You don't want to startle this old fellow. He could kick you from here to thunder, if he cared to, though he'd never hurt a fly on purpose. Would you now, boy? Well, of course you wouldn't. You're a lovely horse, aren't you?"

Hyacinth blinked his rheumy brown eyes and made a sort of wheezing sound.

I heaved a small sigh. I don't know how anybody could have heard it; I hardly heard it myself. But the half-a-nun rested her pitchfork. "Now, now, none of that, Julia." She put a hand on my shoulder. "There's no need to be worrying. They'll take good care of them, I promise you. Your sister *and* your brother."

I fought down the lump that brought to my throat. What was she now, a mind-reader?

She studied her boots while I wiped my nose. And then she speared another forkful of hay and plopped it into the stall. "I'll tell you what we'll do, girls. We'll put Saint Hyacinth on the case. There's not a worry in the world you couldn't hand right over to him. You only have to ask, that's all. He'll have the entire family patched up in—oh, no, no, I don't mean the *horse*!" she added, seeing the look on my face. "*Saint* Hyacinth. The miracle worker. You've heard of him."

"No, Sister."

"The patron saint of those in danger of drowning?"

"No, Sister."

"The Apostle of the North? The Confessor of Crakow? Saint Ceslaus's brother?"

"No, Sister."

"Ah, well, that's all right." Sister Bridget went back to her hay-pitching. "You'd know him if you had a bit of Polish in you, like Betty and me. Isn't that so, Betty? We're both Brickeys, you see, Julia. Betty's father was my brother Harry—well, sure, you knew that already, didn't you? It's no secret. Your father and he were friends, you know. And a fine brother he was, too, no matter what you've heard. Brickey was Brickowski, of course, back in Poland, before our grandfather came to America. And then he settled in St. Louis and married my grandmother—she was a Walsh from County Mayo, and his sister married a Cullen from County Kildare, and later another sister came over and married a Doyle—ah, sure, they're all our cousins, and now . . . well, you know, half the Kerry Patch is kin to the other half. So here's our granny, you see, on the Irish side of the family, wearing the green and playing the harp on Saint Patrick's Day, while over on the Polish side here's our grandpa—our Dziadzio—always swearing by Saint Hyacinth. He used to say that he had cured him of his liver trouble on twelve separate occasions. Of course it killed him in the end, but not until he was nearly ninety. Don't be chewing on that hay straw, Betty. And even when he was an old, old man, if we asked him loud enough, he would tell us *the story*."

"The story?"

"The miracle story." Sister's eyes danced. "Oh my, it was marvelous. He'd wait for the darkest night of the year, or a rainy day like this one, when the wind was howling—do you hear that now? And then he'd sit in his creaky old rocker by the stove and put a finger to his lips—like this—and we'd gather close around him. And the clock would tick, and the fire would crackle, and just when we'd be wondering if he'd fallen asleep, he'd say three words real low and whispery: *Chop . . . chop . . . chop* . . . and our blood would start runnin' cold. Remember, Betty? Ah, no, what am I thinking? You weren't even born yet. It's the light in here, that's all. When it catches you that way, you look just like your daddy."

Betty grinned at us through the hay dust. Was *that* what Two-Bits Brickey looked like? If that was a gangster's face, I'd start eating hay myself. And what in the world did he ever do to get himself murdered on the church steps? The whole Patch knew his name, of course, but what did that have to do with Papa? Maybe Sister was thinking of someone else—

Chop . . . chop . . . chop . . . Betty's left hand stabbed the air, while her right hand tugged on the half-a-nun's sleeve. *Chop . . . chop . . . chop*. . . .

She was asking for the story.

"Well, all right, if you insist," said Sister Bridget, with a bogus sigh, as if she wasn't dying to tell it anyway. She sat right down on a bale of hay and tucked her legs under her like any five-year-old, and patted the straw beside her, so we'd do the same. "If you promise it won't give you nightmares. Do you hear me, Betty? I know how you love it, but you can't be getting all keyed up. This happened a long, long time ago, a million miles from here. And there's a happy ending, remember?" She leaned in closer and closed one eye. "At least, for *some*," she added. And then she dropped her voice to a whisper:

"*Chop . . . chop . . . chop . . .* From miles away you could hear the sound of the battleaxes falling, as the bloodthirsty Tartars came chopping right and left, and the heads began to roll. Like a cursed wind out of hell they came, leaving nothing but corpses in their wake, making straight for the ancient town of Kiev, on the bank of the River Dnieper.

"'Heaven help us!' cried the terrified townspeople as they huddled in their houses, trembling. 'Deliver us from evil, O Lord!'

"And still the hoofbeats thundered and the drums pounded on, and flaming arrows rained against the great wooden gates, and the skies grew dark with smoke and blood, as the Tartars breached the walls.

"*Chop . . . chop . . . chop . . .* 'To the church!' cried the quivering townspeople. 'The Polish priest will help us!' And they ran with all haste to find the holy man, who wasn't a full-fledged saint yet, being alive and all, but had traveled far from home to preach the gospel in this godforsaken city. 'Save us, good Hyacinth! The bloodthirsty Tartars are upon us!' And he looked up in surprise from the altar, where he was saying Mass, as usual, so rapt in his prayerful worship that he hadn't heard a thing.

"But now his kind heart filled with pity. 'Fear not,' he said. 'We'll go to the river, just as soon as I'm done here.' And the townspeople rolled their eyes at one another, being far less saintly than he was, and also having noticed on the way to the church that the river was having its annual spring flood. But Hyacinth never wavered. He finished the Mass as always, right down to the last Deo Gratias (which the altar boy just managed to squeak out before he bolted for the door), and then he took up the sacred ciborium with the Blessed Host, to guard it from the terrible Tartars, and began to lead his flock to safety.

"But just before they left the church, he heard a sweet voice calling to him: 'Hyacinth, my son, why dost thou leave me behind? Take me with thee and leave me not to mine enemies.' So Hyacinth turned around, of course, to see who it was had spoken, and lo and behold, there was no one there at all—not a regular mortal, anyway—only a statue of our Blessed Mother Mary, with the Holy Child in her arms. And the statue was twice as big as Hyacinth, and at least three times as heavy; no earthly power could have lifted it. But to him it was light as a feather. He picked it up as if there were nothing to it, and led the astonished townspeople to the river, with the Tartars right behind them, still up to their old tricks, jeering and drooling and waving their baleful blades.

"*Chop . . . chop . . . chop . . .* And sure enough, when they came to the riverbank, there was the mighty Dnieper in full flood, raging and tumbling and carrying off entire trees and houses. And the poor put-upon townspeople grew discouraged. 'We shall die now,' they sighed, and kissed one another goodbye, and asked Hyacinth to give them the last rites quickly.

"But the saint only smiled, and beseeched God's blessing, and our Mother Mary's blessing, too, and set her down on the bank beside him for just a minute. And then he stretched out his hands over the wild white waves. 'In the name of the Father, and of the Son, and of the Holy Ghost,' he commanded, 'be . . . thou . . . STILL!'

"And all at once the river *was* still—as calm as a summer millpond—and then not only still but as hard as stone: a great silver ribbon of rock beneath his feet. And Hyacinth led the jubilant townspeople to the other side, where they rejoiced exceedingly.

"But as for the bloodthirsty Tartars, when they ventured out to chase the crowd, the river became soft, soft, softer. It sprang to life once more. It woke with a vengeance and dragged the marauders away, shrieking and wailing, until they disappeared for all eternity in its thundering depths.

"And even today, they'll tell you in Kiev, when the sun is shining brightly on the Dnieper, you can still see the good saint's footprints on the quiet blue water.

"But if you're ever by the river at midnight, in the light of a bloodred moon, it's the Tartars you'll hear complaining, sniveling and moaning and gnashing their mossy teeth. And all around you in the darkness, everywhere and nowhere, there's the sound of the battleaxes falling.

"How's that go again, Betty? Ah, sure—*Chop . . . chop . . . chop . . .*"

"That's it to a T, Bridgie," said a deep voice from the open door behind us. "You tell it as well as the old man himself."

If I'd jumped any higher, I'd have knocked the roof clear off the place. But Betty and Sister Bridget were already turning around and smiling at the intruder. The intruders, that is. There were two: the policeman in front—Officer Doyle again? Was there any place he *wasn't*? And Father Dunne just behind him, closing his big umbrella.

But then he'd promised he'd come.

Chapter 14

I was off the bale so fast, the barn spun. "Is Bill— Did you see—" But before I could get the words out, Betty had run past me to Officer Doyle and was hugging him around his big blue-coated middle.

"Well, now," said the policeman, smiling down at her. "And how's my best girl?"

Betty grinned up at him with her slyest, crookedest grin, then commenced rifling through the pockets of his patrolman's jacket.

"Ah, no, Betty," said Sister Bridget. "Go easy there; don't be greedy. Uncle Tim's not made of jelly beans."

But Betty had already found a purple one, and then a yellow, and popped them both in her mouth. And then she saw me looking and popped the first one out again, and offered it to me.

"No, thank you all the same," I said.

The half-a-nun's lips twitched. "That's very generous, Betty. But she doesn't want to spoil her appetite; isn't that right, Julia? It's only half an hour till dinner. Have you had your dinner, gentlemen? I'm sure Sister Maclovius would be honored if the two of you—"

"Did you see Bill, Father? Did he wake up? Is he all right?" I knew I was interrupting, but I couldn't help it; once my voice got unstuck, the words poured out on their own.

"He's been better," said the priest. "He's black-and-blue all over, and lost a good bit of blood, and his left arm's fractured in two places. Still, he's a tough one, that brother of yours. They say it took three orderlies and the head nurse to hold him down for the morphine, when he opened his eyes and saw where he was."

My heart leapt. "So he *is* awake?"

"Well, he was, till they gave him the medicine. He was sleeping like a baby when we left him just now. But you don't have to worry, Julia. They never built the hospital that could keep Bill Delaney for long."

I should have said, "Thank you, Father," but it

wouldn't come. A sob came welling up out of my chest and strangled me all over again.

"You see, Julia," said Sister Bridget, "what did I tell you? He'll be out of there in no time. Whole as a fish, fit as a fiddle. And then—" She stopped and looked from the priest to the policeman.

And then *what?* I wondered. Why was everyone so quiet?

"And then all of this will be behind him," she finished. "Isn't that right, Uncle Tim?"

Officer Doyle cleared his throat. "I wish it were as simple as that, Bridgie. It's the juvenile court judge who has the final say in cases like these. But he's a good man. A fair man. Unlike some I could name. He'll take all the circumstances into consideration."

Dear God. We were talking about *judges*?

The officer was looking at me now. "And that's where you can help us, Julia, if there's anything you might be able to tell us—anything at all—about what happened yesterday. You'd be helping us to help Bill, you see, and the other boys, too. For their own protection."

Mickey, he meant. Mickey, his son. He wanted me to help him find Mickey. He didn't care a whit about Bill or the other boys.

It was only Mickey that mattered, wasn't it?

Sister Bridget knew it just as well as I did. She put a hand on the officer's shoulder. "You don't have to worry about Mickey, Uncle Tim. He can take care of himself."

Pop the Cop shook his head. "They fancy themselves a gang, there's the rub. No one gave them a thought when they were only a bunch of wild kids. But since this harebrained stunt with the car—no, Bridgie, I've got to speak frankly. I know she's only a child, but she was there; she needs to hear the truth. You understand what I'm saying, don't you, Julia? The streets aren't safe for these boys anymore, after the hornets' nest they've stirred up. Bill's one heck of a lot better off *in* the hospital than out of it. Don't they know there's a gang war in the works already? They'll be trapped, that's what, between the Rats and the Nixie Fighters. What in the world were they thinking?" Officer Doyle took off his police hat and ran his fingers through his gray hair, as if it was paining him somehow. "The D and Ds, for God's sake, thumbing their noses at Thomas Egan himself! I'm sorry, Father Dunne; I know the tune he's singing these days. We've all heard about his generous contributions to the widows and orphans. But d'you ever think who made 'em widows and orphans in the first place? This is a dangerous man, Father. He'd just as soon shoot you as look at you, if you get in his way."

"Or have one of his mugs do it for him," Sister Bridget muttered. "The almighty Mr. Thomas Egan." She picked a straw out of one of Betty's braids. "I hope he chokes on his own spit."

"Ah, now, Sister Bridget," said Father Dunne.

The half-a-nun blushed. "Excuse me, Father. Of course the boys were foolish. But great gobs, after the damage that man has done . . ." She broke off there, and drew Betty closer. "You know they only thought they were Robin Hood and his Merry Men, stealing from him who's robbed us all blind."

"Careful, Bridgie," said Officer Doyle.

"So we lock them up, is that it? For their own protection?"

The cop's jaw was set. "If that's what the judge says."

"And what if he says Boonville, Uncle Tim? You know the hard types they have there."

"Don't you hear what I'm telling you, Bridgie? There are worse things than Boonville, believe me. The farther from St. Louis these boys are, the safer they'll be."

"It's a reform school, Sister Bridget. It's not a jail," said Father Dunne. "The state doesn't mix juveniles with hardened criminals."

Sister Bridget heaved a sigh. "God bless you for

your faith, Father. But are you acquainted with the O'Banion brothers?"

Officer Doyle had turned to me again. "I'm asking you once more, Julia. You could be saving these boys' lives. If Bill ever mentioned a place, a name, if there's anything at all you can tell us . . ."

I shook my head. *Watch out for the con. . . .* "They'd rather be dead than locked up."

"Then they might get their wish," said Officer Doyle, looking me straight in the eye.

I must have made a gasping sound.

"*NO,*" Betty said, quite clearly. She stepped between us and pushed the policeman away, taking him by surprise, so he wobbled a little.

"It's all right, Betty," said Sister Bridget, pulling her back. "No one's trying to hurt Julia. They're only talking to her, you see? So they can find your cousin Mickey. You remember Mickey, don't you? Well, of course you do. He gave you your dancing shoes."

The creases in Betty's brow smoothed over a little. She stuck out a slippered foot, to show us. But then she latched on tight to my left arm, just the same, and hid her face from her uncle.

Officer Doyle cleared his throat again. He tucked a

braid behind Betty's ear. Then he studied his cop hat, dusted the brim, and put it back on his old gray head. "Well," he said, "I suppose that's all for now."

"You won't be staying for dinner?" asked the half-a-nun.

"Thank you, no. But of course if Father Dunne—"

"No, no, thank you, Sister," said the priest. "My boys will be waiting. Please give our best to Sister Maclovius."

"I will," said Sister Bridget.

Hyacinth gave a loud snort.

Betty raised her head.

"Well, now," said Officer Doyle, giving her a wink, "look who's puttin' in his two cents. Hello there, Hyacinth, old fella. Did you think I was ignoring you? Don't tell me you're lookin' for jelly beans too?"

Betty laughed out loud, forgetting her grudge. Then—tugging me with her—joined the cop by the stall, where he was petting the horse.

"Not *the* Hyacinth?" said Father Dunne.

"The one and only," said Officer Doyle. "You wouldn't know it to look at him now, would you?"

The one and only *what*? I wondered.

But Father Dunne was already at the barn door,

opening his umbrella, and Officer Doyle was just two steps behind him.

"Anything at all, Julia," he said again.

And then he and the priest both lifted their hats to us and walked out into the wet.

Chapter 15

But I didn't know where Mickey had gone, and I didn't give a rooster's rip, neither. He'd run out on Bill when he was knocked cold and bleeding; I hoped he'd gone to the devil.

Two nights later, in the newspaper Marcella had fetched from the trash pail, still reeking of the fish heads Sister Genevieve had wrapped up in it the day before:

CAR THEFT BUNGLED
OUTSIDE BALLPARK

THOMAS EGAN'S AUTO DEMOLISHED AS BROWNS LOSE YET ANOTHER

FOURTH WARD businessman Thomas Egan was rudely routed from his box seat in the American League stadium yesterday, when police entered the stands to inform him that his Chalmers auto-mobile had been wrecked by a gang of would-be car thieves.

The incident occurred at half-past three in the afternoon, in the thirty-six hundred block of Dodier Street.

Of the brazen delinquents, whose attempt at larceny ended abruptly when the car collided with a lamppost, only the driver, William J. Delaney, fifteen, was taken into custody. Immediately following his arrest, Delaney was moved to the City Hospital, where he is being treated for injuries sustained in the smash-up. Police say he is thus far refusing to name his companions, who remain at large.

Mr. Egan, well-known throughout this city for his many political interests, told reporters that he is "both surprised and saddened by the remarkable lack of judgment these heedless youths have exhibited." He said he is personally

> offering a reward of five hundred dollars for any information that leads to the apprehension of the rest of the gang.
>
> The Browns lost to the Detroit Tigers, 1-0.
>
> When asked if this unfortunate experience had dampened his enthusiasm for the St. Louis team, who are finishing their second consecutive season in last place, Mr. Egan, also well-known for his jocularity, said not in the least. He told reporters he was planning to return to the park for the doubleheader on Sunday. "I have another car," he added. "And I'll give another five hundred dollars—make that top-o'-the-line silver—to any Brown who can apprehend home plate."

"Would you do it?" asked Marcella, when I was done reading, by the dim yellow glow of the oil lamp. It was just before lights-out, and she was sitting with Hazel and Winnie on Mary's bed, since Mary herself was still stuck in the infirmary, and I didn't have the energy to kick 'em off.

I shrugged. "Do what? Hit a home run?"

"Ah, come on, Your Majesty, you know what I mean. Your brother's gang—tell the truth, now. For five hundred dollars, right there in your fist—would you give 'em up?"

"I would!" said Hazel. "I'd do it before breakfast. I'd take every red cent and ride the train to New York City and spend the rest of my life eating oysters with the Rockefellers."

"You would not," said Marcella.

"Yes, I would! Why wouldn't I?"

Marcella narrowed her eyes at the lot of us. "Because we don't do favors for Thomas Egan. Because he's the scum of the earth, that's why. Because he'll break your daddy's legs and torch your mother's house, if they stand up for the union. Don't you dare cry, Winnie. And the next thing you know, you're living with the nuns, reading the funny papers to a bunch of nitwits."

In the hall below, the clock struck nine. Orphans scattered to their rightful beds. Marcella lifted the lamp to douse the wick, before Sister Bridget's boots came tapping up the stairs. But first she turned and held it near me, so the light shone full in my face. "So would you do it?"

"In a pig's eye," I muttered.

What did she take me for, anyhow?

There were rules, if you were a Patch kid, strict as any commandment. We could rattle 'em off before we lost our milk teeth:

> Never throw rocks at a union man, or a boatyard boss, or his cousin, or anyone north of Biddle Street named Brophy.
>
> If you take what ought to be yours already, how can it be stealing?
>
> Look out for your own.
>
> Stick up for your mother.
>
> Don't swap at Doc Monaghan's unless you're desperate.
>
> And NO SNITCHING. EVER. Not even to priests. Better to die unconfessed and do your time in hell like a good sport than to shame yourself for all eternity by naming names.

Of course, it was true there was a bit of a loophole in that last one. If you *had* to clear your conscience, just keep it simple: "Bless me, Father, for I have sinned; it has been one hour since my last confession; I committed attempted murder, due to extenuating circumstances."

Not "Me and Spud Murphy knocked the stuffin' out of Jerry Sullivan 'cause the son of a gun kicked me cat."

But none of that changed the point of all points, the rule of all rules:

Never rat on a friend.

Or an enemy, neither, if he was from the neighborhood. Though that just got you a few years in Purgatory.

For traitors, hell starts NOW.

Still . . . five hundred dollars!

It made me weak in the knees just thinking about it. And I couldn't stop thinking about it. Lucky for Mickey I *didn't* know which rock he'd crawled under. All that endless October, every dull-as-dirt day, that bleedin' reward sat in my head, hissing at me: Hazel was right! She was right, wasn't she? Well, not about the Rockefellers. And who would eat an oyster on purpose? But the other part—the train part—oh, sweet mercy, if we had five hundred silver dollars jangling in our pockets, we could hop right aboard any train in Union Station and go anywhere in the world, wherever we wanted! Just the three of us—me and Bill and Mary, too (she'd been over her pox for a week now and was down in the laundry, drudging away; I wouldn't have any trouble getting her to come with us). Not New York City; I was sick to death of cities. Somewhere out West, maybe? "Home on the Range" . . . Papa used to like that one. He'd make us laugh when he sang it with his Edenderry accent—"*Ah, give me a hoom where the buffaloo room*"—oh, wouldn't it be wonderful? Far, far away out West, where the Rats would never find us. And then—why, then we could build our own house, couldn't we? And raise our own chickens—Gran always said you couldn't go wrong with a chicken—and eat scrambled eggs every morning and custard every night. And milk—we'd need milk for the custard, of course. . . . How much would a cow cost? I wondered. Never mind, we could afford it. We'd have to use our heads, was all, not go off half-cocked, like some people. Even five hundred dollars wouldn't last us forever. But once we got the cow, why, then we could *sell* some of the milk, and butter, and cheese, and ice cream—ah, sure, the whole world liked ice cream—and then maybe we could get *two* cows, and—

"Julia Delaney!"

I slammed shut the cover of my Big Chief tablet, where I was supposed to be doing long division, not drawing the sun shining on a house with a half-open door, and a chicken coop, and cows peeking over. But

Sister Sebastian didn't seem to have noticed my artwork. She wasn't looking my way at all, really, only calling out names from the list that Sister Gabriel—waiting beside her—must have just brought in:

"Agnes Crouse! Geraldine Mulroney! Hannah Hogan! Put your books away quickly, girls, and get your coats and hats from the cloakroom. Then report to Sister Maclovius in the front hall."

Ah, crikey. What now? I turned to the others, hoping for an explanation, but they kept their red-cheeked faces to themselves.

And then I saw Marcella Duggan leaning back in her desk, winking at me. She lifted her right hand in a salute. "Beggars' Brigade," she whispered, as the four of us trudged away.

Chapter 16

"Great jumping Jehosaphat," Geraldine Mulroney muttered as we clattered down Lindell Boulevard, packed tight in the orphan buggy, and lurched at last to a bone-rattling halt.

"Close your mouth, Geraldine," said Sister Maclovius. "You look like a mackerel."

And who could blame her? We were going in *that* place? Up that tall stone stairway, with the huge dark door at the top, and the ten-ton, mile-high, curlicued columns towering over it?

THE ST. LOUIS CLUB, the sign said in small, polished letters on the brass plaque attached to the hitching post. I hoped the members weren't expecting us anytime soon.

We'd be four to five hours just climbing the front steps.

"All right, then, ladies, follow me," said Sister Maclovius, once the half-a-nun had hopped down from the driver's seat, hauled her up, helped her out, got her safely on the sidewalk, and handed her her cane. "Thank you, Sister Bridget. And no slouching, girls!" she added, frowning down at the lot of us. "Chins up, now! Heads high! You have nothing to be ashamed of. These people are no greater than the least among you. 'And again I say unto thee, it is easier for a camel to pass through the eye of a needle than for a rich man to enter the kingdom of heaven.'"

So we were here to help squeeze 'em in, was that it? The Beggars' Brigade, for Pete's sake. Me and Geraldine and Aggie and Hannah Hogan, no bigger than a minute, and Betty, of course, holding tight to my hand. (She'd let out such a mournful wail when she'd seen us leaving in the buggy, the boss nun had breathed a long-suffering sigh and let her come too.)

And now we were trooping up toward the clubhouse in our itchy brown orphan coats, with Sister Maclovius leading us on—*tap-thump, tap-thump*—and Sister Bridget guarding the rear, so there was no escape. *Please, God,* I prayed, *don't let any of my old friends see me. I would die of mortification. . . .*

But just then a pair of crows flew over us, flapping—right over our heads, I swear—and I remembered: Ah, what was I thinking? It was the thirty-first, wasn't it? The thirty-first of *October*! Well, sure it was. I was safe for now. You wouldn't catch a Patch kid out of the Patch, today of all days. The whole neighborhood would be too busy carving the pumpkins, by this time, and building the bonfire on Carr Street, and getting out their ghoul clothes and bogey beards, like normal people. And smelling that grand smoky smell in the air—the Halloween smell—not so cold and plain in their noses, like this air here, like somebody scrubbed it with yellow soap, but . . . browner somehow, spicier . . . with the wind blowing the leaves off the mulberry trees by the priests' house, and the boys splitting apple boxes for the burn pile, and the barmbracks baking in all the ovens—you know the grans would be baking the barmbracks—the good warm loaves with the favors in 'em, for telling the future.

Ring for the bride-to-be, penny for riches . . . unless you swallow 'em first. Don't gobble so, Julia!

Ah, we'd never know the future without the barmbrack. . . .

"Good afternoon, Sisters," said the man at the top of the stairs, doffing his hat and swinging the door open for us. He was nearly as tall as it was, and decked out like a first-class swell, what with the hat and the gloves and the pearly gray suit with the tail to it.

"Is that the king?" Hannah Hogan whispered.

"I don't think so," I whispered back. "It ain't a castle; it's a club. He's prob'ly just the president."

But Sister Maclovius only nodded at him and marched on past, so we all marched right behind her.

And then we were standing inside, blinking, and every one of us had the fish-mouth now, because you never in all your life saw such a place as this. Sweet Mary and Joseph. You could've put a circus in here. I couldn't half tell you what all I was looking at, but whatever it was, there was plenty of it. Gigantic pictures in gorgeous gold frames and crystal lights hanging down from the ceiling and little naked angels standing tiptoed on three-legged tables, shooting arrows at one another, and a palm tree in every pot and a pot in every nook and cranny and then the whole shebang all over again, in eight or nine million mirrors. Not to mention *another* enormous staircase—this one right dead ahead—reaching halfway to heaven at least.

Hazel and the Rockefellers would have loved it.

But before we could even dream of taking it all in, a couple came hurrying across the marble floor toward us: another tall man and a lady in black (black dress, black hat, black feathers on it, with a little net half-veil hanging down) and both of 'em with their hands reaching out, all ready to shake ours. Smiling up a storm, too—well, the lady was, anyhow; you couldn't really tell about the man so much, with his moustache in the way—but even from a distance you could see *her* beaming, just like we were all old . . .

Oh dear Lord.

Oh no.

The handsome man and the hat lady? Mr. Hanratty-Ma-Who's-It and Miss Cora—Cora Downey?

Ah, sure it was, of course it was. Of all the rotten-imp Halloween tricks . . .

"Hello, Sister!"

"Good afternoon, Sister. . . ."

"Thank you so much for coming," said the lady. "And Julia—how lovely to see you again. To see all of you. Oh my, what a fine group. Wasn't it good of them to come, Daniel? And on such short notice!"

My face was so hot now, you could have fried an egg on it. And the other girls seemed fairly miserable, too—

Well, all except Betty, who took one look at the smiling lady, lit up with a happy grin herself, and threw her arms around her as if she'd found her only friend in the world.

"Oh my," said Miss Downey, gasping a little, but looking pleased at the same time—or as pleased as a person could look with the breath knocked out of her. "And who is this? Will you introduce us, Julia?"

"Her name's Betty," I began, but before I could add the "Brickey," Sister Maclovius was leaning in and looming over and aiming *her* smile at us—I could have told the lady that was never a good sign—and with her eyelid hopping again too, and a kind of purplish look to her. "Now, now, Miss Brickey," she said, trying to tug Betty away, "behave yourself; stop that at once. STOP THAT AT ONCE, MISS BRICKEY! I'm terribly sorry, Miss Downey. . . . Ah, for heaven's sake, Sister Bridget, she has hay in her hair. Will you see to your niece before she smothers the poor woman?"

"Oh dear," said Sister Bridget. "Come on, now, Betty. You wouldn't want to hurt the pretty lady, would you? Well, of course you wouldn't. That's right, now; that's better, isn't it? We shake hands; we don't squeeze the life out of people. . . . I'm so sorry, Miss Downey. It's only her way, you see, when she likes someone. Her heart—well, it brims right over. I think it's what they call 'unbridled enthusiasm'."

"Oh, no, no, please, I'm fine," said the hat lady,

keeping the grimy little hand in her own elegant gloved one, while Betty kept right on gazing up adoringly. "So you're a Betty, are you? Well, now. Short for Elizabeth? My favorite aunt was a Lizzie. And Daniel's mother was called Eliza—isn't that right, Daniel?"

The handsome man smoothed the corners of his moustache. "She was," he said quietly.

He'd backed up so far to make room for *our* Elizabeth, I'd almost forgot he was there.

And then the two of them led the lot of us to the foot of the second great staircase, where Sister Maclovius paused, looking doubtful.

It seemed even taller now, up close.

But when Mr. Hanratty-Maguire turned, and offered her his arm, she held her head high and took it.

Her eyelid seemed to be settling down some, too.

"Ladies and gentlemen," said Sister Maclovius, "benevolent friends and esteemed members of the Optima Petamus Society, let me begin by saying, in all humility, what an honor it is to be here today, by dint of your kind invitation, as we endeavor to fill the large shoes of Father Peter Dunne, who requested us to do so. . . ."

Geraldine snickered softly in the seat beside me.

". . . and to speak from our hearts—as would he, no doubt, had duty not called him elsewhere—of the plight of the motherless children of St. Louis, such as these you see before you. . . ."

So there we sat, and nothing to do about it, in the club inside the other club, right up front on the left, fiery-faced, staring out at a room full of rich people. Row after row of 'em, with the men all straight-backed and neat-whiskered, and the ladies right beside 'em (not counting the hat lady, who was sitting next to Betty, her hand still trapped). And all of 'em decked out in *their* hats and gloves, though they were older than Miss Downey, mostly—the ladies, not the hats—and tending more toward the hatchet-faced.

". . . the poverty . . . the ignorance . . . the moral degeneration . . . from which, at times, though it pains me to say it, we struggle in vain to shield them . . ."

It wasn't so awful as some things, I told myself. Like being boiled in oil, maybe. As long as you paid no attention to the pitying glances or the crawling feeling in the pit of your stomach. If you thought about the chickens, and the ice cream, and the good, warm Halloween barmbrack, and counted up all the baked-in favors again . . .

". . . and on that dread day, which ye know not, when the fateful hour is upon you, will you say to your Maker, 'Have mercy, O Lord. I once was a friend to—'"

. . . the penny and the ring, the old maid's thimble, the little paper boat, for traveling. . . .

"And so to conclude, with heartfelt thanks: 'Give and it shall be given unto ye. . . . The generous man will himself be blessed, when the mighty trumpet sounds. . . . And as you're drawing your last breath, may heaven swing wide its gracious portals and crown you for your kindness to the poor, whom we e'er strive to serve, and have always with us, unfortunately.'"

And then it was over—at least, she sat down, finally—once the rich people had finished applauding and the ladies were done dabbing their eyes. And I thought we had got through the worst of it.

But nobody had warned us about Mrs. Horace Merriweather.

". . . our musical guest today, admired by all who have had the privilege of hearing her," said the Optima Petamus president—he had taken Sister's place at the podium—not the man in the tailcoat from the front door, after all, but a little string bean of a feller with an enormous Adam's apple that bobbed up and down when he spoke: "And to our further (*bob*) delight, Mrs. Merri (*bob*) weather will be accompanied on the piano (*bob*) by Miss Cora Downey, who has recently become the fiancée of that fortunate (*bob, bob*) man, our treasurer, Mr. Hanratty (*bob*) Maguire."

I slid my eyes toward Geraldine, who had just made a small strangling sound.

So then the club members applauded again, and Miss Downey blushed a bit, and gave Betty a little wink so she wouldn't worry, and patted her on the shoulder with her free hand, meaning she'd be right back. And then she got up and went over to the piano, which was off to the right, just across from us, and sat down there to wait for Mrs. Merriweather—

Who came walking out slowly now from behind a palm tree and a purple curtain, put her hand to her heart, and bowed.

She was two or three times as big as Miss Downey, with the grandest bosom I ever did see, and red lips, and black hair, and her eyes sort of half-closed and dreamy-looking, so you knew she meant business. She just stood there for a minute, staring out over our heads, till I started to sweat a little. But finally she nodded at the hat lady, and waited for the music, and breathed in deep through her pinched-in nostrils . . .

and when she opened her mouth—oh my—you never heard such a marvelous racket. I only wished Gran could have been there. She always cried her eyes out over that style of singing when we had it in church. Not that this was "Ave Maria," exactly, but it was real loud and strong-sounding, and you couldn't understand a word of it, with that same type of wobbling on the high notes that sort of made your teeth ache.

And the crowd—why, they just loved it. They sat there clapping up a storm and hollering, "Brava!" when it was over, though they didn't stomp their feet, like they would have done back home, and Agnes Crouse got so excited, she forgot herself and whistled, and the Sisters didn't know who had done it and shook their heads at all of us, and Miss Downey peeked over her shoulder and gave us another wink, and Mrs. Merriweather smiled and bowed and held on to her bosom with *both* hands, and said, Thank-you-thank-you-so-much-oh-dear-me-you're-too-kind.

And then it was time for the second number.

We all knew this one right away, of course. The whole world knew "America the Beautiful." Sister Sebastian made us sing it every morning at breakfast, between the oatmeal and the Pledge of Allegiance. So when Miss Downey played the opening chords, we rolled our eyes at one another and sighed just a little, and sunk down an inch or two lower in our seats to wait it out.

And then Mrs. Merriweather came in again with her fine big wobbly voice:

O beautiful for spacious skies,
For amber waves of grain,
For purple ma—jes—steeeeeee . . . ste-steez . . .
Above the fruited—

What?

Purple *what*?

It was the pause that did it. The half a hiccup, when we all heard it sinking in on her. That tiny little crack in the middle of the wobbles, in the long, dying "steeeeeee . . . ste-steez . . ." when you knew she was thinking, *Ah, hell, I've left out the mountain.*

America! America!

Mrs. Merriweather was still up there singing away, but it was too late. There was no going back now. I tried not to look at anybody, I swear, but I couldn't help it. Eyebrows were shooting up all around me, and then—

oh Lord, there it was, a snort, a definite snort—I was staring at the carpet at the moment, so I couldn't say for certain it was Geraldine, but by the time I looked up she had a hand over her mouth, like she was fit to bust, and a tear sliding down her left cheek. And then there was Agnes, wild-eyed, in the seat right next to her. She was trying her best to hold it in, but there were pitiful little bleating sounds coming out of her nose and that was all it took—one snort and a couple of bleats, and then I was gone, too, and all of us were gone, and the entire Brigade was done for. We were giggling like loons, like a gaggle of geese, and no way to stop us. It didn't matter that Sister Bridget was shaking her head again, or that Sister Maclovius was fixing us with the eye of doom, or that Mr. Hanratty-Maguire and the Adam's-apple man looked like they wanted to kill us. It didn't matter that we were biting our lips and sticking our fingernails in the palms of our hands—at least, I was—till they were near bleeding. We'd get hold of ourselves for a second or two, and then Geraldine would wheeze out another "steeeee-ste-steez," and that would set us off again—Betty too, of course, and even tiny Hannah, though neither of 'em seemed to understand the pain we were in and just thought we were all having a wonderful time.

And it wasn't only us, neither. You could hear it spreading through the rest of the audience now—a gasp here, a choking fit there—one stricken Optima Petamuser after another, and meanwhile Mrs. Horace Merriweather kept right on singing, verse after verse—I never dreamed there could be so many of 'em—and by the time she got back around to the second set of shining seas, even poor Miss Downey was going under. She was still pounding away on the piano keys, but her shoulders were heaving and her head was bobbing and her little black hat feathers were shaking, like mulberry leaves in the wind.

Well.

If you thought the applause was loud after the *first* number, you should have heard it after this one. There must have been nine or ten times as much clapping and carrying-on, and a good deal of eye-wiping and nose-blowing, what with all of us being so glad Mrs. Merriweather had got to the end, finally, and hoping we hadn't hurt her feelings too much, and wondering if there might be even a whisker of a chance she hadn't noticed our situation. You couldn't tell for absolute sure and certain, because she was already back to bowing and heart-holding, only now there were little beads of sweat catching the light on her upper lip, and I suspicioned her smile had a clenched look to it.

But there wasn't time to be worrying about Mrs. Merriweather, because Sister Maclovius was standing up now. She was coming our way. She was bearing down on us like a steamboat with all the stacks smoking, and there wasn't any question about whether or not *she* had noticed. She'd left her cane behind her so as to have both hands free, and now she was pulling me and Geraldine out of our seats by an elbow apiece and hauling us over to the podium, where the president was standing again, leading the last of the applause and thanking "our gracious (*bob*) and gifted guest for delighting us yet again (*bob*)—"

But when he looked up and saw the two of us getting plunked down in front of him—still weak from fighting off the snorts, even while we were shaking in our shoes—he left off being delighted and peered squinty-eyed at us through his spectacles, while Sister spoke to him in a voice too low for even my good ear to catch.

"Oh yes (*bob*)," he murmured, as if she'd reminded him of something. And then he reached under the top of the podium to the shelf beneath it and took out—what *was* it he was taking out?—a couple of plates, it looked like, a pair of silver plates, so shiny you could see your face in 'em, and handed one to Geraldine and the other to me.

Were we having refreshments? I wondered.

The president turned back to the audience. "And now (*bob*), once again," he said, "let us re(*bob*)double our best (*bob*) efforts to help those who cannot help themselves. I give you the Mercy (*bob*) girls."

Still I stood there, staring at him, not understanding—

Until he reached in his back pocket, took out a ten-dollar bill and a couple of quarters, and dropped the whole mess in my plate: *clink, clank*.

Saint Chris on a crutch.

He didn't mean . . .

They wanted us to *pass* the plates?

I looked at Geraldine. She was froze up stiff as I was.

The audience applauded. Sister Maclovius smiled.

Well, let her smile.

I wouldn't do it.

I just wouldn't do it, that was all.

I would stand there till my hair turned gray and my teeth fell out, but I would *not* go trotting around that room like a dog itself, begging for whatever scraps the millionaires felt like tossing my way. I would not, I would never, not if they dragged me kicking and screaming. . . .

"There's a letter that came this morning," Sister Maclovius said quietly. She was leaning down between us now, so no one else could hear, her iron claws gripping the pair of us by our outside shoulders. "It was from a farmer's wife in Jefferson County; a Mrs. Lenahan, poor woman. It seems she's just given birth to her third set of twins in four years. And of course with help so hard to come by these days, and six small children to care for, she says she would be most grateful for the assistance of one of our girls."

Geraldine flashed me a look of stark terror—she was second from the top of eleven Mulroneys, after all—and then she wheeled around to face her side of the crowd and went straight to work with *her* plate:

Clink, clank . . . clank, clink . . .

Still I didn't move. I wouldn't move. *Go on, why don't you, send me to the farm with all the babies, what's so bad about babies? I ain't passing this damn plate. I will not, I will never . . .*

"Presuming, of course," Sister Maclovius whispered on, "that our laundry has a girl to spare, just now."

Our laundry?

Oh, dear God in heaven.

She was talking about Mary, wasn't she? It wasn't *me* she was threatening to send to the twins—

Clank, clink . . . clink, clank . . .

"'For he maketh his sun to rise upon the good, and bad, and raineth upon the just and unjust. . . .'"

And she was smiling worse than ever now, because she knew she had won and she knew *I* knew, and there wasn't a thing in the world I could do about it but take the bleedin' plate to the bleedin' rich people on my side of the room and pass it among 'em with my mouth clamped tight, *clink, clank,* went the coins, *clank, clink, clinkety clunk,* another ten and change from the handsome man, four dimes from a fat lady on his left, a whole fistful from Mrs. Merriweather, who gave me a look of pure pity when she dropped 'em in, and I thought again of the five hundred silver dollars and how they'd jangle in my pockets like music itself, and how quick I'd be on that train if I ever had half a chance, and Mickey Doyle had better stay lost if he knew what was good for him.

They gave us cake when the meeting was over. Miss Downey cut me a piece with her own hands. "It's coconut, dear," she said when I couldn't eat it. "Don't you care for coconut, Julia?" She looked worried about it for some reason, so I guess she had baked it herself, and I didn't mean to make her feel bad, but I couldn't help it; even the sight of it made me gag, so Betty ate it for me.

And then we were rattling back to the Bad Lands in the orphan buggy, finally, all of us just as mum as the grave, and not a soul daring to look at me—well, except for Betty, who was watching me like a hawk, as usual, and holding fast to my hand again (I'd kept it in my pocket till she started to cry, so I had to give it to her). But nobody said a word. Dark was coming on already. There were jack-o'-lanterns glowing in the windows on Morgan Street, and ghouls and goblins lurking about in the shadows; they grinned at us from the corners with their burlap bags, waiting to be filled. But we paid 'em no mind. Sister Bridget kept her head down and held tight to the reins, and Hyacinth clopped along, same as ever. And as for Sister Maclovius, she was still so disgusted with the lot of us that she didn't need to say a thing. You could feel it rolling out of her in waves, like coal smoke.

So when we pulled up in front of the House of Mercy, and I saw the ghost in the sheet on the porch, waiting for us, half-hidden behind the hibiscus, I could have told him he was wasting his time. He could have stood there calling for apples and nuts till he was blue in the face, for all the good it would do him. But it was too late; there he was, though no one else seemed to have noticed him, till we were up the steps and nearly to the door—

When he hopped out from his hiding place and hollered, "Julia Delaney!"

And that was when I saw his crutch.

Chapter 17

"Jimmy? That's you, ain't it?"

"Jimmy who?" said the ghost.

"Ah, for crying out loud," I groaned. "Jimmy Brannigan, that's who! I know it's you, ya numskull. What in the world—"

But I didn't get to finish, because Sister Maclovius had swung back around already and was coming right at him, shaking her cane: "Shoo!" she shouted. "Scat! Go 'way! Get off my porch, ye jackanapes! We'll have none of your tricks and your treats at the House of Mercy!"

"But Sister," said Jimmy, "I wasn't—I was only—"

"Only what? What were you only? Putting the horse

in the kitchen, like you did last year? Stealing the laundry off the line itself?"

"But Sister, I didn't—"

"Don't you but-Sister *me*, ye scoundrel! Off my porch before I pitch you off, or I'll call the police! And that better not be my sheet you're wearing!"

She was poking him with her cane as she spoke, backing him down the stairs, one step at a time. But he was game; I'll give him that much. No sooner had his boots hit the sidewalk than he came hopping right up after her again, waving a battered-looking envelope over his head and shouting as loud as his pipsqueak pipes would let him:

"S'cuse me, Sister, beggin' your pardon, I swear I wouldn't touch your horse, he's a grand horse, it's only a message for two of your inmates—please, Sister, I promised—I have a letter from City Hospital!"

Oh dear God.

My heart came crowding so fast into my throat, I could scarcely get a sound around it. "Bill!" I croaked, trying to fight my way back to Jimmy, but Sister Maclovius was blocking my path, and I couldn't say the rest: *What is it? What's wrong? Is he worse? It's Bill, ain't it?* And now she was taking the envelope from Jimmy's outstretched hand and there wasn't a thing I could do but stand there and watch while the wind went out of my lungs and the earth stopped spinning, and I don't know if my legs would have kept me up if Betty hadn't got hold of me again. But she did, so they did, and Sister lifted up the envelope at arm's length and squinted at it for a while, and then she took her spectacles out of some secret pocket in all those yards of black stuff and studied it some more—*Oh, for the love of God, come* on, *will you?*—and finally she turned it over and slid a fingernail under the flap and tore it open—slowly, oh so slowly—and stood there reading with her thin lips pursed, like she'd swallowed something sour.

"Hmmph," she said at last. It seemed like forever, but maybe it wasn't; you couldn't really tell with the world standing still. And then she took off her spectacles and took her sweet time folding them—one stem, two stems—and hid them away again, and looked me in the eye.

"It's for you," she said, and handed me the letter.

Tuesday Morning, Halloween

Dear Mary and Julia,

Well hello and how are you, in good health I hope, I am sorry for not writing sooner.

Sometimes its a puzzle finding a stamp around here but Jimmy's a good man. Anyhow never mind, no need to worry, everything will be O.K. just like I told you, the doctor says I am much improved so you see that's a good sign. Well I hear it might rain tonight no use going to the bonfire but by tomorrow we'll be saying well that's water under the bridge and if we're lucky it will be clear in time for the All Saints Mass in the morning, I bet by ten or eleven at the latest.

Sincerely your brother,
William Joseph Delaney

Well then.

All right, then.

I choked back the tears. He wasn't dying or anything; he hadn't taken a turn for the worse. He was better. Bill was better. *The doctor says I am much improved*. . . . So it was good news, the best news. Well, sure it was. I ought to be setting off firecrackers. It was only relief making me feel a little—well, limp, that was all. Sort of hollow in the middle, as if I was—oh, not disappointed, oh no, of course not, not with a letter from Bill himself right here in my hand. How could I be disappointed? Just—limp. Like the letter itself. A little smudged around the edges, with splotches spattered all through it, as if Bill had been in a hurry, writing.

Well I hear it might rain tonight no use going to the bonfire . . .

After all this time, he was talking about the weather? Surely there was more. There must be more—

"That ain't all, is it, Jimmy?"

But the ghost with the crutch was gone.

The whole House seemed limp that night. Not like Halloween at all. Not on the inside, anyhow—never mind the wind keening at the windows, and the rain pattering against the panes, and the candles flickering outside in the dark, in the hands of passing strangers. Never mind the rabble-rousers carousing through the streets, not a stone's throw away from us. Limp, was what we were. Too limp to care. And still we mumbled our rosary at supper, like always, and chewed something greenish, with lumps, while the gangster boys and the floozy girls laughed and sang and smashed bottles on the sidewalk, and shouted out cheerful-sounding curses, and Sister Gabriel's cheeks kept getting pinker, and Sister Sebastian's eyes kept burning blacker, until

Sister Maclovius broke off praying, finally "*—And lead us not into temptation*"—and thumped to the window and raised it—"Mind your tongues, ye pack o' pagans, or I'll tear 'em out by the roots!"—and slammed it down so hard, our teeth rattled, and thumped back to her place—"*but deliver us from evil, amen.*"

I don't know how long I lay awake that night, thinking about Bill's letter. I didn't have it with me to look at anymore. Sister Maclovius had slid it out of my hand on the porch before I half knew what she was doing. "I'll see that your sister gets it," she'd said. I might have fought her for it, if I hadn't been so limp. But I didn't. It was Mary's letter too.

Besides, I had it in my head already, splotches and all.

Well hello and how are you, in good health I hope. . . .

Had Mary read it yet? I wondered now, as I lay there staring at the ceiling. I hadn't seen her since breakfast. Sister Bridget had told me they'd be working late in the laundry tonight, since they'd have tomorrow off, for the holy day. Even laundry girls weren't allowed to work on the first of November. But I'd see her when I woke up, anyhow, once this rain was done spitting. She'd be walking to church with the rest of us, if it cleared up in time—

. . . for the All Saints Mass in the morning . . .

And then—

Why, by then—

Oh, sweet mercy.

Sincerely your brother . . .

And I sat straight up in my bed then and I wasn't limp anymore. My heart was pumping and my head was exploding because I understood—ah, sure, all at once I understood—well of course, of course anyone could see it blindfolded, and how could I have been so thick? And thank God the other girls were dead to the world already and didn't hear my bare feet hitting the floor by my bed and run padding past them in the slant-walled room, out the dormitory door and down the stairs—I was quiet as a creeping cat, quick as a flea—and in less than a minute I was down, down, all the way down and tiptoeing past Sister Maclovius's office, where a line of yellow light still showed under the door, but I held my breath and she never heard me, and then I was creaking open that old creaky door in the kitchen and scurrying down to the cellar, down and down through the dark again, past the tubs and the tables and the red-glowing furnace, all the way to the alcove where Sister Bridget and the laundry girls were snoring away, same as ever. And I knew Mary right off, from her Mary-shape lying there, with one arm flung over her head, and the good warm Mary-smell of her, and thank God she didn't yell bloody murder when I shook her by the shoulder, but only opened her eyes and sighed. "Ah, for pity's sake, Julia, what now? Are you sick?"

"The letter," I whispered. "Get the letter."

And she got it—oh, thank heaven—it was under her pillow, right next to her ribbon and her rosary—and then she slid out of bed herself and followed me from the alcove and across the laundry and back to the Sin Room, which was luckily empty of sinners that night, at least until we got there. And in that dusty half-light from the streetlamp out the window, she turned around to me and folded her arms. "You'd better be dying of something," she whispered, "because if you're not, they'll kill us."

"Just look," I whispered back, snatching the envelope out of her fist and the letter out of the envelope. "Look again, Mary! Look what he's saying—" And I shook it at her, and pointed, and read along with her:

Tuesday mOrning HallOween

Dear Mary and Julia,

Well hellO and hOw are yOu, in gOOd health I hOpe, I am sOrry fOr nOt writing sOOner.

SOmetimes its a puzzle finding a stamp arOund here but Jimmy's a gOOd man. AnyhOw never mind, nO need tO wOrry, everything will be O.K. just like I tOld yOu, the dOctOr says I am much imprOved sO yOu see that's a gOOd sign. Well I hear it might rain tOnight nO use gOing tO the bOnfire but by tOmOrrOw we'll be saying well that's water under the bridge and if we're lucky it will be clear in time fOr the All Saints Mass in the mOrning, I bet by ten Or eleven at the latest.

Sincerely yOur brOther,
William JOseph Delaney

"You see?" I whispered. "I knew it! The sign—" I could hardly breathe. "He promised to send it, and he's sent it!"

"What sign?" Mary's eyebrows puckered. "You're seeing things, Julia. It's just a letter, that's all. There's nothing there but words."

"But it's not only the *words* that matter! It's what's hidden inside 'em, don't you see? Look there—all those perfect round *O*s—"

"You mean the splotches?"

"They ain't splotches. They're moonstones!"

"Moonstones?"

"You remember—my birthday present—the one Bill gave me . . ." I reached in my pocket and pulled out my lucky marble. The magic was in it again. It was cold to the touch, as smooth and white and comforting as a good front tooth. "Just look—he even *says* it: *Sometimes it's a puzzle . . . so that's a good sign. . . .* A *sign*! Ah, come on, Mary, don't you understand? When did Bill ever give a hoot if it cleared up for Mass? Why, anybody might've read that letter! He couldn't just spell it out plain in a place like this, with nuns galore poking their noses in."

Mary's eyes were round as Bill's little ink moons. "But what on earth does he mean by it? What's he trying to say?"

"He's waiting for us, that's what! Well not yet, not tonight—*no use going to the bonfire*—but in the morning, that's what he's telling us, at the meeting place, just like always: *that's water under the bridge . . . ten or eleven at the latest* . . . Oh, Mary, just *look*—he's got it all in there—it has to be the sign!"

Mary didn't answer right away. She took her sweet time, thinking it over, reading the letter again, syllable by syllable, squinting so hard at it that there were two deep furrows between her eyebrows, exactly like Gran's.

And meanwhile Halloween wasn't even half-gone yet; it was only just getting warmed up. I could still hear the rowdies howling away out there in the streets above us, hollering and laughing, cursing the sun and the moon and themselves and one another and the pavement under their feet for pitching so. . . .

"Ah, for the love of Mike, Mary, *say* something!"

At last she sighed, and folded the letter, and put it back in the wilted envelope. "I guess we'd better start packing," she said.

Chapter 18

But we had to get through the night first.

There was no use packing in the pitch-black, I told her—no use packing at all, for that matter. We couldn't just walk out the front door in broad daylight, lugging our boxes. And we had to wait till daylight. We didn't have a ghost of a chance of getting out till then. The whole House was locked tight after dark now; even the coal chute had a latch on it.

"But we can't wait till morning, Julia. If they see us running, you know they'll stop us."

"Only we won't *be* running! It's All Saints', remember? We'll be walking to church with the rest of 'em. That's closer to the bridge, anyhow; it's practically on our way. We just march in the same as ever, you see, and wait for communion, when the line splits. And then we mix in with the crowd, and slide over to the side door—"

"—and slip out while they're all still praying?"

"Easy as pie."

Even Mary had to admit that it wasn't such a bad plan, really, seeing as how it was the only plan we could think of. Still, it was hours till sunup; we'd better try to get some sleep, she said. So she tiptoed back to her bed in the alcove, and I tiptoed upstairs to mine, though I knew it was purely useless. I was sure I could no more sleep than fly to the moon.

But I was wrong. I must have been wrong. I didn't think I was sleeping, but maybe I was, because all the wrong people kept walking in and out of my head. . . . The scissors grinder took a coconut from behind my ear, and Mrs. Merriweather sang a song about a shortstop, and then there was a loud *bang!* like a firecracker going off—*What was that? What was that noise?* And I thought I woke up then but maybe I didn't—

Oh God, it's them, it's the bloodthirsty Tartars. . . .

Ah, pipe down, Your Majesty, you're dreaming again. . . .

But I heard 'em!

Quiet, ladies. . . .

Why are the nuns here?

They're counting us, that's all. . . .

They always count us when the police come. . . .

Did Jimmy put Hyacinth in the kitchen?

Jimmy who?

Go back to sleep now, Julia. . . .

And then it was morning. Real morning, with sunshine pouring in the window, and all the bad dreams over and done with—not just for now, neither, but forevermore and always—and me so full of what was coming that I thought the whole world would see it in my face. But no one noticed a thing—except Betty, maybe, who couldn't know what was up, of course; she hadn't heard a word of any of it and wouldn't have understood even if she had, would she? And yet when I fumbled my buttons, getting dressed for church, and made a hopeless tangle of my bootlaces, there she was with her brown eyes, watching me, her head cocked to one side, as if a little bird was singing in her ear.

"Don't stare so, Betty. You're making me nervous. I can't do a thing with you staring at me like that."

But then her grin faltered and her eyes filled, and my throat went thick because it only that second came to me: Ah, crikey, I'd never see her again, would I? Not after this morning. And I hadn't expected it, but my whole chest ached all of a sudden, so I gave her a hard hug and said, "Ah, no, now, Betty, don't cry; I didn't mean it. I didn't mean a thing by it. It's just these—these laces, that's all; they're nothing but knots. How'd you ever get yours so neat? Come on, now, what's your secret?" And then she was all smiles again. She brightened right up and showed me. She undid her own lumpy laces and tied them from start to finish, though it took her quite a while, and I followed along, step by step. And finally we were both ready.

So of course by the time we got downstairs, everyone else was there before us, though they weren't lining up by the front door like I expected, or getting their coats and hats from the cloakroom. They were standing in a great clump in the hall, whispering among themselves and waiting for—for what? For something or other. Not their morning mush, I told myself; we always fasted before Mass. So then—

What?

I caught Mary's eye and she shook her head at me, but I didn't know what she was trying to tell me. She was away on the other side of the crowd, too far for me to take her meaning.

"What's up?" I whispered to Marcella, who was leaning against the banister across from me, next to Hazel and Winnie, and looking bored to death, as usual. "Ain't we going to church?"

Marcella shrugged her shoulders and studied a hangnail on her left pinkie. "Not unless they catch the murderer first."

Winnie burst into tears.

"That ain't funny, Marcella," I said, glaring at her to ward off the cold feeling in the pit of my stomach. "You shouldn't tease about a thing like that."

Marcella arched an eyebrow. "And who says I'm teasing? Did I say I was teasing?"

"She ain't teasing," said Hazel, leaning in darkly.

"You heard it yourself, Your Majesty. That racket in the middle of the night, remember? That wasn't just kids playing pop guns in the alley. That was some mug from the Nixie Fighters getting himself shot."

"Shot *dead*?"

"Dead as a hammer."

"A h-h-hammer," sobbed Winnie.

Marcella heaved a sigh and handed Winnie a handkerchief. "So of course the nuns are all up in arms, and the cops are all over the place, and now we'll never get out. We'll be stuck in here till we rot, holy day or no.

Look there—d'jya ever see such a boatload of sour-pusses?"

She pointed across the hall to the door of Sister Maclovius's office, which had just opened to let out another crowd: the nuns and Father Dunne and three policemen—though not Officer Doyle, for once—and all of 'em looking fit to spit nails.

Thump! Thump! Thump! went the cane. "Silence!" Sister Maclovius thundered, and there was silence, quick as that. "All right, then," she began. "As some of you no doubt will have heard by now"—she let her scowl fall on each of us, eyeball by eyeball—"there was a disturbance last night, outside this house—a shooting, the police have informed me—resulting in the unfortunate, if unsurprising, demise of one our local criminals. Should his friends, if he has any, still wish the pleasure of his company, they can find him in the city morgue."

"What did I tell you?" Marcella muttered.

Thump! Thump! went the cane. "SILENCE!" said Sister Maclovius, pointing it directly at the two of us. "'Whoso diggeth a pit, shall fall therein.'"

And why would she be looking at *me*, when I hadn't done a thing yet?

"Be that as it may," she went on, her eyes still

narrowed, "though I have assured these good officers that at the time of the crime in question, all residing within these walls were safely abed; still we at the House of Mercy will be delighted, of course, as always, to assist the police department howsoever we can. If there should be those amongst you, then, who noticed anything—in anywise—last night, of a light-shedding nature, you are to report to my office immediately after Mass, which our kind friend Father Dunne has offered to celebrate here in the chapel, due to the inadvisability of leaving the House, at present."

Marcella cocked her other eyebrow at me. I was white as Jimmy's sheet, most likely. It felt as if every drop of blood in my head had gone crashing to my boots. Could we have worse luck?

"What's the matter?" she whispered.

I paid her no mind. I was searching out Mary again. *What now?* I tried to ask her with my eyes, but she was still too far away to talk to and it was too late anyhow; the Sisters were already herding the lot of us down the hall to the chapel door and I was swept along with all the others and there was nothing to do but pray, so I prayed, *Dear God in heaven, Bill's waiting at the bridge, you know he's waiting, you've got to get us out of this, just get us out of here and get us there please, God, and I'll never bother you about anything else, I swear, I'll go to Mass three times next Sunday but not now, dear Lord, I can't go in there now. . . .*

That was when I felt the big hand on my shoulder.

"Julia," said Father Dunne.

So I turned and there he was, and he had Mary with him too, and now he was taking us aside, to the right of the door, while the crowd parted again and trooped around us into the chapel. And even the cops tipped their hats as they passed us by. Even the nuns—even Sister Maclovius—left us alone. They gave one another sideways glances and nodded respectfully at Father, but they all kept moving and went inside without a word.

And now my heart was pounding again, and Mary had me by the hand and was squeezing the life out of it, but I didn't mind, and neither one of us made a peep but only stood there, waiting for whatever it was Father Dunne was about to tell us—

But all he said was, "Right after Mass, girls, will the two of you come to the office? I'll need just a bit of your time. No, now, don't look so worried; it's not as bad as that. Just a bit of your time, that's all."

And then he was gone too. He was through the door and in the chapel with the rest of 'em, and for one second, two seconds, three and change, Mary and I were alone in the hall, staring at each other.

"What do we do now?" I asked her.

"Run," she whispered.

And then we were running, we were flying, we were tearing down the front hall where we'd first come in, like a story reel playing backward, past the empty classrooms and the beanstalk roses and the sad-eyed pictures with the fiery hearts. We were out the front door, which God himself must have unlocked for us, or maybe it was all the policemen going in and out but we didn't stop to ask. We only held on tight to each other's hands and took out like hell's blazes down Morgan Street, right past another clump of cops milling about by their cop wagon and a lady with a little dog in a shopping basket and a boy on a bicycle and another one on stilts—stilts, for Pete's sake—and a feller in an apron sweeping up broken glass in front of Kelly's Entertainment Parlor—"Watch it, there! What's your hurry?" he hollered when I half-tripped over his broom—but we didn't answer. We just kept running and running all the way to the trolley stop at Twenty-First, where a car was pulling away in front of us, just that minute. "Now!" I shouted—"One, two, three, *jump*!" and we jumped, both of us jumped—the trolley clattered on the tracks below and the blue sparks showered from the line above and we held hands and jumped and we made it, we made it, we were out, we were free, and even Mary was smiling.

And we crouched low on the platform, panting for breath, and hanging on to each other for dear life, and only when we were safely under way did we turn around to look back—

And there was Betty, running after us, too far behind to ever have a hope of catching up, getting smaller and smaller in the distance.

Chapter 19

Ah, no, Betty . . . Ah, hell . . .

Go back! I tried to tell her. I stood up on the platform and waved my arms at her: *Go back! You have to go back!* But Mary pulled me down again, before the motorman saw me.

"She'll be all right, Julia. She's not two minutes from the House. Sister Bridget will be looking out for her, like she always does."

I gritted my teeth, trying to believe it. "I know," I said. "I know she will."

But the ache was there again, just under my rib cage, and I was shivering, all of a sudden. "Ah, crikey," I muttered. "We forgot our coats, didn't we?"

"Are you cold?" Mary asked.

"Aren't you?"

She shook her head. "I put on all my old things under my orphan clothes, you see?" She pulled back on her collar, to show three more layers of collars beneath it. "Since we couldn't pack, remember? I'll give you half, first chance we get."

And I looked at her again then, really *looked* at her, and saw—good Lord—she was twice her normal size, wasn't she? Plump as a partridge under the old brown plaid, with a bit of mashed-in lace sticking out at her throat. She must've been wearing every last thing Aunt Gert had put in her box, and her Sunday best, to boot. Her arms felt thick when I poked 'em, stuffed in her sleeves like sausages, and her pinafore—tied tight over the whole kit and caboodle—looked fit to bust at the seams. And now there were little beads of sweat popping out in a fine mist all over her face, and little damp curls plastered down at her temples, as if it was July, not November.

No wonder she hadn't missed her coat.

"It doesn't show too much, does it?" She tugged at her collars again, trying to get a bit of breathing room. "I know I look big as a house, but there's no one but Bill to see, and I don't care if he teases. It's only for a little while, till he takes us wherever he's taking us. He'll have enough to do, I figured, just feeding us all, without having to worry about our clothes, besides."

She seemed so anxious about it that I didn't say what I was thinking: that she looked like a mattress with the tick about to split. I told her it was a fine idea, and I wished I'd thought of it myself, and no one would ever even notice. (Which maybe a blind man wouldn't, so it wasn't *all* a lie.)

And meanwhile the trolley kept clattering east, closer and closer to the river, deeper and deeper into the Patch: past the dime museum on Twelfth Street and the billiards parlor across Eleventh, past the boys on the corner by the Ninth Street newsstand, smoking like always; past Mr. Patrizi, whistling away at his sidewalk stall, putting out the potatoes, as usual, as if this was a day like any other and we'd never been gone at all.

Was it really only two months now? Had all the clocks in the world stopped ticking?

Not long enough, anyhow, for us to forget our way to the bridge, though we couldn't really see it yet, traveling backward. We hung tight to our roost in the rear of the car till we bumped beyond Broadway to Fourth Street, where the tracks turned, and then we hopped off and took ourselves straight ahead down Morgan to the riverfront, which hadn't changed a bit, neither. There were the same grimy old warehouses between Second and First, by the River Arcade and Pawn Shop; the same grumpy old Doc Monaghan, scowling down from his throne in the ticket window with his beady little eyes; the same greasy old hash houses and bars in every alley, with scraps of ragtime tinkling out when the doors swung open—even on All Saints', at nine in the morning—to let in the dockworkers who weren't needed today and the steamboat crews, in between trips, while the stragglers from the night shift staggered by us on their way out, and a man in a top hat started singing—

Oh! You beautiful doll,
You great big beautiful doll . . .

And all at once there was a long, piercing whistle, and the ground under our feet began to shake, and it felt as if the air was shaking too, and then a train was thundering by just ahead of us, on the tracks along the river.

"Look there!" I shouted to Mary, running past her and pointing. A girl in a straw hat was peering out from one of the train windows—right straight into my eyes, as if she knew me. "That'll be us, one of these days now."

"Not if you get yourself crushed to death," said Mary,

catching up as quick as she could—she waddled just a bit, in her mattress getup—and yanking me away.

But I waved at the girl anyhow, and she waved back.

And then I thought of another window, and another face looking out at me. A little round moonface with a crooked grin, crossing its eyes. And there it was again—that ache, like a bruise I couldn't stop mashing.

Ah, Betty. Ah, hell. . . .

Was she home yet? I wondered. Was Sister Genevieve letting her help with the biscuits?

But there wasn't time to stop and think about it. The train was past us now, rattling north, and before our ears were done ringing with the roar of it, there was the ferry whistle shrilling at the landing on our left, and the Mississippi River dead ahead of us, shining so bright in the morning sun, it hurt to look at it. And the whole grand, gleaming span full of big boats with their smoke-stacks smoking and little boats bumping along in their wakes and great flat barges hauling all manner of who knew what; you could smell some of it better'n you could see it: peanuts, for sure—I wished I had some now—and apples and cigars coming in; and barrel of beer after barrel of beer, and shoes by the crate going out, and vast, glistening piles of coal, and long blackened logs from the creosote plant upriver, with that sharp burnt-tar smell that always gave me a peculiar feeling in my stomach; I never could remember why, but I couldn't think about that, neither, because there it was—oh, there it was—looming over us on the right: the great Eads Bridge itself, rising out of the water like a river dragon in one of Gran's stories, a monstrous big dragon with its stone legs planted in the riverbed, and a steamboat chugging under its middle, and another train clattering right through its belly—look there! You could see it plain as day through the steel ribs, while crowds of people and automobiles and horses and buggies and slat-sided wagons and even a couple of streetcars rode its back. And all of 'em acting as if there was nothing to it—the people, not the streetcars—though it gave me the willies to watch 'em, strolling along up there with their parasols or leaning out like fools over the walkway fences or posing together in clumps, while one of their friends took pictures or pointed to something far away. And wasn't that the man in the top hat who'd sung about the doll? He stopped and tipped it to a kid riding past him on a bicycle—but how in the world did Mr. Top Hat ever get up there so fast? I bet he set all the records for the footrace, back in his school days. Or maybe I was wrong; maybe it was another man who looked just like him. You couldn't see his face clearly from way down here.

But where was Bill?

Oh, where was Bill?

I craned my neck to see if I could get a glimpse of him anywhere. He might *be* anywhere, was the thing; he might be coming from any direction. City Hospital was a good two or three miles, at least, but if he'd got away from there yesterday, he'd have crossed the bridge, like as not; the fellers generally went that way when they had to make a run for it. I'd tried to follow 'em there myself, a time or two, but Bill had always caught me and dragged me back. East St. Louis was too rough for girls, he'd said. Didn't I have better sense? He'd skin me alive, he swore, if I tried it again. . . .

"Do we just stand here waiting out in the open, then?" Mary asked. "For the whole world to see?"

I broke off craning my neck. Well, of course she wouldn't know; she couldn't, could she? She'd never been to the meeting place. She was never one to tag after the boys. "No, no, this way," I said, shaking my head and taking *her* by the hand now, pulling her after me to the bottom of Lucas Street, in the shadow of the bridge itself, to a door in a brick wall that jutted out from an old warehouse by the railroad tracks, on the near side of the dragon's far right foot.

"It's locked," said Mary, rattling the knob. "Are you

in there, Bill? It's us! It's Mary and Julia!"

"It's still early," I told her, when there was no answer. "He'll be here any minute. He'll have the key; he always—"

But I didn't get to finish telling her that he always carried it with him, because just then there was yet another ear-splitting whistle, and another train roaring past, even closer this time. So we held our hands over our ears to shut out the noise as best we could—it was easier for me, I suppose—and squeezed our eyes shut, too, to keep out the thick clouds of soot and sparks blowing back from the engine.

And when we opened 'em again, once the last car had rattled away and the smoke had cleared and the earth was done trembling, Mickey Doyle was standing alone on the other side of the tracks, looking right at us.

I don't know how long we stood there staring back, not saying a word. All the sound in the world had got sucked right out of it, somehow. Not a sparrow cheeped. Not a church bell chimed. Not even an eyelash batted.

And then my stomach growled.

Mary blushed bright red. "For pity's sake, Julia."

"What's *he* doing here?" I muttered.

But there was no use asking her what she couldn't rightly know, when she was too busy being mortified to answer. No way to tell which was harder on her, my noisy belly or her mattress situation, but her cheeks were shining like a pair of Rome apples and the sweat was beading up all over her face now, and dripping into her eyes, until she had to stop and fish for her handkerchief in her outermost plaid pocket—I figured that was what she was doing, anyhow—but nothing was there, and God knows *I* hadn't thought to bring one. So she wiped off the wet with the cuff of one of her sausage-sleeves, as daintily as she could manage, and the two of us just stood there waiting some more while Mickey Doyle came unfrozen too, finally, and stepped across the tracks to us.

"Hello," he said. "I'm sorry," he said. "I guess you're waiting for Bill, aren't you?"

"Yes," said Mary, though *her* mouth must not have been working any better than mine, because it came out more like "yase," kind of strangled and foreign-sounding.

"I'm sorry," he said again. "I came as quick as I could."

Shut up, shut up! I wanted to scream. *Stop saying you're sorry; who cares if you're sorry?*

"You're shivering," he said. "We should go inside." And he reached in his pocket and took out a key—

Is that BILL's key? I wanted to ask him. I'd have knocked him down for it right there, if I could have moved. If I hadn't been well-nigh mute and rooted to the ground.

"It'll be a bit warmer out of the wind," he said. And he put the key in the keyhole and opened the door, and put his hand on my shoulder to try and guide me in, but I jerked away as if he'd burned me with a red-hot coal because who needed him, anyway? I could walk through a door without *his* help, when it was all his fault in the first place. Where was *he* at the ballpark when the chips were down, when my brother was knocked out bleeding in a smashed car? And where was Bill now? Oh, where was Bill? Why was Mickey here and Bill wasn't? Why couldn't he be where he was supposed to be, for once in his life?

But Mary only turned a shade or two redder and let Mickey show *her* inside without the least objection, as if they were just stepping into the Ritz for a cup of tea, or dancing a reel or two at the Waxie's Dargle, though he'd have to be daft to be thinking *she* needed warming up, what with the sweat all but dripping off the tip of her nose. And what was the matter with her, anyhow? Hadn't I told her that he was no better'n a chicken-livered traitor? Surely I'd explained it to her, hadn't I?

Well, if I had, she hadn't been paying attention, because there it was on her face now: that look—the sucker look—the one half the girls in the Patch used to get any time Mickey Doyle flashed his dark eyes in their direction or favored 'em with a smile. *Get ahold of yourself!* I wanted to shout at her. *Watch out for the con, for Pete's sake!*

Though he wasn't smiling now, was he? Oh dear God, why wasn't he smiling? Bill was coming; he was still coming; he would be here any minute. It was early yet, remember?

So I followed the two of 'em inside and we stood there blinking in the shadows, while feeble shafts of light sifted down from the gaps in the roof, a million miles over our heads. It wasn't much warmer in here, after all, wind or no wind—it was only a meeting place, not a staying place—and dark as dungeons, to boot, though I'd have known it blindfolded just the same, from the moldering sawdust smell of it. They used to store lumber here, Bill had told me, back in the bridge-building days, and bricks, too, and mortar-making supplies—you could still see the gigantic tubs where they'd mixed it—and wheelbarrows and cans of whitewash and crusty old spades and picks and shovels and all manner of rusting junk. I'd never known where the key had come from in the first place, but before I could get my mouth open to ask Mickey how *he* happened to have it, there was a pounding on the door—

"Bill!" I cried. And I swung around to run to it, but Mickey grabbed my wrist with one hand and put a finger to his lips with the other: *Don't move, don't say a word,* he was telling us, and I blushed that he'd had to remind me. Well, sure, I knew better. You couldn't just throw a door open without checking first. It could be anyone, the police even, his own father after him. Or the Rats—oh Lord—it might be the Rats; Egan's Saloon wasn't but a few blocks over, and—

"Hey, Mick! Are you in there?" a pipsqueak voice shouted. "It's all right; it's me—it's Jimmy! Open the door, will you?"

Ah, crikey. . . .

"Jimmy who?" Mary whispered.

"Come on, Mick, open up; I know you're in there! I heard the whole thing down at the newsstand! Don't worry, it ain't a trap; they never even saw me!"

Mickey sighed. "All right, all right, hold your horses, Jim. I'm coming."

And then he was opening the door again and Jimmy Brannigan was barreling in through it—hopping-busting-barreling—and talking a mile a minute, while Mickey pulled it shut behind him: "Thanks, Mick, I figgered you'd be here, once I heard about Bill. I knew you would. I knew you'd remember. Ain't a one of 'em knows squat about this place, not even Mr. Thomas Egan himself. Ain't that rich, Mick? That's the genius of it, ain't it? Here we are right under a dozen Rats' noses, and they can't smell a thing!"

"Heard what about Bill?" Mary asked in that strangled voice—better than I could manage, sure, what with my heart stuck in my throat again—but still so low even I could hardly hear her, just an inch away. And anyhow Jimmy wasn't listening to anybody but himself. He was still too busy spouting off:

"But we can't stay here, can we, Mick? We'll have to go across the bridge now, won't we? Back to the camp? You got spotted, that's the trouble. That's what the boys were sayin' at the newsstand—they say you saw the whole thing; is it true, Mick? Last night in the Bad Lands, when the feller got shot—were you there? Was it Eddie who done it? I bet the boys two bits it was Eddie. It's always Eddie, nine times outta ten. And now they're all sayin' you were there, Mick—the Rats, too—the whole world's sayin' it. They'll be wanting to pin it on you next; I bet 'em a half-dollar on that one. We'll have to get out of town for sure now, won't we? I'm ready, you see? Just say the word; I got my kit all packed, see here, Mick? Whenever you say!"

And I figured Mickey would say, "Ah, shut up, Jimmy." Or kick him across the room. But he didn't. He sighed again, and nodded, and took a look at the raggedy bundle Jimmy was holding up in front of him, and double-checked the knot that was keeping it all together. And then he handed it back to him and said, "Good man, Jim. That's fine work, that is. You hold on to it now, for the time being, and when we're ready to—"

"Heard *what*?" said Mary, louder this time. I was numb again, half-paralyzed, but she was trembling all over. "Heard *what* about Bill?" she said for the third time, giving Jimmy's arm a ferocious shake.

And the look in her eyes must have scared the living daylights out of him, because he didn't dare answer her himself. He turned to Mickey with his own eyes all wide and worried and said, "Ah, Mick, they don't know? Didn't you tell 'em yet?"

"I was just about to," said Mickey, "when you knocked on the door."

"Tell us what?" Mary said, turning to him now too.

He just stood there for a second, looking at her square-on. And then he took a deep breath. "Bill's not coming," he said. "My dad—" He cleared his throat. "They've taken him to Boonville."

Mary gasped.

My ears started roaring.

"No they haven't," I said. "You're lying."

"I'm sorry," said Mickey. He shook his head. "It went all wrong—the whole plan. They put handcuffs on him. Houdini himself couldn't have got him out of those things. And then my dad—I never figured—" He stopped a second time and cleared his throat again, as if the words had got jammed there.

But I didn't want to hear what his dad had done. It was too late; I was seeing red again, and now I was flying at him headfirst, like I did with the Rat Man that other time; I was butting my head into his chest and kicking with my boots and pounding with my fists. "You're lying, you're lying, where's Bill, you big liar? He promised, he sent the sign, where's my brother, you liar?"

And he didn't do a thing about it. He just stood there letting me pound him like a punching bag, while Mary tried to pull me away:

"Stop it, Julia! Stop it! It's not his fault—"

"How do *you* know it's not his fault?"

"He's our friend; that's how I know. Let him tell us what happened, Julia!"

But I kept swinging. And then another train was thundering past outside and the walls were shaking and the air was shaking and Jimmy Brannigan was trying to push *his* way between us, and I shoved him away and he bumped into Mary, so hard she staggered back and stumbled over an old broken box behind her. And Mickey shook me off then, like it was nothing, like swatting away a mosquito, and trapped both my arms with one of his and went to help Mary up with the other, dragging me with him. "Are you all right?" he shouted to her, over the god-awful din of the train, and she nodded, so I knew she was, but her cheeks were apple-red again, even worse than before.

"Let go of me," I growled. I'd have bit him if I could, but he had me clamped so tight I couldn't swivel around to get a good chunk.

And still he stood there holding on to me while I thrashed and kicked and Mary kept saying, "Stop it, Julia, stop it, stop it! Will you listen for once in your life? How can he tell us what happened if you don't stop?"

Chapter 20

It wasn't as if I had a choice. He was double my size, easy, with a grip like glue. The more I squirmed, the tighter he stuck. So I slowed down some, after a while. I quit kicking—at least for the time being—though my teeth were still gritted and my jaw was clenched.

"Have you stopped?" Mary asked, when the racket from the train had died down.

"If he's stopped lying," I muttered.

"Mick ain't lyin'!" said Jimmy.

"It's all right, Jim. She's all right," said Mickey, letting loose of me, finally—slowly, at first, then altogether. "I wish it *was* a lie. I wish I was making it all up."

I was shivering again. Mary put an arm around me.

But it was Mickey's face she was studying. "Bill's gone, then," she said quietly. "They've taken him to Boonville. You're sure?"

He nodded. "I saw 'em put him on the train. I followed 'em to the station after the hearing—"

"There was a hearing?"

"Yesterday afternoon. I got there quick as I could, soon as Jim brought me the message. . . ." Mickey stopped and fished in his pocket and brought out a folded-up letter, even limper-looking than ours had been, and handed it to Mary.

We read it together:

Tues Morning, Halloween

Dear Mick,

Father Dunne's taking me over to City Hall at three, they just set my hearing, be ready I'll make a brake when its over if they try to keep me. You be decoy again like at the ballpark, dont worry I wont hit any lampoles this time. Just get their attention so theyll chase you a while, I'll run the other way and meet you across the river like we planned before, I got some ideres for after that but if anything goes wrong you have to look out for Mary and Julia. I told them come to the bridge in the morning, you have to stop them if I cant get there tell them stay with the nuns til I figure it out, I wont let them down.

Your friend Bill D.

"I'm sorry," said Mickey—for what seemed like the millionth time—when we were done reading. "I was there before the hearing started. I was right across Twelfth Street, waiting. I saw the priest taking Bill inside. It was only just the two of 'em, going in. But when they came out, maybe an hour later, my dad was with 'em." Mickey took off his cap and pushed his hair out of his eyes, as if he was still trying to see it all. "I should've known. I should've figured he'd be there. He must've guessed we'd be planning something—that Bill would run, first chance he got. He had him locked right to him: one cuff on Bill's good wrist, one on his own, so neither of 'em could go anywhere without dragging the other with him. And Bill saw me. I'm sure he saw me—I stepped out of the shade on purpose and he looked right at me. But then he shook his head, because what was the use? We never counted on the damn—excuse me, the handcuffs. Ah, cripes, I should have known. . . ."

"How could you have known?" asked Mary.

"I know my father," said Mickey. "He couldn't just walk Bill to the station and turn him over to the conductor. He had to get on the train with him. He must have stayed with him all the way to Boonville. Any other cop would have seen him to his seat and gone home to his own supper, but not him. Not Tim Doyle. That's just how he is. He took a bullet once, guarding a prisoner. He wouldn't have trusted anyone else to get him there safe."

"For his own protection," I muttered. I felt sick to my stomach, remembering.

There are worse things than Boonville. . . .

They'd rather be dead than locked up. . . .

Then they might get their wish. . . .

"I'd have followed 'em, if I could've, if it'd done any good. Hung on to the caboose, maybe. I don't know. I stuck around till the train pulled out. Then I remembered Bill's letter—what he'd said about the two of you. I had to stop you from leaving the nuns' place. So I went over to Morgan Street, but it wasn't any use. I knocked on the door, but they wouldn't open it. I guess you couldn't really blame 'em. It was dark by that time;

half the world was in the saloons. So I figured I'd just wait outside, keep watch, you know, till morning—catch you, if you came out, and tell you what had happened. Only then all hell broke loose with the Rats and the Nixies, and Fat Eddie shot that loudmouth in the alley—"

"I knew it!" Jimmy broke in. "I knew it was him! And he saw you, was that it? Was it Eddie who spotted you?"

Mickey nodded. "He wasn't more'n five yards from me. I should've had more sense. I'd backed up by the dustbins at the fence there, when his gun went off. I was just tryin' to stay out of the way. I didn't think he'd seen me, at first. But then he pointed it right at me. You could still smell it smokin'. 'How's your pal with the broken arm?' he said."

"Dear God," Mary whispered.

Jimmy's eyes were bright as firecrackers. "What d'jya do then, Mick? D'jya knock the gun out of his hand? I bet you gave him what-for, didn't you, Mick? Boy oh boy, I wisht I'd been there! Howjya ever get away?"

"I ran," said Mickey. "I got lucky, that's all. Don't be making me into some kind of hero, Jimmy—"

"But he had the bead on you, Mick! He had you backed into the corner there!"

"Till I tripped over one of the cans, scramblin', and it rolled right into him. It was nothin' but dumb luck, Jim; it gave me time to jump the fence, that's all. And I never looked back, neither. I could hear shouting behind me—people coming outside, I guess—but I just kept runnin'. I got out of there. Bill had asked me just the one thing—to watch out for his sisters, that's all. And what did I do? I ran."

He looked so miserable, I'd have felt almost sorry for him, if I hadn't been so used to hating his guts.

"You couldn't help it," said Mary. "What else could you have done?"

Mickey shook his head. "I don't know. Something. Anything. I wasn't thinking straight. I got all the way back to the camp before my head cleared. And then I took out the letter, and read it again. You were coming to the bridge in the morning, it said. So I figured you'd be here, if you could get here."

"And here we are," said Mary.

Mickey nodded. "Here you are." He started to say something else. "I wish—" he began, then stopped and stared at the cap in his hands. There was a torn place by the rim, where a patch had come loose. "I'd give anything in the world to change it all."

Mary lifted her chin. "You did what you had to do.

You told us what you had to tell us." She looked older than herself, even older than he was, though he had a good two years on her, easy.

"And you'll go back now, then?" said Mickey. "They'll have you back, won't they?"

The hackles rose at the nape of my neck. "Go *back*? Go back where?"

"To the nuns," said Mickey. "Like Bill said."

Mary nodded. "I suppose we'll have to. Where else would we go?"

"*Anywhere* else!" I grabbed her by the arm. "Anyplace but that place! I don't know—the camp, maybe. Is that what you called it?" I looked at Mickey. "Ain't that where Bill would have taken us?"

"He never told me," said Mickey. "There was only the letter. But I don't think he'd have taken you to the camp. It's not just us over there, Julia. It's strangers, mostly. Rough men—hoboes and such."

Jimmy stuck out his chest. "It ain't a place for girls," he said.

"Or for kids," said Mickey. He put a hand on his shoulder. "You have to go back, too, Jim."

"Go where?"

"To Father Dunne's."

"Ah, Mick . . ."

"Just for a while, till we get our plans made. You're our eyes and ears, remember? We need you there."

"But I can't go back now, Mick; I brought my kit!"

"Shut up, Jimmy," I told him. My throat was starting to ache. But I wouldn't cry. I wouldn't. I sank down on the edge of the broken box and covered my ears. "Shut up, shut up, shut up, shut up. . . ."

Mary knelt beside me. She took hold of both my arms, shook me a little. "You know we have to go back, Julia. You saw what Bill said. We've only been gone a couple of hours; it won't be so bad. And Betty will be looking for you."

I wiped my nose with the edge of my sleeve.

Mickey knelt down on my other side. "I'll get him out of there, J. Somehow or other. I swear to you I'll get him out."

I sucked in a ragged breath. That was Bill's name for me. Only Bill could call me J.

But this was his friend Mick, offering me his hand.

He got back on his feet, and held it out, and stood there waiting to help me up.

So after a moment or two, I swallowed hard, and took it.

Chapter 21

Whoso diggeth a pit, shall fall therein.

Whoso diggeth a pit, shall fall therein.

Whoso diggeth a pit . . . shall spend two hours of every day of the next two weeks in the head nun's office, writing "Whoso diggeth a pit" a thousand times.

But that wasn't the worst of it.

That was nowhere near the worst of it.

"The *farm*?" I'd said to Mary at the end of the second Saturday, when Sister Maclovius had finally brought her in to tell me. The room had gone icy all of a sudden. Nobody had lit the fire yet. November kept changing on us—on again, off again. Three days ago it had snowed half a foot; just this morning it was hot as August. And now it was winter all over, not three hours later, and getting colder by the second. The wind was rattling the window frame like a wild thing, when Mary came through the door.

"Be quick now," Sister was telling her. For nearly two weeks, she'd watched me with her hawk eyes, scarcely saying a word beyond "Come in" and "Sit down" and "Work away, Miss Delaney." Nobody was allowed to talk to me while I scribbled on and on; not even Betty could get past Sister Maclovius. So it was only Mary she was speaking to, when she said "Be quick."

"Just say your goodbyes and have done with it. Mr. Lenahan will be here any minute. No doubt he'll be wanting to get back to the farm before dark, with the weather in such a state." And then she narrowed her eyes at me and left us alone and closed the door behind her, and all the time I stood there, gaping.

"The *farm*? Ah, no, Mary—not the farm with all the babies!"

She nodded. "Twins, mostly. The little ones are still fresh."

"But it ain't fair! How could she do that? I passed the damn plate, didn't I?"

"It's all right, Julia. There's no use cussing. I don't mind babies, really. I'll take babies over laundry any day. And Sister says these people are paying a bit, too. It's not much, but it's something. It's not as if they're adopting me, like they might if I were younger. So if Bill *does* get out—"

"*When* he gets out, you mean—"

Mary sighed. "When he gets out. We'll need money then, won't we? You know we'll have to have money. Even Gran knew that—look here, now—I've got her purse, you see? It was in my box; it's been there all along. Aunt Gert must have put it in. There's two dollars and fifty-eight cents, all in change. Gran must have had it from her sewing—her button money, remember? 'Every penny counts,' she always said, 'when you're saving for chickens.' And if they pay me—well, then it's not charity; it's a job, isn't it? It's nothing to be ashamed of."

"How much will they pay?" I asked, taking the little black purse in my hand. It was stitched out of quilted cloth, soft as silk and frayed at the seams, with a bent metal clasp that used to be shiny. If you squinted you could make out bits of goldish paint clinging to the edges. It looked like Gran, somehow; I could still see her patting it in her pocket. And when you opened it, it smelled like her too—like talcum powder, maybe? And something else—I couldn't think what it was. . . .

"A dollar a week," said Mary. "Ah, sure, roll your eyes if you like. I know it's not much. But I'll save every dime, you see; I won't spend a cent of it. They'll give me my meals and a bed to sleep in and a roof over my head. What else will I need? Not a thing. So when Bill gets out—"

"Ah, crikey, Mary. A dollar a week?" The tears were crowding my throat again, so it came out in a growl. "That's nothin', is what that is. That's a spit in the Mississippi."

Mary lifted her chin. It trembled, just a little. She took back the purse and turned away. "I guess a spit's better than no spit. It's not like they're letting me choose."

Caraway seeds . . . that was the other smell. Gran used to like those little brown buns from Patrizi's market, with the caraway seeds on top. . . .

I threw my arms around Mary's waist. "I'm sorry, I'm sorry, I didn't mean it. It's just—you'll be *gone*, don't you see? How will I ever find you? You'll be away out there in the sticks somewhere, a million miles from here. It took us two months to get to the *bridge*, remember? And that's just down the street, Mary; it ain't nothing at all. . . ."

She didn't pull away. She held on tight, till I settled down some, and put the purse back in my hands. "You keep it," she said, "in case you see Bill first." And then she took the blue ribbon out of her hair and bit it, and tore it in two, and tied half of it back in hers, and the other half in mine. "It's not a million miles, you know. It's only Jefferson County. You couldn't ever lose me, Julia, even if you wanted to."

Whoso diggeth a pit, shall fall therein.
Whoso diggeth a pit, shall fall therein.
Deeper and deeper . . .
Colder and colder . . .

That night, when Betty heard me crying into my pillow, upstairs in the slant-walled room, she climbed in bed beside me and hugged me, and patted my back, and made soft clucking sounds, as if she was comforting a colicky child—a Lenahan, like as not—or Hyacinth, maybe, in need of an apple. Until I was worn-out and raw-throated from so many tears, and I fell asleep finally, or halfway asleep, anyhow. . . .

And here's Gran, all of a sudden. She's sitting by Betty, tilting her head at us and taking something from her pocket—is it the purse? Ah, sure it is—her little black purse. And she opens it and turns it over, and coins spill everywhere, and Betty catches them and laughs, but Gran pays her no mind. It's not the coins she cares about. And still she's looking and looking; she peers inside and gives the purse another shake, and now a piece of yellow paper comes floating out, and she snags it in the air and hands it to me. It's folded twice over, so I can't see what's written on it, but I start to sweat when my fingers touch it, and the hair stands up on my neck and my arms. Dear God, ah, no, I've seen it before, haven't I? I've dreamed it a thousand times. I know what it is but I don't want to know; I don't want to remember; I don't want any part of it. I throw the paper down, but Betty picks it up and opens it for me and hands it to me again, and I squeeze my eyes shut, because I won't, I can't look, but still she pushes it at me. . . .

And quick as that, I'm home again, and it's summer; it's always summer. . . . The kitchen window is open, though it's dark outside, and the fog horns are blowing on the river. I can hear them calling to the ferry by the landing, long and low in my good ear. And there's that sick-sweet smell in the air, the burnt-tar smell that makes my stomach pitch. "Never mind," Gran says, when she sees me trembling, "it's only the creosote barges." And I know I'm still dreaming—it's the dream inside the other dream—"*Oh! Fair Thomas*

Egan, too bad you're going to hang. . . ." But I can't wake up; I can never wake up. *Please, Papa, oh, Papa, can't you make it stop?* It's that night again, all over. We're done with the Fair and the Fair's done with us and Gran's tearing up rags for my blistered feet when the note comes. It always comes. There it is slipping under the door now—you see?—the piece of yellow paper with the circle at the top, like the one on the union banner, the circle inside the other circle, that used to make you sing:

The union will butter our beans now!
The union's a marvelous might!
I'm the poorest man here, but I'm buyin' the beer,
And fartin' through silk tonight!

Only this time you don't sing when you read it. Why ain't you singin', Papa? You shake your head like it hurts you and pass a hand over your eyes; they're all red and wild-looking and your hand is shaking again too. "The bridge," you mumble. "They're waitin' at the bridge."

And you turn to leave, and Bill gets hold of you—"Who's waitin', Pop? What's wrong?"—but you won't listen, you never listen, you shove him away so hard, he loses his balance and trips over backward, and you help him up then and stand there swaying like you might fall down yourself.

"Sorry, son, sorry, sorry," you keep saying. "It's the Rats, don't you see? They're swearin' they'll bust the union. . . . I promised your mother I'd stop 'em, don't you see, son?"

And we all grab on to you then and Gran takes the yellow paper out of your hand and wags a finger at you and says, "That's enough now, Cyril. Will you listen to yourself? Have you lost your wits entirely? You're in no condition to be traipsing about on bridges on a night like this!"

But you go just the same. You always go. You put on your coat and your hat and you kiss Gran's cheek. She's mad as a hornet and won't look at you, but you go out the door anyhow, and the fog snakes around you, and the dark swallows you whole.

"Don't stand there gaping like a pack of jackfish," says Gran. Her green eyes are snapping at us. "Go off to bed this minute or you'll live to regret it."

"Let the girls go to bed," says Bill. "I'm going after him."

"You are not, sir!" she says. "You'll catch your death in this damp. Don't you take the first step, do you hear me?"

And he says, "Yes, Gran," but I know he don't mean it. He's only waiting till she's stomped off to her own cot and shooed the rest of us to ours. And then he slips out the door, soft as a shadow. He thinks I'm asleep, same as Mary, but I'm not. I'm watching him like always and I run quick and follow. "Go *back*, J," Bill says when he catches me, but I won't. He can't make me. I know the way to the bridge just as well as he does.

But when we get there, it's no use; we can't see you, Papa. We can't see the tips of our own noses. The fog is even worse here, so close to the water, so thick that the streetlamps can't shine their light through it. They make milky little circles with a million tiny white drops floating in 'em that dot the dark in a long line at the edge of the bridge—it must be the bridge—though they don't show a thing. And somewhere in the soup ahead, there are footsteps and rough voices, but I can't make out the bodies they belong to. They move through the fog like muttering ghosts, the ghosts of ghosts, grumbling and shoving. "Pop!" Bill hollers. "Are you there, Pop? Are you all right?"

And the next thing I know, somebody's got me tight around the shoulders and someone else is grabbing Bill and pushing him back, pressing him flat against the rail of the bridge itself and snarling, "What are you shoutin' about, ye tomfool kid? Close your mouth or I'll close it for you. Your pop ain't here. He never was here. Do you see what I'm sayin', boy?" And he boxes Bill's ears and I want to kill him for it but the other one has me pinned so tight, I can't move; I can hardly breathe; I can't make a sound. All the air's gone out of my lungs and I want to wake up, but I can't wake up, and I don't understand, I don't understand anything, what with the fog and the fog horns and the muttering and confusion and the water making the slapping sound down, down, way down in the river below us—it must be the river; I can smell it now—the fish smell and the smokestack smell and the burnt-tar smell from the barges. . . . Oh, Papa, I can taste it now, too; the bile's rising in my throat, and I know it, I know the river's down there in the milky dark, waiting to suck me under, and still you don't come, you never come.

"Pop!" Bill keeps hollering. "Where are you, Pop?"

Whoso diggeth a pit, shall fall therein.

Whoso diggeth a pit, shall fall therein. . . .

"PAPA!"

"Ah, for the love o' Mike. . ."

"There she goes again."

"Wake up, Julia!"

"Who's that yellin'?"

"It's you, ye dope."

"You're havin' another nightmare."

"Go shake her, Hazel."

"I ain't shakin' her. You shake her."

"Is she sick?"

"I ain't touchin' her."

"Her bed's wet. . . ."

"PAPA!"

"Ah, crikey, she's burnin' up!"

"Somebody get Sister. . . ."

Chapter 22

White.

All white.

Holy hell, my eyes hurt.

I closed 'em again, and lay on my back, breathing.

How long had I been here?

"Measles," the doctor had said, a million years ago. "Have you ever had the measles, Julia?"

But my pillow had been swelling just then, so I couldn't answer. It always did that when I got a fever. It swelled up like an elephant's head with a trunk as long as a fire hose that wrapped around my neck and squeezed and squeezed—

"Definitely the measles," said the doctor, snapping

his black bag closed. "You'll be in for it now, I'm afraid, Sister. They're spreading like wildfire already. I saw four cases just this morning, down by the river."

And Sister Gabriel had laid the back of her cool hand on my hot cheek and said, "Ah, well, we'll manage, won't we, Julia? You see now, it's nothing serious. The whole world gets the measles sooner or later."

And once the whole world got 'em, they put the whole world in the infirmary—that was this place here, remember?—though you couldn't see the others but only heard 'em every now and again, coughing and sneezing or calling for Sister, while you lay alone in your single cot in all the white: white sheets and white pillows and white curtains all around you but for one white wall, with a single window looking out on the white, white snow. And the pigeon brought you broth in a steaming cup, though you threw it up mostly, and sips of water with bits of ice in it, and a cool cloth for your burning eyes, and said, "Ah, no, now, Julia, you mustn't cry. You don't want to make them worse, dear. Thank God that it's only the measles. You'll be right as rain in no time." And so you stopped crying after a while, a day or a week or a million years, maybe, because what was the use? Bill was gone, and Mary was gone, and Mama and the twins and Gran were gone, and Papa was lost in the fog forever, but you were still here; here you were, Julia Delaney. It was only the measles, thank God.

Plink, plink . . . plink, plink . . .

What was that sound?

I pulled my pillow over my ears—the good one and the bad one both—but I could hear it still somehow, from down below me in the house:

Plink, plink . . . plink, plunk . . .

From the parlor, maybe?

There was a piano in the parlor off the front hall, wasn't there? The infirmary was on the second floor, just above it. Nobody had ever played it, that I knew of, in all the time I'd been living here, but—

Plink, plunk . . . plink, plunk . . .

Well, sure, that was it. Someone was tuning the piano. I'd heard the piano man in the Patch doing the same, plenty of times, when the windows were open at the Brannigans', down the street. They'd had a lovely old upright in the house they rented, before it burned down. . . .

Plink plink plink plink plink . . .

I took the pillow off my ears, and opened my eyes again. They still ached, but I was awake now. I couldn't just lie here forever. I sat up and sneezed twice, then climbed out the left side of the bed and used the chamber pot that was under it, and then the room started to spin a little, so I climbed back in and listened to the *plinks* and stared out the window at the falling snow. Was it still November? I wondered. My skin was afire with itches, paper-thin where I'd scratched and dry as dust, but the sheets were cool against it. I stretched my arms and my legs till they tingled—

And then my right hand touched something in the bed beside me.

A lumpish something or other.

I sat up, trembling, with my head pounding and my heart bumping (because you never knew—it might be anything; all manner of creatures crept inside when the cold came). I gritted my teeth and took hold of the edge of the covers by the tips of my fingers, but with a good strong grip, and pulled 'em back an inch at a time: little by little, thread by thread, all ready every second to pull 'em down again and yell bloody murder if the lump moved or squeaked or bared its teeth at me (Gran had killed a rat in the pantry once with two swift swats of her broom) . . .

But it was only a doll.

A *doll,* for the love of mercy.

I started to breathe again.

If you caught the measles, they gave you a doll?

Didn't they know I was *eleven*?

Still and all, though . . . as dolls went . . . this one here was a beauty, wasn't she? She was a lady, not a baby. I picked her up. Oh my. . . . Harriet Bocklebrink, that was who she looked like. Aunt Gert's dead husband's rich niece—the Harriet who used to come to the house with her stuck-up mother to bring the baskets at Christmas. The mother was an old bat no better than Gert herself, but the daughter was next door to an angel from heaven, with her sweet smile and little white teeth. I always figured she must've been stolen from her cradle when her real ma wasn't looking. She used to give me a wink and then slip me some secret treat, peppermints or gingersnaps or a gingerbread man with candy buttons or—on one unforgettable occasion—an entire jar of sweet gherkins she'd put up with her very own hands. And now as I lived and breathed, here she was again, only shorter: same gray-blue eyes and goldy locks and the pink of her cheeks like roses on cream—china, was that it? Was that what her head was made of? I'd once heard Doc Monaghan spouting off in the River Arcade and Pawn Shop about a doll that wasn't half as good as this one. "Bone china," he'd said. "Best there is to be had."

Oh, bless her little bone head, what was *she* doing in the House of Mercy?

She had a string of pearls wrapped double around her neck, and pearly buttons on her sky-blue dress, which was made of some soft, shiny stuff that surely must be satin. It had little puffed sleeves and a soft net overskirt shot through with flowers, all purple and green and peach-colored, like a fruit stand in summer. And there was lace dripping from the edges, and a shiny ribbon—pale green—tied around her tiny waist, ending in a pair of miniature roses, one yellow, one blue. And her hat! And her parasol! Why, they were blue, too, trimmed with more lace and soft white feathers and another teensy rose, and every last bit of it made to match, just so.

I wondered if they'd given her regular legs, or balanced her on a cone of wax, or stuck her on the top half of an umbrella, like some I'd seen. So I checked. But she was as perfect as perfect could be, right down to her snow-white bloomers and stockings, right down to her two little feet in their dainty dancing slippers.

"Hello, Harriet," I whispered. She was so beautiful, she made my chest ache.

I half expected her to shut one eye and offer me a pickle.

Plink plink plink . . .
Plink plunk plink . . .
Plinkety plunk plink plink—

Oh! You beautiful doll!
You great big beautiful . . .

"Good afternoon, Julia! Well, now, are we awake yet?" Sister Gabriel sang out from the curtain on my left, as she pushed in backward with a loaded tray. "Look here what a feast your friends have brought us all! Happy Thanksgiving!"

It was Thanksgiving?

What friends?

I turned even redder than the rash had turned me already, and shoved the doll back under the covers. Ah, crikey. Had she seen me holding it? Marcella would make no end of fun if she ever got wind of such a thing. A great girl of eleven, playing with dolls . . .

But Sister didn't say a word about it, if she'd noticed, only bustled into my little white box of a bedroom, all smiles, and propped the tray on my lap. "And what's this? Sitting up today, are we?" she chirped on, checking my head for fever. "Well now, that's more like it. That's a grand sight, Julia. And just in time for the turkey, too! Oh, do have a taste, dear. Miss Downey made the stuffing herself—see there? With the lovely oysters in it? She was ever so concerned when you weren't downstairs with the others. It seems you've made quite an impression. Oh my, yes. And on the gentleman too, I believe. They'd have come right up and brought your tray themselves, if I hadn't mentioned the measles. Mr. Hanratty-Maguire hasn't had them, you see, that he can recall. And though Miss Downey is quite sure *she* has, still he begged her not to risk it, since there's always that chance, as he pointed out: What if she's mistaken? And then of course she'd be catching them, and he'd be catching them, and there they'd be in a fine fix. They're to be married in the spring, you know. Oh my, such a handsome couple! Won't you have a bite, Julia?"

"No, thank you," I croaked, feeling dizzy again. I'd have said it louder, if I could have, but my throat was still ragged.

"Oh, do try, dear. Just a taste or two. Miss Downey has taken such an interest. And there's more she's planning, on top of it all—not only this good dinner. Listen, now. . . . Do you hear that?"

Plink plink plink . . . plunk plunk plunk . . .

I sighed and nodded. "The piano?" I said.

"Exactly!" said Sister. Her eyes were bright as berries. "Well, you'll never guess our luck, Julia. Miss Downey has promised piano lessons to all the girls who want them! Now, isn't that marvelous? So I thought of you right away, of course, what with the musical talent on your father's side. 'Julia might have the gift,' I told her. 'They say it often runs in families.'"

"No, thank you," I said again. Louder this time.

"Oh well," said the pigeon, putting her head to one side. "You don't have to decide right now, of course. There'll be plenty of time later, when you're better." She lifted a hand to smooth my hair, but I bristled and pulled away. I didn't want Miss Downey's music lessons or her charity turkey (never mind my traitor stomach, growling again). I didn't need her stupid oyster stuffing or—my knee brushed the lump under the covers and jerked back—or her dressed-up lady dolls, neither. Ah, sure. It was them that had brought her, wasn't it? Blue-eyed Harriet with her little white teeth. It was them that had brought it all. The millionaires, that was who, the Optima Petamusers, with their hats and their gloves and their fancy binoculars and their nickels and dimes clinking and clanking on their fine silver plates. I burned with shame, just thinking of it. Well, I'd never take another crumb from any of 'em, ever again. They couldn't make me take it, could they? I'd smash the piano first. I'd hock the damn doll. I'd buy a one-way ticket to Boonville and find a way to get Bill out and then—

Plink . . . plink plink plink plink plink . . .

I sat up straighter.

Sister Gabriel was smiling.

Plink . . . plink plink plink plink plink . . .

I covered my ears. Oh no. . . . She wouldn't dare, would she?

"Julia?" The smile was gone now. "What's the matter, dear? Don't you like the music? We thought for sure you'd like it. I told Miss Downey about your father, you see, and asked did she happen to know the tune, and—ah, no, now, Julia, don't get up. You're still on the mend, remember? Is it the lavatory you're needing? It's too far, dear; use the chamber pot. You're not up to all those stairs yet. . . . Don't you hear me, child? You can't be going out there. . . . Come back this minute, Julia!"

But I was gone already. She was grabbing at air again like she did the day I met her, and I was climbing out of bed and ducking under her arm and running along the cold linoleum with my two bare feet, and I didn't care who saw me. Billows of white from the other patients' curtains blew around me, and startled faces came and went (was that Marcella in the bed by the door there, grinning from ear to ear?) and now Sister Gabriel was running after me; I looked over my shoulder and saw her puffing along with the turkey tray still clutched to her pigeon breast in one hand and the other hand waving over her head—"No, no, come back, Julia! Your fever's not gone yet, dear; you'll be spreading the measles all over the—"

Only I didn't hear the rest because I was too far ahead now and the room was spinning again and my head was pounding and my eyes were burning like hellfire itself but it didn't matter, none of that mattered. I couldn't stop to think about it. I was out of the infirmary and down the stairs before I knew it, and then I was lunging through the parlor door and pushing my way through the crowd of nuns and orphans that were sitting in chairs, all facing the piano, where the handsome man was standing, turning pages for Miss Downey, who didn't see me coming but was pounding away on the black-and-whites—

"Stop it! Stop! You can't! It ain't yours. . . ." I meant it to be a shout, but my nose was running and my throat was all in tatters and I couldn't do more than croak like a hop-toad: *Stop it, stop it, stop it. . . .*

And then the music *was* stopping and Miss Downey was turning around and looking at me with her beautiful, puzzled face, and Mr. Hanratty-Maguire was staring at me, round-eyed, holding his handkerchief to his nose, and Sister Maclovius was all purple-cheeked again, heaving herself to her feet and shaking a gnarly finger, while Betty came barreling through the crowd and Miss Downey took me by the elbows, saying, "Child? . . . Child, child!" and then someone was tugging me away from her and the voices were all jumbling together. "She means no harm, Sister," and "I wouldn't bet on it, miss; best mind those teeth," and I knew they didn't understand, none of 'em understood, but I couldn't help it. I couldn't help it. It wasn't theirs, was it, Papa?

Oh, come with me, my love!
Come away, come afar. . . .

No one else in this bleedin' world could play "Julia Delaney."

December

Chapter 23

Lucky for me, they told me later, when the shouting was over mostly, that I had been sick as a dog that day, and looked it. And that Sister Gabriel had come puffing into the parlor right behind me, apologizing every step of the way—*Sorry, sorry, sorry, the poor child doesn't know what she's saying; it's only the fever talking.* And that Sister Bridget had elbowed *her* towering self through the crowd then, and peeled Betty off me, and carried me upstairs, kicking—*Beg pardon, Miss Downey; excuse us if you will, sir; for heaven's sake, hush now, Julia*—before Sister Maclovius could clap me in the Sin Room for the next million years.

"And your face was all scabby and wild-eyed," Hazel informed me, her own little pea eyes glittering. She'd had a front-row seat by the piano, she said, and enjoyed every minute. "I wouldn't have gone near you, if I was a nun. Not even if the Pope said I had to. I wouldn't have touched you with a ten-foot pole. And I've already *had* the measles."

She leaned across the refectory table and tapped my plate with her fork—*ding-ding!*—as if she was expecting me to . . . to what? Congratulate her? Or smack her one, maybe.

But I wasn't up to fighting yet. It was only just that morning they'd let me out of the infirmary on purpose, two weeks after I'd got away the first time. I'd been telling 'em I was fine for the past five days, but the doctor had made me wait. "I don't like the sound of that cough," he'd said, and Sister Gabriel's eyes had gone wide with worry, though she had more than she could do as it was, what with the flood of fresh cases that kept pouring in.

The white room was full to busting when I finally left it, jam-packed with wheezers and sneezers, and Sister Bridget was down on the front porch with a mouthful of nails, hammering a large yellow sign on the door:

MEASLES WITHIN
ENTER AT YOUR OWN PERIL
STAY OUT UNLESS YOU'VE HAD THEM

"Do you see what you've started, Your Majesty?" said Marcella. She'd got sprung before I did and was sitting next to Hazel now at the half-empty table, pointing *her* fork at me. "You're the Queen of the Epizootic, that's what. You'll be the top-liner in the morning edition: 'Typhoid Mary Loses Crown to Measles Delaney'!"

Hazel laughed so hard at that, she gave herself a choking fit, and Marcella had to pound her on the back, which would have set Sister Sebastian's eyebrows dancing if she'd been there to see it. But Sister Sebastian wasn't on dinner duty today. She'd caught the bug herself last week and was laid up now, they told me, in whatever secret place it was nuns went to be sick in.

"So who teaches our lessons, then?" I wondered out loud.

"They're taking turns," said Hazel, when she'd finally got her breath back. "Sister Genevieve was the first. She taught us cooking in the kitchen on Monday. We all blubbered like babies, chopping onions. And Sister Bridget came Tuesday and Thursday both, and made us learn a monstrous long poem about the Light Brigade getting slaughtered. She said it would give us backbone."

Marcella rolled her eyes and saluted. "*Theirs not to reason why, theirs but to do or die. . . .*"

"But that wasn't the worst," said Hazel. "Friday was the worst. We had Sister Maclovius in the classroom for two solid hours, trying to teach us Latin."

"Speaking of slaughter," said Marcella.

"*Amo*, *amas*, a mouse, a moose—"

"The piano lady comes on Wednesdays," said Winnie, tapping softly on my left shoulder. And Betty, on my right, lit up like a lamp then (she hadn't left my side since they let me out of the infirmary) and started playing the table with her fingers, as if it was a keyboard.

My stomach tightened a little. Miss Downey, they meant. She'd kept her promise about the piano lessons. It was old news now, even to me; there was no way *not* to know it. I'd spent my last two Wednesdays in the white room with my ears stopped, gritting my teeth till the torture was over, while her pupils down in the parlor plunked out sour notes for hours at a time.

"Don't look so glum." Marcella grinned at me. "These charity ladies never last for long here. They get sick of it quicker'n we do. Trust me; she'll be callin' it a lost cause by Christmas."

But December slogged on and on, and still Miss Downey kept showing up, which was more than you could say for most of the world. We'd look out front and count the neighbors crossing clear to the other side of Morgan Street when they saw our stay-away sign. Only the doctor would come near us now—McGill was his name—and Father Dunne, as a favor on Sundays, so we could have Mass, since there was no use dragging such a sickly looking lot to church. And Jelly Donahoo, the milkman—at least he didn't desert us—though he'd wrap his muffler 'round his face three times, so only his eyes peeked out, and leave the full bottles on the back stoop, then rush back double-quick to his horse and wagon, toting the empties by the woolly tips of his thick-gloved fingers. I met him by accident, one frostbitten morning, as I was coming back from the lavatory, and he let out a little yelp and tripped all over himself, scampering past me, looking as if he'd seen Old Scratch himself.

But aside from the Fearless Four—Doctor and Dunne and Donahoo, and Downey, on Wednesdays—the world gave us a wide berth mostly, and minded its own business, and the nuns minded ours, same as ever.

And all this time, Harriet the Doll waited mute as

a stick under the mattress of my old bed in the slant-walled room, still wrapped in the pillowcase I'd borrowed from the infirmary when I smuggled her out. Not a soul besides me knew a thing about her. I hadn't breathed a word to any of 'em. I was waiting, just like she was. I'd had days on end to think it all through and now I was biding my time, this time, till I was good and ready—till I was well enough and strong enough and steady enough on my feet again to beat it back over to Doc's, to hock her.

I hadn't forgotten.

I couldn't have forgotten.

My plan had swelled and swelled inside my head till it was so big and bright and clear to me that not even Mary with all her worrywarting could have found a flaw in it. Why, she'd said it herself, hadn't she?

Every penny counts when you're saving for chickens. . . .

Oh, wouldn't Bill be surprised when he saw us coming? I'd have Gran's old purse brimming over by then, stuffed full as a little black turkey. I just had to catch Doc in the right mood, that was all; he was no use to anybody in the wrong one. But if I got lucky—if it was a good day (even Doc had a good day, every now and again)—why, I bet he'd pay ten dollars, easy, for a doll like that! More than twice what Mary made in a whole month, taking care of a hundred Lenahans. He might even go as high as twenty dollars, or thirty—well, you never knew; he *might*—once he saw what a peach of a doll she was. What an elegant doll, really, with the china being bone and all. Enough for a boatload of train tickets, when the time was right: to Jefferson County, to start with (I'd need to stop and pick up Mary, of course), then straight from there to Boonville, for Bill. And then I'd send him a note, all in code, like the one he sent me, and he'd slip away to the depot, quick as he could. And once we had him safe aboard with us, why, no telling how far we'd go then . . . to the sun itself, maybe!

First class, right up front—just us three, with plenty of legroom—and an ice cream bucket, and a couple of hens, besides.

Chapter 24

"O God," prayed Sister Maclovius, "on this holy night of nights, when in thy infinite mercy thou saw fit to send a Savior amongst us, pour down thy light and healing grace on these thy children, in this house of contagion, whilst we commence celebrating this joyous season, as best we can."

She heaved a large sigh.

"Amen," we all murmured—what was left of us, anyhow—the cluster of nuns and plaid girls who weren't upstairs itching at the moment, but were gathered around Sister at the parlor window, for the Christmas Eve candle lighting.

"Hannah Hogan!" she called out now, stretching

forth a craggy hand. "Come forward, child!"

All the eyebrows in the room went shooting up, as usual, and all the eyes turned to Hannah, who'd gone pale as a ghost. She was off to the right a bit, next to Betty and me, looking minuter than ever.

But Sister Bridget, just behind us, leaned over to her, smiling. "Don't worry, dear. You've done nothing wrong. It's a very great honor to be chosen. It's because you're the youngest in the House, you see; only you can light the candle for the Christ Child. And only a girl named Mary can blow it out—"

Betty's eyes lit up. She tugged on Sister's sleeve.

"Yes, Betty. I know. You're Mary Elizabeth. But that's not till later, remember? Go ahead, Hannah dear. . . ."

"Come along, Miss Hogan!" said Sister Maclovius. She'd put down her cane by this time and picked up a box of matches with one hand and a tall white taper with the other, and was beginning to look a little thin in the lip, waiting for the kid to get moving.

"Yes, Sister," Hannah whispered, soft as a bird's peep. It made her seem even smaller, if that was possible. Still, she took a deep breath and inched her way to the window, one teeny-tiny footstep at a time. And after four broken matches and a good deal of fumbling, and a great deal more sighing from Sister, they managed to get the thing lit.

"All right, then," said Sister Maclovius. She pulled a handkerchief from her sleeve and mopped her face—it was beaded up slick with sweat now—and then she squared her shoulders and tried again: "Will you tell us, please, if you can, Miss Hogan, for whose sake we light this candle? Whose dear family traveled afar, midst the cold and gloom, that first Christmas Eve? And just as they trusted in the True Light to shield them from the Power of Darkness, when the inn was full and the road was rife with peril, whose bright coming do we await in utter confidence, Miss Hogan, this drear winter's night?"

Hannah's eyes grew even wider. "Santa Claus?" she whispered.

Winnie gasped.

Hazel tittered.

Only Betty gave a glad little whoop and went running to the window, and she and Hannah pressed their noses to the pane, and the two of 'em stood there all aquiver, squeezing each other's hands—looking for what? Flying reindeer? On *Morgan* Street?

But there were just the same old garish lights from Kelly's, spilling down on the same old snow, and three or four of the same old customers stumbling about, and a man with a holly wreath 'round his neck, who grinned when he saw us staring, and wiggled his ears at us, and lurched down the sidewalk, singing at the top of his lungs:

I saw three ships come sailing in,
On Christmas Day, on Christmas Day!
I saw three ships come sailing in,
On Christmas Day in the morning!

Sister Maclovius cleared her throat.

"Look out," Marcella muttered, and the rest of us jerked to attention and turned back from the window, expecting all manner of trouble.

But Sister only lifted her eyes heavenward and closed them for a second, as if she had a pain somewhere. And then she breathed in another mighty breath, and kept right on praying:

"Grant us strength, O Lord, that what we lack in understanding, thou wilt rectify in patience, like unto Job's. And make us wary of the devil's snares, lest we doubt—in our mortal weakness—the wisdom of thy ways. And though we might be tempted to wonder, on occasion, why certain of thine enemies among the criminal element might appear to be enjoying no end of the bloom of health and no shortage of Christmas cheer, even whilst the innocent children ask, 'Will Santy Claus come, Sister?'"—she pressed her handkerchief to her brow again, took yet another deep breath, and went on—"Please aid us nonetheless as we attempt to explain that it's highly doubtful, this year, unless *he's* had the measles, which I've never heard mentioned, since he can't be spreading diseases over the entire continent of North America and who knoweth how far beyond. Amen."

Still, it could have been worse, as Christmas Eves go. No one cried herself to sleep, not even Winnie. And Betty and Hannah—who evidently hadn't understood a word that Sister had said—went to bed still beaming about Saint Nick, and woke up happy as clams.

It made me want to punch somebody.

"Poor little chumps," I muttered to Marcella, while we were getting dressed for Mass. "I wish I had something for 'em. They'll be disappointed as hell."

"Ah, they'll get over it. We all get over it, don't we?" She buttoned her top button and gave her collar a fierce tug, straightening it. "When was the last time Santa Claus brought *you* a present?"

I picked up my left boot. Sister Bridget had mended the sole on this one and patched the hole in the other, though they were getting a bit tight in the toe now. "Last Christmas," I said, squeezing my foot in.

But when we came out of chapel an hour later and went to the refectory for our mush, like always, we found the tables covered with long white tablecloths and pots of red flowers, and platters of bacon and eggs, still steaming, and mugs of hot chocolate, and baskets of cinnamon buns and muffins. And on each of our plates there was a huge, fat orange, with a sprig of holly stuck to it, and a bit of green ivy, tied with a ribbon, and a red net stocking stuffed clear to the top with walnuts and great stripedy chunks of hard candy.

"He came!" cried Hannah, grabbing Betty's hand again.

Sister Sebastian—back from the measles—saw my face and closed one eye.

What was she winking about? I wondered.

And then my heart gave a bump, and it hit me—ah, sure, it was *them* who had done this, wasn't it? The meddling millionaires. The Optima Petamusers. They were at it again, weren't they?

"He came! I knew he'd come!"

I fought down the lump in my throat.

Well, what if it *was* them? What did it matter?

Of course I'd sworn I wouldn't be taking any more of their charity—and I wouldn't, neither; I'd stick to that. Except for the chocolate. And the muffins. And a bun or two, maybe.

Since I wouldn't be here much longer.

I slipped my orange in one pocket and my stocking in the other.

I could hock the lot with Harriet.

We all figured we'd had plenty of Christmas, after that. Once that magical breakfast was over. The morning was mostly gone by the time we staggered to our feet, full up to the gills. Still, it was good having the whole day off from lessons, though it was a little on the short side, this being December. It was practically dark by midafternoon, what with the sun going down so early, and more snow starting up, and the backyard too cold to go out in, even if we'd had a mind to. So the Sisters let us rest and read instead—whatever at all we wanted—as long as we could find it on the bookshelves in Sister Sebastian's classroom. I groaned a bit when I heard that part. I was afraid I'd get stuck again with William Wadsworth Longfellow, or the *Lives of the Saints, Part Six*. But I ended up with a grand book about a girl named Gypsy Breynton, who had "a merry laugh and large brown eyes that shone like a whole galaxy of stars," and a peach of an older brother, who was forever taking her on "uproarious adventures." And I sat glued to my seat then, reading and reading, till it was nearly suppertime and I was way down deep in the story—which had some silly parts and some sad parts, but was lovely, mostly—when Betty came in and started tugging on my arm.

"Not now, Betty," I said. "Just another little while; there's no hurry, is there? Look here, you'll love it; they're about to go camping. I'll read aloud to you—"

But she wouldn't listen and wouldn't listen and wouldn't stop tugging; she wouldn't let me be till she'd dragged me all the way to the parlor and flung open the door with a bang—

Only it didn't look like the parlor anymore.

"Oh my," I breathed.

It was all done up in green and white—white satiny ribbons wound through great green branches that smelled like—oh, sweet mercy, what *was* that smell? Something fresh and cold and Christmassy—like snow on the mountains and deep piney forests, or what I imagined forests smelling like, anyhow. And everywhere you looked there were tall white candles—candle after candle—as if our one skinny light from last night (half its old size now, in the window) had multiplied a million times, over and over and over. And right in the middle of 'em all, all lit up with even *more* candles, was the biggest Christmas tree I'd ever laid eyes on, and an easy chair just beside it, and Santa Claus himself sitting in it, with the younger kids all around him: Winnie O'Rourke on his right and Betty tugging me to his left, and little Hannah on his knee between 'em, perched there like a tiny bird, looking like she might faint dead away from happiness: too happy to smile or breathe or move a muscle, but with her brown eyes shining like—well now, wasn't that something?—a whole galaxy of stars.

"Merry Christmas!" said Santa Claus, handing me a candy cane.

"Merry Christmas," I muttered, wishing my face wouldn't burn so. I hoped Marcella wasn't watching. There'd be no end of teasing if—

Wait a minute. That voice . . .

I looked at him again.

I couldn't be sure right away, with the beard and all. Not till Betty reached in his pocket and pulled out a handful of jelly beans, and offered me one.

Ah, crikey . . .

A hundred jumbled pictures tumbled over themselves in my head. The barn in the rain and the priest and the cop . . . *I'm asking you once more, Julia. . . . If there's anything at all you can tell us* . . . and the train smoke clearing from the track by the river, and Mickey Doyle standing across it, looking right at us. . . . *If Bill ever mentioned a place, a name* . . . and the door and the key and the great dragon bridge and the camp on the other side and even the handcuffs—the damn handcuffs—I hadn't seen those with my own eyes, but it didn't matter; they were clear as day anyhow. The damn handcuffs he'd put on my brother's good arm—he himself, Pop the Cop—clearer than all the other pictures put together.

Could he see me seeing 'em? I wondered.

But there wasn't time to think about it. People were pouring into the parlor now—and the laundry girls, too, and even Sister Gabriel and her charges from the sickroom—the ones who were halfway well enough, at least. I suppose the nuns must have figured, what the heck, it was Christmas, and surely the worst was over. Anyhow here they came—a whole crew of 'em, blinking in the candlelight—a dozen or more infirmary girls, still dressed in their nightgowns and wrappers, looking around half-dazed with their splotchy faces, while the millionaires escorted 'em in. So this *was* their party, wasn't it? And now they were milling about all over the place: whiskered gentlemen and white-gloved ladies and the president with the Adam's apple bobbing away, with Agnes Crouse on one arm and Geraldine Mulroney on the other (flashing me a squeeze-lipped, saucer-eyed grin as she passed, looking fit to bust out laughing any second). The whole bloomin' club was there, it looked like—even Mrs. Horace Merriweather, smiling up a storm and clasping her coin purse to her bosom and handing out quarters left and right—why, they'd *all* turned up, hadn't they? Every last one of 'em, except the handsome man, maybe; I didn't see him anywhere. Prob'ly tucked up snug at home with his hot water bottle, dreaming about catching something.

But I guess he hadn't convinced Miss Downey to stay home with him, because here she was now, coming around from the back of the Christmas tree, where she must have been lighting candles. The taper was still burning in the holder in her left hand.

"Merry Christmas, Julia," she said. And she looked me in the eyes with her own steady gray ones, and held out her other hand. So I shook it. But I was blushing red-hot the whole time, thinking of the last time I was in this room with her—that misfortunate Thanksgiving—when I'd stood here howling like a spotted dog.

"I do hope you're feeling better," she said.

"Yes'm," I mumbled.

"Well, that's wonderful news. I'm so glad to hear it."

I would have said thank you—I could have managed that much—but before I could get it out, the door was opening yet again (was the whole *world* coming over tonight?) and this time it was Father Dunne and a crowd of his newsboys who came tramping in, apple-cheeked, brushing snow off their shoulders, with music books clutched in their mittens.

"We've come to sing for our supper," he told Miss Downey, thanking her for the invitation and shaking Sister Maclovius's hand (she was standing beside the hat lady now, looking nearly as dazed as the invalids, and almost as happy as Hannah, for once in her life). "Though it's not the whole group, I'm sorry to say; only the ones who've had the measles already. And Tobin has the toothache, and Tommy's laid up with the mumps, and young McMahon here's hoarse as a crow, so no high *C*. But we'll do our best, won't we, boys?"

And while they were saying, "Yes, Father, we will, Father," I looked over the lot of 'em, thinking, *Ah, no, he wouldn't be here, would he? He'd never be part of* this *gang. . . .*

But there he was, all right—no mistaking that freckled face—poking his nose up over by the door there, looking right at me.

When had Jimmy joined the *choir*, for Pete's sake?

But he only shook his head, once he'd caught my eye, and put his finger to his lips, and waggled his eyebrows, as if—what? What was he saying? Had he brought another message, was that it? Was I supposed to pretend I hadn't *seen* him?

Ah, come on, Jimmy!

Only I couldn't get near enough to ask him what was up. He'd wave me away every time I even tried, or go rushing off somewhere or other. And he wasn't the only one acting peculiar, neither. The whole house was all awry that night, once the boys got there. Even after the music started, and they were chirping out the old songs to Miss Downey's piano-playing—"Jingle Bells" and "Joy to the World" and "fa la la" and all—there was still something odd in the air. Something was wrong, though I couldn't put my finger on it. . . . Dark looks I'd halfway see out of the corner of my eye, and whispers all around me that I couldn't quite catch, and more heads shaking, too, though they'd stop quicker'n they started if they saw you staring. And while Miss Downey and her helpers were putting out supper on the sideboard, Father Dunne crossed the room to the big chair by the tree and said something to Officer Doyle that made him widen his eyes and shake *his* old head, red cap and all a-jangling, and get to his feet right then and there and give out all his candy canes in under a minute (and his jelly beans, too, when Betty ran after him), and make right straight for the door.

So then I started looking for Jimmy again to ask him what in the world, but it wasn't any use. Every time I'd come close, or catch even a glimpse of him, he'd go sliding away slick as goose grease.

Still, supper was a wonder, when they let us at it: not just turkey with the oyster stuffing like the last time, but a huge glazed ham and pickled onions and soft white rolls with butter melting and three kinds of potatoes and four kinds of pies, which Miss Downey sliced herself. And while I was standing at the very tail end of the pie line, wishing I'd got there sooner, someone slipped in just behind me and leaned in close to my good ear and whispered, quick and desperate-sounding: "There's been another shootin'."

"Jimmy?" I started to say, but—

"Don't turn around!" he added, so fierce I could feel

his spit on my neck, his hot breath tickling my earlobe. "They shouldn't see us talking. We're not supposed to know about it. No one's supposed to know."

"Not even the police?" I whispered back, looking straight ahead, as if I was speaking to the mincemeat.

"The police? Are you nuts? It ain't any of *their* business."

"Well, whose is it then? Who got shot? What happened?"

"The Rats were havin' a little party of their own today, and the wrong people came, that's all."

"And now they're dead?"

"*Shhh!* Well, whadd'ya think? And now you watch, just watch, they'll be sayin' it was Mick who done it. You know they will, like the last time."

"*Did* he do it?"

"Well a'course he didn't. Why would he go to *their* party? He never owned a gun in his life. But they'll *say* it was him, that's all that matters. They'll say whatever their boss tells 'em to say. Mick knows too much, remember? He saw Eddie shoot that other feller out there in the alley on Halloween; they'll hunt him down now, for sure. They have to pin it all on *somebody*, if word gets out."

"Who told *you*?"

"Jakey Nussbaum down at the newsstand. His cousin's a barmaid over on O'Fallon Street, not two doors from where it happened."

"But if they're talkin' about it at the *newsstand*—if *Jakey's* talkin'—"

"Then the whole world's talkin'."

"And if the cops find out—"

"We're sunk. Mick's sunk. Every Rat in the Patch'll swear they saw him do it. That's why it's a *secret*, don't you see?"

"So what are you tellin' *me* for?"

"I figured you'd want to know."

"Pumpkin or cherry?" asked Miss Downey, smiling down at the two of us. "I'm afraid we're all out of the others."

"Pumpkin, please," I said, doing my best to smile back, and Jimmy gave her his best gap-toothed-angel's grin and took a large piece of each.

"So I've gotta warn him," he went on with his mouth full, as soon as it was safe to talk again. We'd slipped into the cloakroom with our plates—I'd borrowed the candle from the parlor window—though I wasn't so hungry once we got there. But Jimmy was still chomping and jabbering away: "I'll be goin' across the bridge, first thing in the morning. Mick don't even know what's happened, I betcha. I'm his eyes and ears—remember when he said that? I have to tell him to clear out quick, before the Rats come lookin' for him."

"He hasn't *left* yet? What's he waitin' for?"

"He's savin' up, he says. For him and Bill both. He's got their getaway all planned out, but he's gotta have cash to make a go of it. He's been workin' for more than a month now."

"Workin' where? In East St. Louis?"

"Shhh!"

"Ah, for cryin' out loud, we're in the *cloakroom*, Jimmy. Workin' where? Doin' what?"

"At the levee over on that side—I don't know—whatever they do there. I couldn't find him at first at the camp, last time, but then a feller pointed me back to the river, and there he was, haulin' crates. Makin' two bucks a week, he told me. But it's too late for all of that now. He's out of time; they'll be comin' for him. I know he needs the money, but I got him some tonight—look here—" Jimmy reached in his pocket. "The fat lady gave me two quarters just for standin' there, and I got three bucks from the squinty-eyed man. He was giving out dollar bills to anybody who went near him, but he couldn't tell us apart—he kept calling me Dennis—so I went back twice."

My head was starting to hurt. "That's grand, Jim. That's good work. But—"

"Don't say it. It's no use."

"What's no use?"

"What you're thinkin'."

"You don't know what I'm thinkin'!"

"Yes I do 'cause I thought it first and I already asked Mick that day at the levee and he said, 'No, not yet, it's a one-man job, Jim, it's all in the plan, you've got to stay here for now, we'd never get in if it was all of us but I can do it alone and then we'll send for you later, once I get Bill out, you and his sisters, too, I swear it. You can tell 'em that for me.'"

Good Lord. "He said all that?"

"He did. And that ain't even the half of—"

But I never did hear the rest, because just then there was the sound of more piano music starting up in the parlor and somebody hollering out in the hall: "Brannigan? Jimmy Brannigan! Come on, will you? We're up again!" And Jimmy said, "Ah, hang it all, I'm comin', I'm comin'," took one last bite of pie (he'd started in on mine now), and went rushing away, still dribbling crumbs, banging the door behind him.

In the bleak midwinter,
Frosty wind made moan,
Earth stood hard as iron,
Water like a stone;
Snow had fallen, snow on snow,
Snow on snow,
In the bleak midwinter,
Long ago.

I didn't run after him. Not right away, anyhow. I just sat there for a while, half listening to the carol—I didn't know this one, though I could have sung most of 'em in my sleep—trying not to see all the new pictures he'd planted in my head: guns going off on Christmas Day and Rats on the loose all around us and the dark pressing in again on the House itself, whispering, slithering, bleeding right through the walls—I could feel the weight of it, even in the cloakroom—even while the candles flickered and the little girls smiled and the newsboys kept on singing:

Our God, heaven cannot hold him,
Nor earth sustain;
Heaven and earth shall flee away
When he comes to reign.

In the bleak midwinter
A stable-place sufficed
The Lord God Almighty,
Jesus Christ.

And blast it all to blazes, why did Mickey Doyle's plan have to sound so much like *my* plan? Had he read my mind and *stolen* it?

It's a one-man job, Jim. . . . I'll get him out of there, J. . . . I swear to you I'll get him out. . . .

And who asked him, anyhow? Bill was *my* brother, not his. I could bust him out of Boonville just fine on my own, and I didn't have to hang around levees hauling crates, neither. I already *had* our ticket money, didn't I? Harriet herself, tucked up safe in her pillowcase upstairs, under my mattress, just waiting for me to cash her in, just as soon as—

As soon as—

Was that *Jimmy*, singing all alone now?

What can I give him,
Poor as I am?
If I were a shepherd,
I would bring a lamb;
If I were a wise man,

I would do my part;
Yet what I can I give him:
Give my heart.

Well, hell.

Ah, hell, Jimmy . . .

Who taught you to sing like that?

I wiped my nose on the cuff of my sleeve. I was standing at the back of the parlor now. I'd come out of the cloakroom to see him for myself, that little squirt, just singing away up there like there was nothing to it, like he could do it any day with the whole world watching and *still* take money from the squinty-eyed feller.

Money for Mick. For his friend . . .

So the Rats wouldn't get him . . .

So he could help Bill . . .

Ah, hell . . .

People were applauding now, and saying goodbye, and the newsboys were getting their coats on, and there wasn't time to think about it. Thinking would get me nowhere. If I thought any more my head would explode, so I didn't think. I couldn't think. I just waited till Jimmy was alone for half a second, while the others were busy gabbling, and slipped over next to him and told him what I was going to do. And then I took my candle, what was left of it, upstairs to the slant-walled room, and put it in the window so he'd know where to look for me, and got Harriet from under my mattress, still wrapped in her pillowcase, and took her to the window, too, and pushed open the sash. . . .

And then Betty was standing beside me, watching—I didn't know she'd followed me upstairs—but I didn't mind; I was glad of her company, though she couldn't understand, of course. And we looked outside, and there was Jimmy below us, looking up.

So I took a deep, deep breath, and flung the wrapped-up doll out the window, and Betty and I watched her sailing down to him, down and down and down. . . .

Until he caught her, and waved, and tucked her inside his coat, and ran off to join the others. . . .

And Betty sneezed a great loud sneeze, so hard she blew out the candle.

And then she laughed.

We both laughed, because it was so funny, and we couldn't help it.

We stood there in the dark by the open window, watching the snow fall, laughing and laughing and laughing.

PART TWO

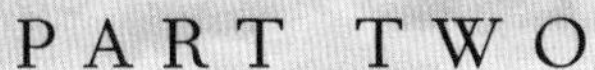

Beyond the Bad Lands
Winter–Spring, 1912

January

Chapter 25

"Jelly Donahoo claims the river's freezing again," said Hazel, kicking the back door closed behind her as she clumped inside with the milk bottles, still stamping snow off her boots. "He says there's chunks as big as boulders pilin' up by the bridge now, and the ferry ain't made it across in four days."

"I don't c-care," I said, pushing past her, bracing myself for the icy blast as I opened the door again, my teeth already chattering.

"Well, lah-dee-da, pardon *me*, Your Majesty," she hollered after me—it was my turn in the lavatory—but I didn't care what she called me, neither. It was too cold to care. Fourteen below yesterday on the back porch thermometer, and no telling how much worse now; no use stopping to read it in this weather. The very water in my eyeballs had been froze up solid for two weeks straight.

Still, it couldn't last forever, could it? Nothing lasted forever. Not even winter, I told myself as I tromped through the hoarfrost, wishing I could feel my toes. Not even the epizootic—now *there* was a miracle—it must be over now for sure, I figured, if Jelly Donahoo wasn't dying of fright when he saw us coming. Sister Bridget had ripped the nails out of the stay-away sign on New Year's Day, when the last bed had emptied in the infirmary, and fed it to the furnace to celebrate, and we'd all said an extra round of the Joyful Mysteries—though we'd been a bit early, as it turned out. Sister Gabriel had scarcely had time to change the sheets the next morning, when I brought Betty in to her. I'd noticed the spots on her back and neck while we were getting dressed for school.

But it was only a mild case, the doctor said. Thank heaven for that much, anyhow. Betty hadn't even realized she was sick, till he told her she was. She'd been cheerful as ever and more surprised than anybody when he'd ordered *her* to bed—the last of the last—"sitting up there in lone splendor, eating custard," Sister Bridget had reported later, “like the Queen of Sheba herself.”

More than a week now, wasn’t it? Tuesday, Wednesday . . . ah, sure. She’d be up and about in no time. And no one else had come down with anything much since then—no more than the usual winter throats and chilblains and stuffed-up noses—so the sign had stayed gone. And good riddance.

Now, if only . . .

If only . . .

Ah, nuts. If only everything. If wishes were horses and pigs could fly and I could feel any part of my left foot . . .

I finished up in the privy (it was even colder inside than out, without the sun to warm it) and closed the door behind me.

I heard him before I saw him:

“*Psssssssssst!* Over here!”

And there was Jimmy Brannigan’s head, poking out of the buggy barn.

I thought my heart would bust right out of my chest, the way it started hammering. But I didn’t say a word till we were both safe inside, where no one could hear us. And then it came pouring out all at once:

“So what happened with Doc?”

“Well, I—”

"How much did he give you?"

"Well, he—"

"Was it enough for Mick's train ticket? Did he make it to Boonville? Did he get Bill out yet? What have you heard?"

"That's what I'm tryin' to—ah, for Gordon's seed, Julia, will you let a person *talk*, for once in your life?"

"So *talk*," I said. "Who's stoppin' you?"

Hyacinth stuck his nose over his stall half-door, blew out a great steaming cloud of oat dust and horse breath, and nudged Jimmy in the shoulder, as if *he* was waiting for an answer, too.

I guess he figured all short people were like Betty, with apples in their pockets.

"Well, say," said Jimmy, laughing. He rubbed the old boy's muzzle. "You're Hyacinth, ain't you? Ah, sure, I heard all about you. And I never put you in the kitchen, did I? That was Little Joe Kinsella, as the whole world knows. I only dared him to, that's all. I never thought he'd go and *do* it. . . ."

I gave his other shoulder a shake. "Don't stand there talkin' to the *horse*! What did Mick say when you saw him?"

Jimmy sighed. "I never saw him."

"But you said you were going the next day—first

thing in the morning—you promised me you were going—"

"And I did, too! Well, a'course I did, straight after I went to Doc's."

"So then—"

"Mick wasn't there, that's all. He'd already gone when I got there."

"Gone where? Gone to Boonville?"

"I don't know. He wasn't *there*, I told you. He musta got wind of the shootin'. Half the town had heard by that time."

"Well, didn't you talk to anyone, then? What about that feller at the camp—the one you saw before—didn't *he* know something?"

"I never found him, neither. Them guys are always comin' and goin'; this was a whole different crowd than the last time. But you don't have to worry. Mick knows what he's doin'. He gave us his word, remember? And just look here—" He reached in his pocket. "I brought you your money, see?" He pulled out a wad of something that smelled like old cigars, then squinted at it and shook his head. "Nah, that ain't it."

Sweet Mary and Joseph . . .

"Hang on, I got it here somewheres. . . ." He started rooting around again. "A'course, Doc took a bit of finagling, like always, but I was ready for him. He didn't even want to *look* at your doll, at first, till I talked him into it. He said, 'Don't waste my time, ye clabber-head, there ain't no market fer it. Nobody buys dolls the day *after* Christmas.' So then I took her out of the pillowcase and showed her to him, like you said—she's a peach, all right—and you could tell he sorta liked her, though he'd never admit it in a million years. You know how he is—ah, sure, here we are—"

But *that* wad of paper turned out to be a pair of ancient-looking tickets to a prize fight between No-Neck Najinsky and Rooster McGee, who'd died of old age, last I heard.

"Ah, for cryin' out loud, Jimmy; I'm freezin' to death here. . . ."

He was checking his inside pocket now. "So then Doc—well, you know Doc—he has to act like he's doin' you all kinds of favors. 'Well, all right, then,' he says. 'I suppose I could spare you a dollar fer your dolly, just this once, seein' as how it's the hand-out season.'"

"A *dollar*?" I gave his arm a thump. "You didn't sell a fine doll like that for a *dollar*, did you?"

"Well, a'course not. Whadd'ya think? I wasn't born yesterday. And I told him so, too. 'Why, just *look* at her,'

I told him. 'With the hat and the pearls and the feathers and all. I'd be the laughingstock of the neighborhood if I sold this doll for a dollar.'"

"And what did he say to that?"

"He said I could save my bleedin' blatherskite breath; them were paste pearls and chicken feathers, dolls like that were a dime a dozen at the corner junk store, and who did I think I was dealing with here, did this *look* like the lunatic asylum, 'Get out before I throw you out, ye cheeky little beggar.' So I tipped my cap and headed for the door and said, 'Well in that case, then, good day to you, sir, I'll take my business elsewhere.'"

I rolled my eyes. "And *then* what?"

"He offered me a dollar-fifty."

My heart sank. "Ah, crikey, Jimmy, she's worth ten times that! You didn't *take* it, did you?"

But he wasn't listening. He was looking in his boot. "Aha! Here you are!" he announced, puffing up proud as a sugar toad, and he pulled out the third wad and handed it over:

Three lousy bucks.

"Three lousy bucks?"

I didn't mean to push him, really. I only thumped him in the arm again—no worse than before—but it must have caught him a bit off balance this time, because he tripped over the hay bale behind him, sat down hard, and dropped his crutch.

"Sorry," I muttered, red-faced, picking it up for him.

He shrugged. "It's all right," he said.

But he wouldn't look at me.

"No, I mean it, I didn't mean to—it's just—ah, come on, Jimmy, you can't even get a good layin' hen for three lousy bucks. How're we ever gonna buy a cow?"

Now he looked at me. "You want to buy a *cow*?"

"I do," I said. And I sat down on the bale beside him then and tried to explain it to him, dollar by dollar—the whole bloomin' plan, cows and all—but the more I talked, the more tangled it got and the sillier it sounded.

"Ah, shut up," he said finally, plucking a straw out of his coat collar.

So I shut up.

What was the use?

It was a terrible plan, wasn't it? Nobody buys dolls the day after Christmas. . . .

My teeth were chattering worse than ever now, like a box of coffin nails, shook up. I blew on my hands to warm 'em, but it didn't do any good.

"You'd better go back in," said Jimmy. "They'll be lookin' for you, won't they?"

I sighed. "Sooner or later."

He nodded and stood up. "Well all right, then," he said, giving Hyacinth a pat on the nose. "I guess I'll see you around, when we get some news."

"See you around," I muttered.

I stuck the three bucks in my pocket. I meant to say more—I wanted to say thank you—but it caught in my throat somehow.

Three lousy bucks . . .

Still, he looked so little all of a sudden, pushing the barn door open.

I ain't little. I'm just short.

"Hey, Jimmy!" I managed to croak out, just before he disappeared.

He turned around. "What?"

"Your song was good. On Christmas night."

He didn't grin, exactly. "Thanks," he said, touching his cap. He started to leave again.

"I didn't know you could sing."

He cocked an eyebrow at me, as if I'd lost my mind. "Well, a'course I can sing. All the Brannigans can sing. They'd be ashamed of me if I couldn't."

Which Brannigans did he mean? I wondered. Wasn't he the only one left, out of all of 'em, when their house burned down?

I didn't ask it out loud—I would never have asked

him—but I guess he must have seen it in my face.

"Sometimes I forget," he answered, before he scrambled over the fence.

All day long I kept trying to put it out of my head—Jimmy standing there holding the money in his fist, so proud of those wadded-up dollars, and Mickey Doyle gone rushing off to Boonville without a single one of 'em, and me just sittin' here stuck again, stopped cold again, like the river, the whole godforsaken froze-up Mississippi.

I could feel it out there still that night, pressing on my eyelids, though we were too far away to see it, really. I looked for it from the window, before we went to bed, but I couldn't make it out with so many houses in the way. But when I climbed under the covers and closed my eyes, there it was, same as ever, just as clear as glass. As clear as the air itself—so sharp and cold, it hurt my chest, remembering.

And there we are, Bill and me, just the two of us—only it's broad day now—in that other frozen time, the winter after the Fair. We're picking our way through the ice shards that pile up along the shoreline, just below the bridge: jagged and dangerous-looking, like splinters of the ice mountains in Gran's fairy book, or broken bits of her good white platter when I dropped it at dinner. . . . *Ah, for pity's sake, Julia . . .*

"Careful, J," says Bill, "mind where you step, now. They could slice you wide open if you ain't careful."

But he ain't scared of 'em himself. He climbs over like they're nothin' and heads for the middle of the river, where the ice is slicker, smoother, whiter, as flat as a tabletop, and I scramble after him, like always. They closed the harbor days ago, after the ice gorge broke loose upstream and crushed a twenty-ton barge, till it was no better than a pile of matchsticks. We'd heard the crack and boom of it all the way from home, like thunder in the clear blue sky. But now there's only the sound of our own footsteps crunching along, and our breath rasping in the sharp-cold air, and my heart beating like a drum in both my ears. . . .

And something else somehow, above all that—a peculiar kind of high-up humming, everywhere and nowhere—all around us and above us and below us, too—as if the ice itself is singing to us. And the closer we get to the middle, and the smoother it is under our boots, the higher and keener the sound gets—like the highest note Papa used to play on his fiddle, the one like a needle in our ears, that made us screech and laugh and run outside, and a glass broke once, though no one was touching it.

"Do you hear that?" I say to Bill. "It's Papa playing! He's teasing us again!" And Bill looks up at me now—all this time he's been trudging along with his hands in his pockets and his eyes searching everywhere, squinting in the brightness—the sun's bouncing off the ice every which way, till you can hardly bear to see. I don't know what it is he's hunting for, but when I say that about Papa, he looks up at me like he's coming out of a cloud, and there's light in his face. . . . But then he listens and frowns again and shakes his head and jerks me back from the smooth part, the lovely white ice in the middle. "Stay away from there, J," he tells me. "It's too thin when you hear that; it sounds higher in the thin spots, where the river wants to break through. If it gives way and you go under the ice, you'll be gone forever, dead as a duck. We'll never find you in a million years, do you understand me?"

And he's pulling me even farther away now, back toward the terrible, sharp ice teeth, the broken-china bits, but I try to get my hand loose; he's holding it so tight, it hurts. "Let *go*, Bill! I know it's him, I heard him, didn't you hear him?"

And for just a split second—a half of a half second—

when I turn my head, I can *see* him; I can see Papa standing there, fiddling. And he sees me, too, I know he does. He looks right at me and closes one eye. But then I blink and he's gone, there's no one there at all, and then there's a cracking sound below me and it's the ice, it's coming apart, it's splitting under my feet, and my left boot goes through and fills up with icy water and I open my mouth to scream, but the cold sucks the breath right out of me and before I can make a sound, Bill is dragging me back; he's got me again. "What did I *tell* you, J? Didn't I *tell* you, for Pete's sake?"

"But he was *there*," I say. "I *saw* him," I say. "He was playing his fiddle and I heard him and then I *saw* him!"

And Bill says I couldn't have, I didn't. "It was only a trick of the light," he says, and he won't listen, he never listens, no one ever believes me, but I know what I saw—I saw what I saw, with that shining ice singing, and the sun so bright in my eyes, and Papa playing his fiddle, same as always.

February

Chapter 26

Quinquagesima Sunday

Dear Mary,

Well hello from your sister in St. Louis, that's me, how are things in Jefferson County, I am in good health and hope this finds you the same. I am sorry I never did write to you before this and by the way why didn't you neither, did the twins swaller your pen? Ha ha. I take this one in hand now because Sister Sebastian says we can either catch up on our New Testament or write a letter to a loved one, so that's you and this is it, I don't know Bill's address in Boonville, do you? Hazel said what do we write about and Sister said the news of the day, so I guess this will be short because nothing intrusting ever happens around here, everything is exackly the same as you remember.

Well I bet you didn't know I could spell Quinquagesima. I never even knew I wanted to but Sister put it on the chalkboard and now I have spelt it twice. She says it means the Sunday before Lent when all the fun starts, so what are you giving up this year? I bet your wondring what we are doing in the classroom on a Sunday but don't ask me because they don't tell us anything exept keep quiet. I saw the docter's buggy out front, I'm afraid its Betty whose got sicker again, she started out with the measles like all the rest of us and I'm worried I gave them to her, I guess I gave them to everybody but we all got well and she didn't, hers turned into something else, Marcella says probly newmonia like dead Cecilia, remember her, or maybe menunjitis or insefa-something but I don't know, nobody knows, they keep saying just another week and then another week, I counted up to six now, they were going to take her to the hospital but it was always too cold for her to go outside and then they thought she was better once so they let her come to the parler on game night, we finely played bunco like they promised, remember on that first day and she loved it, she didn't win anything really but they gave her the most bon bons anyway and she laughed harder than anybody when Sister Gabriel rolled three twos and got the booby prize but then she got sick again, Betty I mean, she was shaking like a leaf the next morning but we couldn't wake her up and that was more than a week ago but she'll be all right don't you think? They don't know how strong she is, remember when she carried that ladder to the coal shute and besides Sister says not to worry, the docter is giving her medicine but shes a sick little girl and it would be good to pray for her so I was thinking maybe you could too, your better at it than me anyhow and you always remember the words. And you still have your rosery right? If you ever have time I mean when all of them babies are asleep, do they ever sleep at the same time, I know your real buzy but if you ever have a chance. Well I guess that's all the news, the sun was out for a coupel of days but the paper says another snowstorms headed this way so I guess Ill be here if you need me, I have no ~~defanit~~ ~~definut~~ imedeate plans at present.

Sincerely your sister,
Julia C. Delaney

The crows were the first to feel the storm coming. The first crow, first thing, Tuesday morning—just the one, to start with—an old feller with a broken wing, pacing back and forth on our window ledge and peering in, like he meant to, squawking us all awake before the sun was done rising.

Hell's bells, what a racket!

How'd he ever manage to get up so high, with a hurt like that? I wondered.

But by the time we went down to breakfast, he'd figured out how to get down, too—unless there was *another* broke-winged crow just like him. He'd sent for his cousins, it looked like. "A murder of crows," Sister Genevieve called 'em, and she stomped to the back stoop, waving her broom, and set the whole flock screeching and flapping away, scattering in a dozen directions.

"And don't come back!" she hollered, shaking her fist at 'em.

It wasn't like her, really, to be getting so riled up. She was cheerful as apples, most days, even if she *was* the world's worst cook. But she hadn't been herself at all this week. I'd stopped by the kitchen yesterday and found her standing over a pan of biscuits, blotting tears with the corner of her apron. "Burnt," was all she'd said, waving a hand at the mess.

And they were, too. Burnt to a crisp: black as tar, with the smoke still billowing.

But I knew it was more than the biscuits, and it wasn't just the crows—who were back in no time anyhow, in case she wanted another crack at 'em. I saw the crippled one pecking around the dustbins not an hour later, and by the ten o'clock bell, the sky was thick with 'em. I didn't know there were so many crows in all Missouri. Didn't they have sense enough to fly South for the winter? *You're too late!* I wanted to tell 'em. *You should have gone with the geese!* But of course they wouldn't have heard me. The air was too full of their cawing. Even with the windows shut tight we could hear it all morning, off and on, though it didn't look much like morning anymore, what with all the black wings shutting out the sun.

Betty would have loved it, if she'd been here. Had they waked her with their caterwauling? She'd be standing right by me at the window, if she wasn't sick. She loved crows like she loved anything that crept or crawled or trotted or flew or had any brand of a heartbeat—Mary'd seen her one time feeding cracker crumbs to the ants in the laundry. Poor Sister Bridget had had a terrible time, getting rid of 'em.

But Betty was still upstairs in the infirmary, so Sister

Bridget was, too, I guess. They said she wouldn't leave Betty's bedside. Everything was topsy-turvy now; the whole House was different. You wouldn't think one little kid with hay in her hair could make such a big hole in the place when she was missing, but she'd been everywhere somehow or other; she was always there like the air we breathed, and I'd never even noticed, till she wasn't.

Maybe the crows knew, too. Maybe they'd come to say goodbye; that was what I was afraid of. That was the thought that sat on my chest all morning, choking me.

But I wouldn't ever have said it. It was Hazel who said it.

"Crows in the coffeepot, coffins at night," she whispered at the noon meal, arching her eyebrows, and I slapped her face and Winnie started wailing and Marcella banged her fork on the table and said, "Shut up, shut up, will you ever shut up, for God's sake?" And then Sister Sebastian was swooping in, quick as a crow herself, saying, "Hush now, Winifred," and "I never heard such rubbish, Hazel. Crows are creatures of the Lord, just the same as the rest of us. It's only this weather stirring them up—the change in the wind—can't you hear it blowing?"

We heard it, all right. There was no way to miss

the moaning in it, rising every minute now. And no sooner had the last black tail feather disappeared, than the snow the paper had promised started sifting down on Morgan Street—only a few lost flakes, long about midafternoon, and then great waves of it, sheets of it, whirling and blowing, with little bits of ice mixed in. You could hear it when it hit the windowpanes, tapping like tiny fingers.

But there was no real change upstairs, they told us. Not that anybody would tell us much of anything. Betty was holding her own; that was all Dr. McGill would say at first, when I saw him heading out the door near dark and went running after him.

"So she's not—she ain't—" I tried again. "She won't *die*, will she, sir?"

He didn't answer right away. He looked about a million years old. Still he took my hand in both of his, steady as can be. "Not if we can help it," he said.

And then it was Wednesday.

Remember, man, that thou art dust, and unto dust thou shalt return.
Remember, man, that thou art dust, and unto dust thou shalt return.
Remember, man . . . Remember, man . . .

Sister Maclovius's voice droned on and on as we stood in the chapel, waiting, while she dipped her thumb in the bowl beside her and marked our foreheads with the ashes in it—little black cross after little black cross—one plaid girl at a time.

Remember . . . Remember . . . Remember . . .

It should have been the priest saying it, really, if only the priest had been here. Or if we'd been at church, like the rest of the world, this first day of Lent. But they couldn't take us anywhere in the middle of a blizzard, and Father Dunne couldn't leave his boys today. The snow was heavier than ever now, with no sign of slowing down yet, piling up in deep white drifts out the downstairs windows. So Sister had burnt the dried-up palms from the last Palm Sunday (they made the best ashes, she said), and prayed over 'em quite a bit, and told us how fortunate we were to be safe here together, especially on Ash Wednesday, which was a day for remembering, after all, she said, the *point* of it all—she stopped there and cleared her throat, as if it was giving her some sort of trouble—and then she asked if any of us could say what that point might be. But we all just stood there, dumb as shoe leather, so she told us the point herself: that life was short in this vale of tears, and our Father in heaven never put us here to stay, but was only waiting for that day of days—known to him alone—when he would call us home.

"Amen," the others answered.

But I couldn't find the wind for it.

She was talking about Betty, wasn't she? She was saying it without saying it and I couldn't stand it, that was all. I couldn't stand around waiting and waiting and never hearing, so I went to see for myself, while no one was watching. I slipped out the back, ashes or no ashes, while the others were still getting theirs, and ran upstairs. We weren't allowed in the infirmary, but I didn't care what I caught; I must've given her the bug in the first place, and I'd take it back, if I could, if it would make her better, and anyhow no one stopped me. They never even saw me go in. The room was white as ever, but dimmer than I remembered, and no one was there at all, I thought at first; there were just two rows of white beds, empty, neat as pins, with the curtains pulled back, mostly—

All but one, at the end, by the window.

I remembered that window.

And sure enough, there was Betty, fast asleep on my old pillow, and Sister Bridget in the chair beside her.

She didn't look so sick, really. Betty, I mean. She was paler than she used to be, and her cheeks were a little thinner, but if you didn't know, you wouldn't know, except for the sound in her breathing—a sort of a rasping, rattling sound it was, not as loud as a snore even. Just a little rougher, maybe—

But that wasn't so bad, was it? Half the House was always snoring, if you woke up to listen. . . .

"Isn't she beautiful?" said Sister.

And she was. But I only nodded, because my voice had stopped working again.

Still, that was enough, I guess. Sister Bridget smiled and held out a hand, and made room in her chair for me, and we sat there together for quite a while, not saying another word.

And just when I was beginning to think that she must have fallen asleep herself, she started talking again, real quiet, so I had to turn my good ear to hear her:

"Look there, now," she said, "how she rests her cheek on the back of her hand. Her daddy used to sleep that way at home. Oh my, just exactly like that—" She smiled and shook her head. "You'd have to shake him awake ten times in the morning, before he'd start moving at all, and if you left and came back two minutes later, he'd be dead to the world, same as ever."

It was an odd thing to say, I thought—"dead to the world"—but I don't believe she even knew she'd said it. Two-Bits Brickey, she meant. The gangster. Betty's daddy was Sister's brother. Though she wouldn't have called him Two-Bits, would she? And I never said a word about it, but she must have heard me wondering, because a moment later she shook her head again, and sighed, just as if I'd asked out loud.

"Ah, Harry. Poor boy. There wasn't a bit of harm in him. You can't believe what they say, you know. He was as good a brother as ever there was. Only got mixed up with the wrong crowd, that's all—that tough gang from Ashley Street—the Rats, they call them now. But Harry was no Rat. He thought Thomas Egan had hung the moon. He'd given him work, you see, sweeping up and running errands, after our father died in a strike bust-up down at the Laborers' Union. Your father would have been there, too; all the workingmen were there. Never mind the whispers that it was Egan's hired thugs who'd *picked* the fight, cracking union skulls for the owners. A job was a job, and times were hard, and Harry was putting food on our table. Even our mother thought it was a gift from heaven. 'You do what Mr. Egan tells you,' she said to him, 'and don't be asking silly questions. No use pokin' your nose in places that aren't any of your concern.'

"And oh, sweet mercy, that face of his! An angel's face, if ever I saw one. Just look at Betty there and you'll have an idea. . . ." A tear slid down Sister Bridget's cheek, and she had to stop and fish for her handkerchief. "So Egan knew he could trust him, you see, like his own right hand," she went on, once she'd blown her nose. "He was that innocent, our Harry was, and loyal as a dog, never saying a thing but 'Yes sir' and 'No sir' and 'Right away, Mr. Egan.' So he'd send him hither and yon, Egan would, with that face like a day in June, and not a cloud in it. And Harry did as our mother told him; he never asked questions, only took this package to one man or that package to another, and never a hitch but a single time when he tripped in a pothole and dropped the bag—

"'And what should fall out,' he tells us at home that night, 'but a roll of cash as big as my fist!'

"'Ah, you knucklehead,' says our brother Jack. 'That's bribe money. What were you, born yesterday? Egan sends you with the boodle so he won't get his own fingers dirty.'

"'That's a lie,' says Harry. 'Mr. Egan's not like that.'

"'Oh no?' says Jack. 'I'll tell you what was in that bag, boy. Grease for the wheels. A hundred for hizzoner the mayor, five hundred for the chief of police, a thousand for his old pals down at the Four Courts. And then the great Thomas Egan does whatever he bloomin' well pleases, and the whole world goes deaf, dumb, and blind.'

"'Stop it, Jack!' Ma tells him. 'You leave Harry alone. He's keepin' us out of the poor house, which is more than I can say for some.'

"But then one day Harry comes home with his face white as eggshells and his eyes popping out of his head, and I say, 'What's wrong, are you sick?' And he claims he's fine, but I know there's something up with him; he's not himself at all. So after supper I whisper, 'Is it your girl, then, Harry? Is it Maggie?' Because we all know he's sweet on little Maggie Meehan. She's in the dance act down at the Standard Theater. Jack's seen him hanging around the stage door, flowers in his fist, standing there with his sheep's eyes, ready for the slaughter. But Harry says, 'No, no, Bridgie, for heaven's sake, you don't know what you're talkin' about. Don't go sayin' a word about her, do you hear me?' Still his face goes from white to red, so I know I'm getting warmer, but now the others have their big ears cocked, too, and he clams up tight. And then finally I'm asleep in my bed and he's shaking me awake and saying, 'Bridgie, I have to talk to you, I have to tell somebody. I need to know what class of sin I've committed and you're the only one knows the whole catechism.' 'Oh Lord, Harry, what have you done?' I ask. 'I went to the track,' he says. 'Well, that's not so bad,' I tell him, though our mother would skin him alive if she knew. Hadn't our pa—rest his soul—had a weakness for the ponies, and run her ragged with worrying he'd bet away our last dime? But what did Harry have to gamble with? Only what Egan paid him—peanuts—a few dollars a week, that's all. Unless . . . oh Lord . . .

"'How much did you lose?' I ask him, though I'm afraid to hear the answer, because now I'm remembering the story he'd told us—the one about the pothole and the cash in the bag. And what if—oh God help him—

"'I didn't lose,' says Harry. 'I won.'

"'You *won*?' says I. 'Well, that's good news! That's all right, then, isn't it?'

"But he says, 'No, no, Bridgie, you don't understand. It was Mr. Egan who sent me with the bettin' money. A hundred dollars—he said to put it on the favorite in the fourth race. Fogarty's Bum. And if I'd done what he told me, that would have been the end of it; I'd have lost the whole bundle when the Bum limped in last. But I was late in line at the ticket window, and I heard this feller talking, you see; he was telling the man next to him about this old nag of a long shot, and how no one but a fool would put a penny on him, and what sort of a name was Hyacinth for a smelly old horse like that? And I say to myself, did he say *Hyacinth*? And it comes at me in a wave, Bridgie, like a sign from heaven, like the river is washing over me and the bloodthirsty Tartars are hot on my heels and I'm in danger of drowning for sure now, if I don't know a miracle when I see one—'

"'So you put Mr. Egan's money on the nag?' I ask him.

"'I did,' says Harry. 'Forty to one.'

"'Forty to one!' Well, of course I think he's pulling my leg. 'You don't mean to say that old horse—why, if Hyacinth came in first—that's four thousand dollars, Harry! You didn't win four thousand dollars!'

"'I did,' says he.

"And still I don't understand him. 'Great gobs!' says I. 'Mr. Egan must have been beside himself!'

"'I didn't tell him,' says Harry.

"'You didn't *tell* him?' I gasp.

"And he shakes his head and grabs on to my hand like he'll sink in that river without it. 'Ah, Bridgie,' he says, 'it ain't such a big sin, is it? I gave him back every dime of his hundred bucks, and I never lied, neither; I told him I got to the window late—which I did, remember? And I never bet on the Bum—which I didn't. And Egan clapped me on the back, and put the hundred in his pocket, and said lucky for him I was always such a slowpoke.

"'But dear God, Harry, he'll hear!' says I. 'You know how people talk. And four thousand dollars—oh Lord, Harry, he's bound to hear!'

"'Well, what if he does?' says Harry. 'It's mine, ain't it, Bridgie? I won it fair and square. It can't be stealing if it wasn't his to start with. If he'd thrown away an apple core and I'd planted a seed in my garden—well, it wouldn't be his apple tree, would it?'

"And I don't know how to answer that, with his face lit up like Christmas, and still he's talking a mile a minute—

"'And now we'll be all right,' he says. 'Don't you see, Bridgie? We'll never have to worry again. You and Ma and the whole family. I'll buy us a house—one of those big ones in Lucas Place, with electric light in every lamp and roses on all the rugs and the terlet right inside with a chain to pull. And a fat silver teapot on the dining room table—can't you see Ma sitting there in a fine new hat, pouring out the tea? And Maggie—well, you know, if she'll only—' He's blushing again.

"'If she'll have you,' says I.

"'She'll have me,' says Harry. 'She's got to have me. I don't see how I could stand it, if she wouldn't. I can't live without her, Bridgie. She's the beat of my heart.'"

Sister Bridget uncrumpled her handkerchief again and wiped her eyes on the only dry inch. "Ah, Harry. Poor boy . . ." She stopped and lifted a damp curl from Betty's brow—it had wrinkled a little, as if she was worrying—but at Sister's touch, it smoothed again. "I never did see a happier bridegroom. Your father was there, you know. Marched 'em in at the start, playing 'Haste to the Wedding,' and out at the end, still fiddling. And Harry beaming like the sun itself, with his girl on his arm, looking like he'd bust with pride."

"And then . . . ?" I breathed. All this time I hadn't said a word, but I couldn't let her stop now. Still, I couldn't finish the question. "And then—" I said again.

"And then they killed him," she said quietly.

"For the four thousand dollars?"

"For the four thousand dollars," she repeated. "Though they never got a penny of it. He'd frittered it all away by then; we never knew how he managed it. All on gifts, just like he'd promised. Well, except for Ma's mansion; even he couldn't manage that much.

But the fine silver teapot and her grand new hat—she had 'em till the day she died—and gold watches for all our brothers, engraved with a *B*. And a piano for me, of all things. It's the one in the parlor now. It came here when I did; I wouldn't part with it for the world, though I still can't play a lick." Sister smiled a little, and blew her nose again. "And the loveliest china doll for Maggie . . . Oh, I suppose it was a silly present to be giving a bride. Jack teased him to death about it. But she loved that dolly, Maggie did. She was only sixteen, you know. And Betty dotes on it, of course, now that's it's hers. It's her pride and joy. She never lets another soul touch it." Sister tucked away her hankie. "You haven't seen an old doll anywhere around here, have you, Julia?"

Chapter 27

No.

No, no, no, no, no, no, no . . .

She didn't mean *that* doll, did she?

She couldn't mean *that* doll. . . .

"A—a baby doll?" I stammered. There was something hard and cold in my throat, wedged in against my windpipe. It felt as if I'd swallowed a block of ice.

Sister Bridget shook her head. "More of a lady, I'd say." She smoothed Betty's covers. "With feathers on her hat and a fine satin dress—oh, now, don't look so worried, Julia. It doesn't matter, really. I just wondered, that's all, if she might like to have it here—as a comfort, you see, when she wakes up. Would she keep it in the barn, do you think? You know how she loves it out there—"

"I'll find it," I said. I was on my feet already. There must be another doll. There had to be another doll. . . .

"Why, thank you, dear. Did you hear that, Betty? Your friend here's getting your doll for you. But put your coat on first, Julia; it's bitter cold. And don't be staying out there too long now. It's only a little thing, really. We can't have you taking sick again too. We can always—"

But I never heard what we could always do because I was out of the room by that time; I was hurtling down the stairs. "I'll find it!" I called back again. It would be in the barn; yes, of course it would—*please, God, let it be there*—and now I was grabbing my coat from the cloakroom and cramming my arms in the sleeves and running at the same time, racing down the hall to the back door and thank heaven no one stopped me. There were *plinkety-plunk*s coming out of the parlor as I passed, and there was Miss Downey giving Winnie her Wednesday lesson, blizzard or no blizzard, but they both had their backs to me and the others were all in the classroom now, so no one noticed me going outside. There'd be hell to pay later for being late but I didn't care. It didn't matter.

None of that mattered. I had to find the other doll, Betty's real doll that wasn't Harriet—*there has to be another one; oh please let there be another one*—so I went tearing into the barn and started searching high and low, in the loft and under the hay and in the boxes behind the buggy and even in Hyacinth's stall, while he snorted and blew smoke at me and pawed the floor under him with his forty-to-one hooves—he looked more like a million-to-one now—there were icicles in his eyelashes and an extra blanket folded up in the corner and I looked under that, too, but there was nothing there, neither, so I slung it over the other one on his poor old back and kept looking and looking—*God help me, oh please help me*—and all this time the stone-cold feeling in my insides was getting colder and colder and heavier and heavier, and what was the bleedin' use of lookin'; I'd hocked Betty's doll, hadn't I? Her pride and joy that her daddy gave her mother. There'd never been another one; I wasn't going to find any other one; there was just Harriet and only Harriet and it wasn't the millionaires who'd brought her, neither, when I was sick as a dog and didn't know anything. It was Betty herself, wasn't it? *Ah, sure it was, ye thickhead*—it was Betty all along, thinking her doll would make me feel better, and now

I had to get it back, was all. I had to go and give Doc the three lousy bucks. They were still in my pocket, weren't they? Sure they were, right here. And Harriet would still be right there at Monaghan's River Arcade and Pawn Shop—well, of course she would, of course she would—nobody bought dolls after Christmas, remember? Not the day after or the month after or—oh Lord, this was *two* months after, wasn't it? Well anyhow, there was no use standing here worrying about it. She'd be there, she had to be there, and I had to go, so I went. I left. I opened the barn door and ran to the fence, and the wind and snow came whipping around me and stung my eyes, my throat, even my teeth, but it didn't matter; I'd be taking the trolley; it wasn't but a ten-minute ride on the trolley from here, and then—

"Julia?"

Oh no.

"What are you *doing*, Julia?"

I was halfway over the fence, was what I was doing, but I turned around and there was Winnie on her way to the lavatory, the bloomin' lavatory; couldn't a person get out of this place for once in her life when the whole world *wasn't* going to the lavatory?

"It's all right, Winnie," I told her. "You go on, now.

Everything's all right. I'm just—I was just—"

She burst into tears. "Don't run away, Julia! You're runnin' away, ain't you? Oh, no, please—you can't—it's too cold; look how cold it is, Julia! You'll get sick again, you'll die, you'll die just like Betty—"

I climbed down and shook her. "No I won't, I ain't dyin'. *Nobody's* dyin', do you hear me? And I ain't runnin' away, neither; don't you go tellin' anybody I'm runnin' away, Winnie! I'll be back, I'll be right back, I'm just *gettin'* something, for Betty, that's all. Her doll she loves, her lady doll. I hocked it accidentally—well, not accidentally, exactly. I sold it to Doc Monaghan—I made Jimmy sell it, that is, but I still have the money, see? I never touched a penny of it! So I'm going there to get her now; you tell Betty if she wakes up—only Betty, do you understand? Tell her I'll be back in no time, an hour, tops. It'll be all right then, she'll get better then, I know she will but I have to go now, don't you see, Winnie? Ah, don't cry! Why are you cryin'? I'll be *back*, ain't you listening? I'm coming right back—"

And still she just stood there with the tears streaming, shaking her head no, no, no, but I couldn't help it; I couldn't wait. I had to get Harriet, so I left Winnie standing there and I climbed back up the fence. It was slick with ice and my hands kept slipping and my boots kept slipping and I gashed one shin on something sharp, a nail, maybe, but that was nothing, I hardly felt it, and then I was over and out and running down the alley to Morgan Street—or not running, exactly, with the snow dragging at my boots and up to my knees in places and still stinging my eyes, my throat, my teeth again but I didn't care, it didn't matter, I was almost to the streetcar stop; I could see it just ahead already and the trolley itself was right there, too—now *there* was a bit of luck—I wouldn't even have to wait, would I? I could jump right on and be on my way, and back with the doll in no time—

Unless—

Ah, for crying out loud—

That car wasn't just stopped. It was stuck, wasn't it? Well, sure it was, of course it was, there were horses and wagons and workers beside it, shouting and pointing and shoveling the track in front of it and around it, throwing up piles of snow to the left and right—mountains of snow, huge walls of it—leaving a great deep canyon in the middle. But the quicker they shoveled, the quicker the wind blew down half their work and new snow came down on top of it all, till it looked as if they'd never be done.

"Hey, little girlie!" one of 'em shouted. "Go home! There's no school today—didn't anybody tell you? All the schools are closed!"

"I know!" I called back, so he wouldn't bother me. "I'm *going* home!" And I guess it worked—he stopped yelling, anyway—so I just kept walking the way I was walking. I couldn't stand here forever waiting for the trolley to get unstuck; I'd freeze if I just stood here. I'd catch it later if they ever got it moving again, but I had to keep going now so I just kept going. I wished I had a hat; I should have thought of a hat. My ears were so cold they were burning hot somehow but never mind, never mind, if I stuck to the shoveled-out places behind the wagons up ahead I could go faster anyway and it wasn't that far to Doc's, really. I could walk it in half an hour on a good day, and anyhow there was one block behind me already now and then there was another and another, three blocks and change; I couldn't feel my feet anymore and the drifts dragged at 'em but they kept moving all the same. *I'm on my way, Betty, just wait, just you wait now, I'll get her back, I'm gettin' your doll. . . .*

There were hardly any regular people on the street anymore, no one but me and the trolley crews, shouting and shoveling—there were more up ahead, all along the track—and a few scrawny dogs, up to their haunches in snow, plodding beside me. "What are *you* doing out here?" I asked 'em. "Scat, now! Go home!" But they didn't even bother barking. They only half looked at me with their eyes all slitted up and their ears blowing back and their tails between their bone-thin legs, and we all kept going and going, block after block, one foot after the other, past the dime museum shut up tight and the newsstand without any newsboys in it and Patrizi's market, right where I left it, but with no Mr. P in sight. No one was anywhere they were supposed to be. And there were great sheets of white stuff coming at me again, so I couldn't see more than a few feet ahead anyhow, with odd shapes looming up out of nowhere in it, swimming at me like big white snow-fish—or was it *me* swimming at *them*? They turned into all manner of whatnot as I got closer: stalled motorcars and blown-over buggies and a stuck steam fire engine with the horses still strapped to it, floundering in the traces—"Damn it all, is that a kid down there? Go home!" the firemen yelled as I pushed through the drifts around 'em, past a half-buried bicycle and an abandoned sled with a crumpled runner and an upended grocery wagon with its crates cracked open and bright red apples spilling out on the snow, and one left-behind crow bent over 'em, pecking—but not *that* crow, surely—not the broke-winged feller—was it? And it blinked a pale eye at me and hobbled away.

"Go home!" yelled the man helping the sobbing lady cross Eighth Street.

"Go home!" yelled the Seventh Street cop.

"Go home, for the love o' God, child!" called the blue-lipped woman lugging the sack of coal down Sixth. "Does your mother know you're out in this?"

"She does," I lied. "I'm on my way."

Go home, go home, go home, go home. . . .

"I'm *going* home!" I told them all. Deeper and deeper into the Patch, closer and closer to the river . . . The white was thicker than ever here, once I got across Broadway—it had to be Broadway, didn't it? It was wider than the other streets and ten times busier, most days, though all its regular street sounds were muffled now. You couldn't hear a thing over here on the far side, only the wind howling like a madman, no train whistles or ferry whistles or steamboats blowing their horns today, just that god-awful wind that cut you to the bone, sliced you right in two, it did, and—ah, crikey, what was *that*, then? A horn, after all—a single car horn blaring at me; or maybe not me in particular, but close, so close I had to cover my ears to shut it out and I didn't see anyone else it might be honking at. . . . I could just make it out now, a few feet ahead of me—another snow-fish, it looked like, another stranded automobile—this one might have been blue once, before the snow. . . . And now there was another man shouting, too, and the dogs beside me were barking their heads off at him, a huge mountain of a man bent over the half-blue wreck, who got even huger as he straightened up and pointed right at me. "And where do you think *you're* goin', miss? Is it freezin' to death you're after? Go home to your house, ye tomfool kid; don't stand there gapin'!"

Oh God, dear God . . .

And my heart bumped harder than it was bumping in the first place because I knew him, sure I knew him, it was Eddie, wasn't it? Fat Eddie Farrell, Eddie the Rat, dear God in heaven, well of course it was, of course it was; no one else in the world was as big as that—*I have another car*, his boss had bragged; this must be it but still—*oh God, please God*—it was all right, it would be all right; Eddie didn't know *me*, did he? He wouldn't remember that far back. October was a million years ago and I was nothing to him, was I? Just some kid, that was all I was, and besides, I was leaving already, I was past him, I was gone, with the dogs still yowling behind me—

I'm going, I'm going. . . .

Fourth Street, Third Street, Second, closer and closer, oh so close now—there was Doc's just ahead on the corner—I could see the ticket booth jutting out, just the same as ever. The wind hadn't blown it away then. I was wet right through by this time, my coat my plaid my socks my boots even my long johns, soaking wet and froze solid at the same time but I didn't care, it didn't matter, I was running again, I was almost there—*almost there, Betty! Just let it be open, it has to be open, please don't let the door be locked—*

But of course it was locked.

Of course it was—

"Open the door, Doc!" I hollered, pounding on it with my fists till the blood came. I could see it seeping out of my knuckles but I couldn't feel it; I couldn't feel anything anymore. "Let me in, let me in! I know you're in there, Doc!" He lived over the shop, so where else would he be on a day like—

"Go away!" came a wheezing old croak from the upstairs window. Doc had shoved it up and was poking his head out. "We're closed, can't you see? It's a blizzard! Go home!"

"I can't go home! I won't!" My mouth was so numb from the cold that it wouldn't bend right around the words, but I kept shouting anyway. "You have my property in there—my friend's, I mean—look here, Doc, I brought money!"

And I guess it was the money that did the trick. The three lousy bucks—but of course *Doc* didn't know it was only three lousy bucks—when I pulled it out of my pocket (still in a wad, so you couldn't tell how much) and waved it at him. "Please, sir!"

"Ah, for the love o' Leo, will ye stop your infernal racket? I'm comin', I'm comin', fer God's sake!"

So I stopped knocking and waited because my knuckles were killing me now, after all—I guess I'd cracked through the ice in 'em—and then Doc was there finally; he was opening the door; he was standing there scowling at me, holding a large gray handkerchief to his bright red nose. "Well, come in if you're comin' in, Julia Delaney. I can't stand here jabberin' all day!"

Chapter 28

So I walked in the door past Doc, who was holding it—it was the odd sort that swung out, not in—and the wind came a-roarin' and rattlin', and slammed it shut behind me.

I took a deep breath.

The old place still smelled like peanuts, just exactly like it always had. The old clocks on the walls—hundreds of clocks—were still ticking away, so loud, even I could hear. It was all just the same, as far as I could tell. I couldn't see too well at first, after the blinding white outside. But little by little the shapes around me turned familiar, even in the dim. I knew 'em all by heart, anyhow: the cardboard strong man who'd swing his fist for a penny and punch a hole in the cardboard wall; the porcupine with the quills that popped out when you put a nickel in its nose; the one-eyed lady fortune-teller who used to blink, when she worked, and creak open her metal mouth, and spit out papers that said *Strike while the iron is hot!* or *Are you SURE?* or *So long, sucker!* Even with no lights and no music and everything stopped dead cold, I could see 'em all staring at me—feel 'em all waiting—Madame Marvella and her camel, too, one row over in the peep boxes, all ready to go galloping off, with just a crank and a spin—

"State your business then, girlie, if ye got any business to state!" Doc had swung around now and blocked my view with a worse one—his long, skinny self wrapped up in a dark blue polka-dot robe, and his long, stubbly chin poking out, and his bony finger pointing and his little red eyes squinting and his tall white head full of spiky bits, like they'd never known a comb. "What's so all-fired important that you'd come roustin' me out of me sickbed in the middle of a blizzard? Have ye lost what little wits ye never had? And don't be castin' your eyes at them picture boxes, Tinkerbell, because we ain't open today, I told you already, and I ain't fixin' ye tea and biscuits, neither, so don't be standing there chattering your teeth at me and dripping snowmelt on me floor when you ought to be home with the nuns—ah, sure, I know you, I know all about ye; I got a memory like a steel trap—and speaking of which, by the by, you owe me at least two dollars in ticket money, which you never paid, now did ye? All them times ye came sneakin' in here, you and your car-thieving brother—don't ye cut your eyes at me, missy; I'm only statin' the facts, is all—so we'll have to be taking that into account, now won't we, regarding this so-called property—your friend's, you were saying? Which you claim that I have, though I doubt that I do, or I'd know it meself, now wouldn't I?"

I gritted my teeth. Crabby old crook. What business did *he* have anyhow, calling my brother names? Still, I didn't say it. I knew I couldn't say it—or kick him in the shin, neither—then I'd never get Harriet back. And I had to get her back, I had to get her back. That was all that mattered now, so—

"It's a doll," I muttered. My lips still weren't bendable, but my tongue wasn't quite as thick now.

"A *what?*" Doc hollered. He grabbed his ear trumpet from behind the counter and held it up to his ear. "Speak up, ye little brat! Are you tryin' to make a fool of me?"

"A *doll*," I said again as loud as I could, leaning around him and searching with my eyes. There were glass-front display cases everywhere you looked, once you started looking, in front of the counter and behind the counter and reaching to the ceiling, some of 'em, and every one stuffed with stuff, crammed to the brim with rings and watches and bracelets and boots and an elephant made of matchsticks and magnifying glasses and earmuffs and bright-beaded ladies' handbags and silver-backed mirrors and teacups and shaving cups and shiny steel razors and footballs and baseballs and leather gloves and penny whistles and crutches and false teeth and a wooden leg with the shoe still on it and oh—oh—just to the right there, behind the stuffed parrot in the golden cage, a whole *shelf* of doll cases, every one chock-full of dolls—big ones and little ones and babies and ladies, too, but none half as fine as Harriet; I still didn't see Harriet—*oh God, someone's bought her; well of course they have, of course they have, she's better than any of these old—*

"There she is!" I cried, when I spied her at last, all alone in a glass box of her very own, in the middle of all the others, front-and-center in her blue dress, with her hat and pearls and parasol and her little white teeth smiling at me—*oh, thank God, thank the Lord*—"That's the one! That's my doll! My friend's doll, I mean—"

"Oh, it is, is it?" Doc lifted a spiky eyebrow. "Your 'friend's' doll, ye say? Would ye be meaning that little beggar with the crutch who brought her here? Brannigan, wasn't it? Little thief in the makin' himself, no doubt. And what would *he* be doing with a doll like that? Lucky for him I didn't call the police. Lucky for *both* of ye, I can see now. Go on, get out of here. Go back to the nuns. That doll's not for sale. I'm waiting for the *rightful* owner to claim it, and it ain't you, me fine lady; you don't fool me for a second. You couldn't afford that doll if your life depended on it."

"But . . . but I *am* the rightful owner!" I sputtered. "I mean—my friend is—Betty, not Jimmy—he was only sellin' it for me, that's all, because—because I didn't *know* it was hers, you see—and—and I can pay, see here? I brought you the money—three dollars—every bit of what you gave him—"

An ugly smile cracked across Doc's large yellow teeth. "Oh, is that what he told ye, the sly boots? Three dollars, was it? And you *believed* him? My, my. Three dollars for a doll like that? Why, I gave him ten, I did, and counted it a bargain. So I couldn't think of partin' with her now, now could I? Not for a penny less than twelve, at least. Eleven at the outside. But of course if you'd care to purchase one of our *smaller*—"

"That's a lie!" I shouted, grabbing hold of his polka-dot sleeve. "You gave Jimmy *three* dollars—three lousy bucks—you know you did; you *know* you did—"

The voice came out of the shadows behind me: "Give the kid the dolly, Doc, if she wants it so much."

All the ice in my hair that was melting on my head started running down my neck, colder than ever. All the birds in the clocks started singing: *Cuckoo! Cuckoo!*

"Why, hello, Mr. Egan! I didn't see ye back there!" Doc squinted into the dark. "And Eddie, isn't it? Well, of course it is. Come in, come in. What can I do for you two gentlemen? To what honor do I owe the pleasure, on a day such as this? I have the kettle on upstairs, on me hot plate, if you'd care for a drop of tea. We're closed down here, due to the weather, of course, for the *general* hoi polloi—you were just leaving, weren't ye, Julia? But of course it's always a privilege—"

"Just get the doll, Doc." Egan stepped in closer.

My own legs wouldn't move at all.

"Well, of course, Mr. Egan, if you say so. Right away, right away—" Good Lord, was the old man *trembling*? He fetched a stepladder from under the counter and pushed it over in front of the cabinet with Harriet in it. "But as I was just explaining to the young lady here . . ." He reached in his pocket and took out a gigantic ring of keys of every shape and size—there had to be forty or fifty, at least—*clinkety-clank*ing all together as he searched through 'em with his knobby old hands. No question he had the shakes now. "Naturally a doll like this is worth a great deal more than *some* people might—oh, yes, here we are, sir, here's the—ah, no, now what am I thinking? Not *that* key; that's for the parrot! Oh dear, I know it's one of these. . . ." The bully Doc was all gone; there was another Doc here now, with a wheedling, whining sound to him, like a dog fearing a kick.

"Take your time," said Tom Egan. He looked at me and smiled. "We don't have any pressing engagements today, do we, Miss Delaney?"

Oh dear God, what's happening, what's he talking about? Why would the Rat of all Rats be standing here smiling at me and why won't my legs move, my fingers my toes my tongue oh God dear God, please, Betty's waiting, I can't just stand *here. . . .*

"Here we are!" said Doc, mopping his damp brow with one hand and turning the key in the lock with the other, and handing down the doll not to me but to Egan—*oh no, oh please, don't touch her*—who held her up high and looked her over.

"Well now, she's a beauty, ain't she?"

And then he put her in my arms, parasol and all.

Thank God. Thank you, God. Do you see that, Betty? I've got her! I've got Harriet!

Now if only I could move . . .

But it was Egan who was moving again, reaching inside his overcoat and pulling a cigar out of his vest pocket and snapping his fingers at Fat Eddie, who came trotting right over, like a good boy, and lit a match from a box in his own pocket.

"Well now," Egan said again, puffing out a cloud of smoke—

And no sooner do I smell the smell, than the October sun is shining inside my head and the flag is flapping on the flagpole and I'm back at the ballpark by the smashed automobile. . . . *Now, ain't this rich? Ah, Eddie, you big lug. We've been robbed by a gang of midgets?*

But then my head cleared and it was winter again, in the middle of a blizzard. We were still standing in Doc's, and Egan was putting his arm around my stone-cold shoulders, saying, "Well now, Miss Delaney, isn't *this* a bit of luck, running into each other like this, when you're just the girl I've been meaning to talk to for the longest time? Wasn't I just sayin' that the other day, Eddie?"

"You were," said Eddie.

"M-me?" I stuttered.

"You," said Egan. "None other. I'd have paid you a visit some time ago, in fact, but I've never had the measles, as it happens. And the good Sisters are a bit thorny about gentleman callers—as they should be, of course—and well, you know how time flies. And then there you were, coming to *us*, right out in the snow just now, when our car was giving us a spot of bother—"

So that was it, then? He was in the stuck car?

"And I said to Eddie here, 'Now there's a little girl who could use a hand, Eddie.' Didn't I say it, Eddie? Those very words?"

"You did, Mr. Egan."

"So here we are, you see, to offer it—and not only to you, but to your brother, too, poor lad. Ah, such a shame! When you know as well as I do what a fine boy he is—well, of course he is, at heart—Father Dunne thinks the world of him. Not the reformatory type atall, atall. That was all a mistake, now wasn't it? One that could be corrected, you see, with a bit of explaining, once the judge is made to see that Bill was tricked, that's all. Led astray, poor boy, by his so-called friend . . . Mickey, I believe it is. Mickey What's-His-Name—Doyle, isn't it, Eddie? Oh yes, my yes, he's the bad apple in that barrel, no question about it. I've offered a substantial reward for that one." Egan took another puff of his cigar and blew a smoke ring around my head. "You wouldn't have any idea where I could find him, would you, miss? Five hundred dollars, you know; that would buy you a lot of dollies. . . . Well, come along now, we can think about all that later. Let's get *you* sorted out, shall we? We ain't but a block or two from my place of business; how would you like something nice and hot to drink? And some dry clothes, too—ah, me, look how you're shivering! Poor little kid, you're wet through. . . ."

And then he was pulling me along with him, and I wanted to pull away, but my legs weren't working right; they were like a pair of dead sticks under me, and meanwhile Eddie had one elbow gripped tight and Egan had the other, but I still had Harriet, I still had Harriet; Doc was watching the whole time with his little kicked-dog's eyes but he didn't care if I took her now, did he? Egan had slapped down a bill on the counter—did that say *twenty*? Saint Chris on a crutch, I'd never even *seen* a twenty-dollar bill—*look there now, Betty! do you see what your doll's worth?*

And I'm hanging on to her for dear life, but what good does it do me when Betty's a million miles away and it's snowing harder than ever when they drag me out the door. . . . It wouldn't matter if I could yell, but I can't yell, I can't make a peep, and I have these stick legs and *oh God, we're outside, and there's only white, white everywhere and the sounds in my good ear are all confused. . . . There's a bell ringing somewhere; is it the Angelus again? Or the ferry, maybe—but there'll be no ferry today; it couldn't get through the ice, could it? The river's froze up stiff, remember, and there's no one out here anyhow; they're all home where they belong where it's warm and it's dry and there's no snow stinging their eyes their faces the lungs in their chests and I want to be home, too, I want to go home—well, not home, but the House—I've got the doll, Betty needs the doll, and if I tell the Rat where Mickey is he'll give me five hundred dollars and we can get on the train and have the chickens and the ice cream but then he'd shoot Mickey, wouldn't he? Oh dear God, I'd be a murderer and Bill would never forgive me, ah, hell, I guess I can't let him shoot Mickey after all but where's he taking me, anyhow? He said a hot drink, I'd like a hot drink but you know what the Rats do, they put the powder in it, Bill told me all about it, and then you're asleep and when you wake up they've already robbed you blind and what if they take the doll, Betty needs the doll, remember? Please God, make my legs work, I can't have the hot drink, I can't go in the Rat's hole, I can't I won't I will not no no no no* NO. . . .

And then I woke up; I jerked awake; I sunk my teeth into the hand on my left shoulder and kicked the nearest knee and then my right foot touched the ground, the snow on the ground anyhow, and twisted under me and oh it hurt, it hurt, but it woke me up even wider now and my legs stopped being sticks and I was running, half running-hopping-running like Jimmy with his crutch, only I didn't have a crutch, just the doll, just Harriet, I had her at least and they couldn't catch us, Betty; the Rats couldn't catch us, they were old and fat and I was fast as a fox but I couldn't see which way to run in the white, the air was all white and I couldn't see, I couldn't see anything, and all I could hear was the sound of the Rats coming after me, *thump-thump* through the snow, and cussing "hells" and "damns" and "Catch the damn kid, you big dope; never mind me, I'm all right, holy shite, she bit me, the little brat," "Oh dear, you're bleeding, Mr. Egan," "Never mind, it's nothing, just get her, get her now, do you hear? Don't let her get to the river, for God's sake," and what did he mean the river? I couldn't see any river; I thought I was going toward the trolley tracks—*oh God, what's that sound behind me? Is it the trolley, did they get the car working, is that it? But I can't see, I can't go back, I can't turn that way now; the Rats are there*—thump-thump—*Don't be afraid, Harriet, don't worry, Betty, I'm coming, I've got your doll now, you'll be all right, I'm sorry, I'm sorry, I didn't know, you know I didn't understand, oh somebody please, oh help, God help me, what's the matter with you anyhow? Are you deaf in both your ears? Did they give* you *the drink with the powder? Please God, help me help Betty help Bill help Mickey too, ah, sweet Mary and Joseph is that the bridge? It couldn't be, could it?*

And still the white blew and shook from the sky like feathers from a featherbed, wing feathers, angel feathers, but then it came apart partway like a great curtain opening and I could see it looming over me again, the monster, the river dragon, the great gray bridge after all, after all, oh God, it was the bridge for sure and then I was on the river, the froze-up river, and there were the sharp bits all around me like that time with Bill, the great broken china bits, and still the Rats were coming; I could hear them breathing hard and thumping and cussing and there was that other sound, too, that trolley sound only not a trolley but a great wheezing and clattering and all the time that high-up ringing in my head like the ice was singing again, and I looked for Papa like before but I couldn't see him now, only white and white and more white and the great gray bridge—*oh dear God, what was that noise?*—that other noise, that God-awful roaring in my ears, all mixed in with the hollering, someone was hollering, more than one voice now; it must be the Rats yelling, "Stop! Stop! For God's sake, stop, Julia Delaney! You're going the wrong way; it's too thin in the middle, the ice won't hold! Come back, Julia! Stop, do you hear?"

And so I stopped then, I turned around, and it wasn't just the Rats behind me, and it wasn't the trolley, neither; it was Hyacinth—oh God, it was Hyacinth—and the orphan buggy with Miss Downey at the reins and one of the nuns standing up beside her with her veil flying black in the wind like a great crow's wing—not Sister Maclovius! Oh no, it looked like her, but it couldn't be, could it? Yes, it could, and it was, great jumping Jehosaphat, Sister Maclovius and the hat lady with her feathers flying, too, and Hyacinth coming toward me like hell on wheels through the terrible chopped-up river-ice, bumping and clattering but still coming and coming, and the Rats had stopped dead in their tracks, watching 'em—they shouldn't be out here; *we* shouldn't be out here—and there was a terrible cracking and booming all around us in the white now and I saw it then, oh God, I saw it, the crack in the river-ice just beyond me, just under the bridge, splitting wider and wider—bloody hell, couldn't they see? It couldn't hold a whole horse and a buggy besides, for God's sake, but still Hyacinth was clattering toward me like Dan Patch smellin' the barn and the Rats were froze-up stiff as the ice, stiffer than the ice now; they must have seen the break in it as well as I did; they didn't know which way to turn, but still the horse and the nun and the lady kept coming and now I was running again, only *back* now, back toward the buggy, away from the bridge, not spittin' distance from the Rats but they never tried to stop me, only stood there gaping—I guess they were the ones with the stick legs now—they were paralyzed entirely and the great split in the ice was moving faster and faster, coming right at the two of 'em but breaking on either side so they didn't know where to go, what to do, and then Fat Eddie's face changed and he started to slip; the ice was opening under him and he slipped and lurched and tried to grab hold of me as I ran past but there was nothing to grab hold of because I was quick, too quick, jerking away jumping flying before the river got me, too, and all the time he was falling down, down, sliding into the water itself—*oh God, oh God*—and his hand reached out and grabbed me by the boot but when I kicked, it came off in his hand, and now it's too late for Eddie, the river has him, and I don't want to look but I can't help it, I have to look, and he's waving at me and yelling, "Go on, go on, get out before it gets you, girl, don't you see what I'm sayin'?" and then he's gone and I'm backing up, I'm turning around, I jump clear of the crack before it takes me down, too, and now I'm flying, I'm hobbling one-shoed but I'm flying all the same, I'm fast as a fox and I still have the doll and they can't stop us, no one can stop us, here's the horse and the buggy and the lady and the nun with their arms out, pulling us in with 'em and we're safe, we're safe, we're in the buggy, Harriet, the ice is still cracking and booming all around us but Sister Maclovius has me fast in her iron grip and Miss Downey is turning the horse around and the bridge is behind us now and there's good hard ice ahead and Sister keeps saying, "You're all right, you're all right, don't look back, child, you're all right. . . ."

Only then the buggy bumps and lurches and jerks around again and we're stopping—why are we stopping? And when I crane my neck to see past the flapping black of her habit, there's Tom Egan standing by the horse's head; he's got Hyacinth by the cheek strap and he looks all wild-eyed and lunatic, like he'll keep us there forever; he'll never let go. . . .

But Hyacinth won't stand for it. Miss Downey jerks the reins, but the poor horse has had enough. He tosses his head and rears up both his front legs and Egan can't hold on; he loses his balance and falls on his knees to the ice itself, and his hat goes flying, and there he is looking at us with the black smudge of ashes on his forehead clear as day, the Ash Wednesday ashes, just above his thick black eyebrows.

And Sister Maclovius sees 'em just as clear as I do. I see her seein' 'em. She's still got me tight in her left arm, but she lifts her right and straightens her back and stands even taller, like a great craggy mountain, and points at the mark on his head with her terrible, gnarled finger: "Remember, man, that thou art DUST!"

And he doesn't say a word—can't say a word—his mouth gapes open like a great gasping fish and works as if he wants to speak, but nothing comes out, only a wheedling "But, Sister . . ."

"Don't you but-Sister *me*, ye scoundrel!"

And Miss Downey gives the reins a good, hard shake, and Hyacinth takes us home.

Chapter 29

I thought we'd never get there. The world had stopped turning again. The blizzard was still blowing and the snow was still snowing and the buggy was still bumping along in it, creaking, lurching, jerking along, until there was no beginning and no end to anything anymore, only snow and snow and more snow. My eyes were blind with it and my brain was thick with it and I was tired, so tired, too tired to think straight. I didn't want to think. I didn't want to see the pictures I couldn't stop seeing: the Rats running and the ice breaking and the river swallowing Eddie—I couldn't think about Eddie now—

Hurry hurry oh please hurry. . . .

"Is Betty all right? Did she wake up?" I kept asking, but my mouth was still numb with cold and I was half smothered under Sister Maclovius's flapping cloak and near crushed in her steely arms. She wouldn't let loose of me for a second and when she finally heard me croaking she only said, "Hush, child, hush, we know of no change." And Miss Downey didn't say anything—if she heard me at all. I couldn't tell if she did, what with the wind still whining and the buggy clattering so. But her back was board-straight and her head was high and I guess she'd forgot her gloves because her hands gripping the reins were all white-knuckled and blue-veined, and she wouldn't say a word—except to the horse, the poor old horse, who was on his last legs, by this time. I opened my mouth once to ask *couldn't he go any faster oh please* but then I shut it because—dear Lord, just look at him—he could hardly lift a hoof now, could he? He'd just stepped into a hole of some sort and now his front knees were buckling and his head was drooping and Miss Downey was handing the reins to Sister and climbing out of the buggy and pulling him up by his harness. "Easy, old boy. Easy, that's the way. . . . You're all right now; I've got you. . . . Come on, just a few blocks more, love. . . . We're almost there. . . ."

And I wondered was I dreaming again, because who in the world was *this* Miss Downey, hauling a horse out of a hole in the middle of a blizzard, tugging him through the muck in her dainty little shoes? But my head was too thick to figure it out, so I just sat there holding tight to Harriet while Sister Maclovius held tight to me, and the lady held tight to Hyacinth, shoes or no shoes, and kept towing him along with her, block after block, till I saw it up ahead, finally—it was almost dark now, but I could just make it out—the old gray House looming through the shadows ahead of us, and the oil lamp flickering in the parlor window. . . .

And the doctor's horse and buggy, waiting out front again.

Oh God. Please, God . . .

I'd have jumped up and gone tearing inside that second, but Sister's grip was still like iron; I couldn't budge at all. "Wait," she said. "Not yet," she said. "Let me talk to the doctor first. I'll send word if . . ." She trailed off there and hauled herself to her feet—you could all but hear her bones creak—and turned to the lady. "If he's allowing visitors," she finished. "I'll leave Julia to you, Miss Downey."

"But the doll!" I began, getting to my feet too. "Couldn't I just— Oh, please—"

"Not yet," said Sister.

I might as well have argued with the Rock of Gibraltar. So I didn't, though it just about killed me. I shut my mouth and held my tongue and told myself that it was all right, it was all right, she said she'd send word, so she would, sure she would. Nuns couldn't tell lies. They weren't allowed, were they? And it shouldn't take long. What was another ten minutes or so? It wasn't as if . . . as if . . .

I tried not to let myself finish the thought, but it was there already, sapping the string out of my legs again, sinking in my gut like a stone: *as if somebody was dying*.

But Betty wasn't dying. Of course she wasn't. I would put the doll in her arms and she would open her eyes and look at me and smile and smile, and this damn day would be *over* finally, for once and for all and for—

TAP . . . thump, TAP . . .

Miss Downey had helped Sister out of the buggy already, and handed her her cane, and now she was helping the old nun make her way through the snow on the sidewalk and up the steps to the front door: *TAP . . . thump, TAP . . .* I'd never seen Sister Maclovius move so slowly. She'd always been old, but now she was ancient all of a sudden—bent in the shoulders and shaky in her cane hand. She looked as if she'd aged fifty years on the buggy ride home. But Miss Downey got her there eventually, all the way up and in, and then she came back to me and the horse. I'd climbed out of the buggy by now and was standing there with him, petting his poor old trembling neck, not knowing what else to do. "We should see to him first," she said, taking hold of his halter, "if you're up to it. Are you up to it?"

And I said I was, so we led him to the buggy barn, and I found the lantern and lit it and put on the rubber barn boots Sister Bridget kept by the door (they were big as boats on me, but better than one wet shoe). And then I did whatever the lady told me to do, still hanging on to Harriet, while Sister went about getting Hyacinth unhitched and settled in. She was still the other Miss Downey now, not the elegant millionairess but the sure-handed stranger who'd lugged us home, the one who looked as if she'd done this sort of thing a thousand times—mucked out stalls and watered horses and rubbed down their shaky old haunches, as if there was nothing to it at all. She didn't say much, or look at me much. She was more tight-lipped and business-like than I'd ever seen her. And when she was tending to a bloody patch on the old boy's left cheek, where his throatlatch had rubbed him raw, and he jerked at her touch and tossed his head, I saw a muscle jump in her own jaw, and heard the sound of her breathing in sharp and hard, as if she felt the sting too. "Easy, dear, easy. . . . I'm sorry, I know, it hurts like the devil, doesn't it?" And he calmed right down, and let her do her work, and shivered with pleasure while she brushed him—that horse kind of shiver that was like goose bumps—like a wave of ripples under the hide. And I was glad to see him so happy, the poor old thing, but God in heaven, we must have been in here a good *hour* now—it felt like an hour anyhow—and still no word from the sickroom. So I got up from the hay bale where I'd been sitting for a while, watching Miss Downey work, and asked if it would be all right to leave her now, since she was doing so well and all, and seemed to have everything she needed.

"Not yet," she said quietly. "We're not quite done here."

I was already halfway to the door. "But I thought I could just go check inside, you see, in case they've forgotten—if it's all right with you—"

"It is *not* all right," said Miss Downey—this other Miss Downey, the stranger holding the horse brush. She was still brushing the old boy down with it in sure, hard strokes—getting harder now, though he didn't seem to mind at all—and speaking in that odd, quiet voice, so as not to frighten him, I guess. But quiet or not, there was a sound in it *I'd* never heard, and a look on her face I'd never seen, and tears—were those *tears?*—streaming down her cheeks all of a sudden, while I stood there, stopped in my tracks, listening to her: "It is not all right, Julia. None of this is all right. We're here and you're safe, by some miracle; you're alive and standing in this barn with me, but you must *never* do anything like that again. *Never again*, do you hear me?"

I just stood there, gaping at her.

"Do you hear me, Julia?"

"Yes, miss, I—I hear you," I stammered, but it didn't do any good. She was wound up so tight now, there was no stopping her.

"You might have been killed out there today. A man *was* killed; I don't know what sort of a man he was, but he'd be alive right now if you hadn't left this house without permission this morning, as usual—if you hadn't run away *again*, Julia—how many times is it now? You can't take it into your head to leave whenever you like and then just *leave*, free as a bird. You might not always understand the rules but you have to follow them; we *all* have to follow them, whether we like it or not. They're there to *protect* us, don't you see? You might have died a hundred ways today, a thousand ways—"

"But—but I—"

"And not only you, Julia, not only you. Did you see what it took out of Sister? She'd have died ten times over to keep you safe, but she's an old woman, a *sick* old woman at that. Think what you will of her—I know she's not well-liked among the girls—but she'd give her life for any one you, if that's what it took to protect you; she'd take on every gang of thugs in St. Louis before she'd let them harm a hair on your heads. Though she might save herself the trouble, for all the thanks she gets. Not that she's doing it for that, mind you, but she'd do it all the same. And when I think of those men out there today on the ice—when I think what might have happened—"

"But it *didn't* happen," I tried to tell her. She was crying so hard now—brushing and brushing and crying and crying—that even Hyacinth was starting to look alarmed, rolling a worried eye at her, and I couldn't stand it anymore; I had to go over and pat her shoulder and try to comfort her as best I could. "It *didn't* happen, Miss Downey—"

"But it might have, Julia! It might have, don't you

see? I know we all have an allotted time on this earth; I know we know not the day nor the hour, but that doesn't mean you have to hurry the clock *along*!" She put the brush down and took tight hold of my shoulders. "You have to promise me, right now—no more foolishness, do you hear? No more running off. There are people trying to keep you safe, but how can they do it if you won't *let* them, if you push us all away? You're eleven years old; you *don't* always know best. I know you were trying to help your friend today, but how would it have helped her if *you'd* died, Julia? You have to look before you leap, child! You have to promise; you have to swear to me that you'll never do any such fool thing ever again. Do you swear it?"

"I . . . I . . ."

"*Swear* it, Julia! Say the words: 'I'll look before I leap, Miss Downey. I give you my solemn word.'"

"I'll—I'll look before I leap, Miss—"

Just then the barn door opened.

"Excuse me, ladies. . . ." It was Sister Gabriel, putting her head in.

And all of a sudden I didn't want to hear any more. I'd rather die not knowing. I covered my ears with my hands because it hurt too much; it all hurt too much. . . .

But my eyes were still open, and Sister was smiling.

Betty was sleeping again when they let me see her. She didn't look all that different from how she had looked when I'd left her that morning—just a shade or two less pale, maybe—was it *only* that morning? It felt like weeks ago, years ago. . . . But she was better, the doctor promised. The worst was over. They all promised. She'd woken up, said Sister Gabriel, not an hour ago. Sat up, and knew us all, said Sister Maclovius. Had herself a bit of soup, said Sister Bridget. Chicken soup, Sister Genevieve had added. "With gizzards. You know how she loves me gizzards."

And then she'd gone back to sleep.

But I wouldn't believe a word of it till I'd seen her with my own two eyes. I wouldn't leave her till I'd tucked Harriet in beside her. (They'd tried to pry her out of my hands before, but I wouldn't let go.) And once she was lying there safe on the pillow by Betty, my legs had gone all rubbery without any warning, and my head had turned thick again, and the doctor had taken a good look at me and checked me from top to toe, then turned me over to Sister Gabriel, who hustled me out and up to my own bed in the slant-walled room. And Miss Downey came with her, but I didn't mind, really. I was too tired to mind. I sat there like a lump—

like Hyacinth under the brush—shivering a little while the two of them pulled off my stiff, wet clothes, and *tut-tut*ted over the bruises on my arms and the gash on my shin, and brought a basin of warm water to wash away all the dried-up blood and half-froze sweat, and the tears that started falling now, steady as rain, when there wasn't a reason in the world for 'em.

"Hush, now. Hush," said the lady, holding me fast. "You're all right now, love. I've got you."

And then I heard it through my hiccups—or *didn't* hear it, that was more like it—the roaring that had been in my ears all day.

It had stopped.

The wind had stopped.

I lifted my eyes to the window.

The snow had stopped falling.

And away up high, past a thousand chimneys poking out of a thousand rooftops, the evening star was winking at me.

March

Chapter 30

Saturday the 2nd

Dear Julia,

What the devil???

I just got your letter from last week yesterday but before I could answer it Henry the Hired Boy who's from the Patch too told me that he'd been to town for his cousin Ed's funeral, only there wasn't a body to bury because he'd been drowned under the ice in the Mississippi River and washed away to kingdom come in the middle of *the blizzard while himself and Thomas Egan were trying to save some little kid from the nuns house with the same last name as me and God help us, Julia, I know it was you, who else could it be? No one, that's who, and what in the world were you doing out there, for pity's sake? Henry says it's all anybody's talking about all over town, only one says one thing and another says the opposite and all he knew for sure was that this kid didn't drown too, so that was a relief anyway. But now you listen to me, Julia, there's things I never told you because you were too young and it was none of your business but if you're going to be cavorting on the ice with Thomas Egan and that crowd of hooligans you should know we Delaneys want no part of them, do you hear me? Not Egan or any of his mugs neither, though I guess there's one less now that Eddie's under the ice. And I suppose it's Egan himself spreading the big hero story, which I don't believe for a second, though God knows I'm glad you're alive, even if you don't deserve it.*

Yours truly from your sister,
Mary P. Delaney

The letter got to me first thing Tuesday morning, three days after the Saturday she wrote it, and by dinner that noon I'd read it maybe fifty times. And I knew I should answer it right away, but there was too much to tell and no way to tell it all, and my blood boiled up so red-hot every time I even *thought* about Thomas Egan making himself into some sort of hero that I couldn't think of even the first word to say about it.

Still, it sounded as if Mary knew it was all lies anyhow, smart girl that she was. And a good thing, too, with the whole world blabbing about it from morning to night, and no way of guessing what manner of eyewash she'd be hearing next.

So I put it all out of my mind for the time being, and watched Betty getting better and better, just like the doctor had promised. She was sitting up every day these days, when they let me visit, and hanging on tight to Harriet, and smiling like her old self for longer and longer stretches. Sister Genevieve was still claiming it was her gizzard soup that had turned the tide—she wouldn't stop making it now—we all but drowned in the awful stuff, gallon after gizzardy gallon. But I didn't mind much. I'd have clucked from here to Christmas if it was that doing the trick, though I didn't really think it was the gizzards—or Harriet, neither, or Sister Gabriel's mustard and boiled onion poultices, or even Dr. McGill and all his medicine. Maybe they helped, and maybe they didn't; I guess they couldn't have hurt. But I knew a miracle when I saw one.

And then there were cats.

It was Winnie who found 'em, out in the barn. Nothing wrong with *her* ears, catching their scrawny little mewing even from outside, early one morning. The mother cat had 'em hidden away, up in the loft. She'd come in from the cold and had 'em there, and then disappeared somehow or other—died in the storm, or was gobbled up by something bigger, or got herself killed in a cat fight, maybe. What was that old limerick Gran used to recite when Mary and I started fussin'?

There wanst was two cats of Kilkenny—
Each thought there was one cat too many—
So they fought and they fit
And they scratched and they bit
Till instead of two cats, there weren't any.

But instead of none, this poor old cat had left six more like her to take up where she'd left off—six tiny bits of fluff, tussling with one another and crying for their mama in a hay-nest, scarcely big enough to sneeze at. Just a handful of fur apiece—five hungry little stripers with the teensiest claws I ever saw (sharp as knives, even so), and one small black lump with his eyes hardly open. "Little Bear," we all called him—L.B. for short—when Winnie brought the lot in a basket to the infirmary, and begged Sister Gabriel to let her show 'em to Betty, who fell in love straightaway, of course.

"Glory be to gracious—cats, is it?" said Sister. "Cats in the sickroom! What next? We'll be covered in fleas! Ah, no, Betty, don't let it—look there, now, oh dear—not on my clean sheets!" But it was too late; Betty was already in cat heaven. She was awash in cats. She had taken every one out of the basket and now there were kittens in her lap and under her chin and climbing up her braids and sitting on Harriet's hat, and you have never in all your life seen anyone look so happy as Mary Elizabeth Brickey. It would have taken a harder heart than Sister Gabriel's to take those raggedy cats away, and dim that shining face. So that was that; they were Betty's cats now, for good and all. Though she shared, of course, being Betty. We all took turns feeding 'em—milk with eyedroppers at first, till they learned to lap it—and cuddling and chasing after 'em and taking out their everlasting cat box, morning after morning. And trouble though they were, I swear they were better than any tonic, finer than an ocean voyage to the South Seas themselves, for putting the pink back in Betty's cheeks and the sparkle in her brown eyes. And I could have kissed Winnie—well, almost—and every cat ever born, from first to last, for making her laugh again. Making us all laugh till it hurt, with their solemn little pipsqueak faces and sweet, silly tricks.

"Good work," I told Winnie. She'd been keeping her distance ever since I got back from the blizzard, glancing at me sideways with jittery eyes and skittering away if she saw me coming, and I knew she was afraid I was mad at her for tattling that day, when she caught me climbing the fence, and telling Miss Downey and the Sisters where I'd gone. It had to be Winnie; who else would have known? Still, I might be dead now if she hadn't, and I knew I should tell her so, when I got the chance. But I never could find the right moment, till now. "Good work"—that was all I could think of—and "Thank you, Winnie." But I think she understood me. "It's all right," she said, blushing clear up to the roots of her wispy brown hair.

Sister Maclovius, in the meantime, had caught a cold in her head that day in the storm, that got stuck in her chest somehow, and now it wouldn't turn loose, no matter what the doctor tried. She'd lost her voice altogether just before Saint Patrick's Day—now *there* was a miracle for you—we hadn't heard a peep out of her since. But it didn't stop her from waving her cane at all and sundry, of course, or showing up at the coroner's inquest the next morning, which he'd agreed to hold in the parlor—*our* parlor, piano and all—since Sister wasn't well yet.

"The *coroner*?" I said to Sister Bridget, when she told me my presence was requested. "You mean the feller from the *morgue*? He doesn't think I *murdered* Eddie, does he?"

"Oh, no, no, no, Julia, don't worry yourself. It's only a formality, you see, when a thing like this happens. An informal formality, you might call it, just for the record. It's some sort of law, I believe. He wants to talk to you, that's all—you and the other witnesses—just to make sure he understands what happened that day, so they can put it on the death certificate. To be certain it was only an accident, you see—which it *was*, of course—don't look like that, Julia; no one's blaming you for Eddie! It was no one's fault—well, not *your* fault—not on purpose, anyway. And you won't be alone, of course; we'll be right there with you."

I didn't care much for that *not on purpose*. . . .

"But there's no body!" I reminded her. "They never found him, did they? He's halfway to the Gulf of Mexico now, if the fish didn't eat him first. How can there be a death certificate without a body?"

But Sister Bridget didn't know, and neither did anybody else—not even Marcella, who knew everything. "I'd have my bags packed, just to be safe," she advised me. "In case they ship you off to Sing Sing right after."

I knew she was only teasing. But that night I dreamed I was on the ice again, and Eddie was rising up out of the river, reaching for me, and I was shaking like a leaf the next morning, when the inquest started—or *didn't* start, actually—which it didn't, for a full half hour, because Miss Downey was late.

Miss Downey, who was *never* late.

"I'm sure she'll be here any minute now, Doctor Bracy," said Sister Bridget, smiling a nervous smile at the white-haired gentleman with the coal-black eyebrows, who was sitting in the same large armchair that Santa Claus had favored, three months earlier. Betty had checked his pockets for jelly beans, just in case (though he didn't look a thing like Officer Doyle, really), and he did seem a bit . . . surprised. Still, he patted her head, which made me like him, and she patted his right back, and fortunately Pop the Cop arrived just five minutes later anyhow and let her clean him out, first thing, so she started the day smiling.

I could have told 'em they were pushing their luck, having Betty at a coroner's inquest.

But it couldn't be helped. "We'll have to explain about the doll, you see. It's part of the evidence," Sister Bridget told me. "And where the doll goes, Betty goes. She won't let loose of her now." The poor half-a-nun was so flushed under her freckles I was afraid she was feverish. I'd never seen her so fidgety about anything in all the time I'd been here. Sister Maclovius was right beside her, looking like her old self again—her *regular* old self—having mostly recovered. But her speechifying voice hadn't recovered with the rest of her, so it had been decided that Sister Bridget would do whatever talking was needed, seeing as how she had the knack for it, and knew the whole story, besides. "It'll be fine," she went on explaining now, to anyone who might happen to be listening. "You've *promised* to behave, haven't you, Betty? You understand me, don't you? Well, of course you do. . . ."

I wasn't so sure. Not so much about whether she *understood*—I was fairly sure Betty understood everything she chose to. But at the moment she seemed mostly interested in the left pocket of her pinafore, which had a suspicious-looking lump in it. Only one, thank heaven, as far as I could tell—most likely L.B., since it was still as a stump, this lump, and more than likely fast asleep. But the little bear was getting bigger every day, and was apt to wake up and yowl when he was hungry. Should I warn Sister Bridget? I wondered. She'd have spotted him in a second any other time, if she hadn't been so busy worrying about everything else. But I didn't want *Betty* to start yowling, neither, if we tried to take him away from her. So I kept my mouth closed and hoped for the best.

And the room was filling up now, anyway: Father Dunne was here, of course—Sister had told me he was coming—"just as a friend," she'd said, in case we needed him. He'd gone right over and started talking and smiling with Dr. Bracy, as if they'd known each other forever. And then there was a tall boy with his cap in his hands—near as tall as Bill, but more bashful-looking—red right clear to the tips of his ears, which were at least two sizes too big for his head, though that seemed smaller than it really was, I suppose, due to his hair being cropped so short. He looked relieved when he spotted the priest. "Henry!" said Father Dunne, waving him over, and I heard him introduce the kid to the others as "an old friend of mine—Henry Tyborowski. One of our boys, till he grew up and left us. Just last fall, wasn't it, Henry? Eddie's cousin," Father went on. "We thought the family should be represented." And Sister Maclovius bowed to him, and Sister Bridget said he was welcome, and the gentleman-doctor-coroner (who had got up already to greet the priest) kept standing and shook Henry's hand. "I'm sorry for your loss, son," I heard him say, in a lovely deep roll of a voice, like a king should have, or a lion maybe, if only a lion could talk. Henry? I wondered. Not Henry the Hired Boy, was it? Why, sure—Eddie's cousin—Mary's friend from the farm. And he looked like an okay sort of feller (I liked those fiery ears, though I worried they might hurt him), so I made up my mind to talk to him first chance I got, and ask him about Mary, and tell him what to tell her for me when he got back to Jefferson County. But it would have to wait for later, because the door was opening again now—

And my stomach went crashing to my boots, heavy as lead, because there was Tom Egan himself coming through it, taking off his coat and hat and handing 'em to the skinny little weasel of a man next to him—scarcely bigger than Jimmy Brannigan, that one; Fat Eddie could have fit *him* in a pocket—and smiling at the room in general, as if there was no question in his mind whatsoever that we'd all be thrilled to see him.

"Good morning, Sisters," Egan boomed, putting out a hand (which they both ignored), "and thank you for your kind hospitality. I do hope it's not too much of an imposition, busy as you are. And look here, now—why, here's the little girl again, isn't it? Well, well, no hard feelings, young lady. No one's blaming you for that unfortunate day. Not atall, not atall . . . just an accident . . . These things happen. . . . Rotten weather, that was what it was. Had us all in a state, now didn't it? Such a sad day, a terrible day . . . But that's all behind us, isn't it? Good to have a bit of sunshine for a change, hey? Spring at last, do you think? Glad to see you all up and about, while we clear up any little misunderstanding among us. Our friend Eddie wouldn't have wanted that, now, would he? No, indeed. Ah, me. 'Twas a brave man, Eddie was. And who's this with you here, Father Dunne? Part of the family, is it? Well now, of course it is, of course it is; I remember you from the funeral, don't I, lad? And such a touching tribute it was, too. . . . Are you getting all this, O'Hara?" he said to the weasel, who was following him around like a puppy now, hanging on every word, scribbling on a notepad with a stub of pencil he'd taken from behind his ear. "And what's the holdup, Doctor Bracy? Weren't we supposed to be starting at nine sharp? Not that I'm hurrying you, of course, but the Knights of Columbus are waitin', you see; I do have a meeting in half an hour. So if we could get started in the next few minutes—?"

Dear God, wouldn't he ever shut up? The bile was rising in my throat again. I was going to be sick, if he kept on. I'd known he was coming; I guess a part of me had known it all along, but I hadn't let myself think about it. I couldn't let myself think about it. Oh Lord in *heaven* how I hated him—

But then Miss Downey was rushing in, pink with embarrassment, and Mr. Hanratty-Maguire was right behind her, looking as if he'd just swallowed a prune, pit and all, and meanwhile the both of 'em were trying to explain at the same time, their words tumbling over one another:

"Oh dear, so sorry to . . ."

". . . keep you all . . ."

". . . motorcar . . ."

". . . never seen such a stubborn . . ."

". . . traffic . . ."

"Oh, for heaven's sake, Daniel, it wasn't just the *traffic*! If you'd only just turn *left* for once in your—"

"Remember yourself, Cora!"

Miss Downey closed her lips tight then, and looked

as if she was *trying* to remember herself, and having no luck, and I wanted to tell the handsome man he was wasting his time here. The Cora he was looking for was long gone, since the blizzard. And *this* one didn't care to be bossed. She flashed him a look that would have withered his moustache, if he'd been paying better attention. But he was already busy bowing and shaking hands all 'round (though he skipped Thomas Egan, who hadn't offered his anyhow), and Sister Bridget was ushering the whole crowd into their seats, and now Dr. Bracy the Kingly Coroner was clearing his throat and looking around the room and thanking us all for our time:

"I'm sure that many of you had obligations that might have appeared more pressing than this one, under the circumstances, but I find it to be of great comfort to the family, you see, in a case such as this, to assure them that no harm was ever intended. So would each of you now describe to us, if you will, to the best of your recollection, your acquaintance, if any, with Mr. Edward Farrell, and your own best memory of the events prior to and culminating on Wednesday, February the twenty-first, 1912, that might be, in your opinion, in any way associated with his death."

We all just sat there for a minute. And then Sister

Maclovius gave Sister Bridget a small poke in the shoulder with her cane (she was sitting just behind her), and the half-a-nun jumped and blushed some more and got to her feet.

"Sister Bridget, isn't it?" said Dr. Bracy, checking his notes. "Thank you for getting us started. Would you begin?"

"I'll do my best, sir. To the best of my knowledge. Though I wasn't actually at the scene of the incident on that *particular* day."

I gritted my teeth and waited my turn and tried to think of pleasanter things—getting a tooth pulled, maybe—while the telling commenced, sort of, bit by little bit at first, person by person: the snow that wouldn't stop and Betty sick in bed and trolleys stuck and broke-down cars and the doll that had to be found to make her better—

"A doll, did you say?" Dr. Bracy asked. He was adding to the notes on his own pad, while the Weasel Man scribbled madly on his.

"A china doll," said Sister Bridget.

The doll that had been a gift from a boy to his bride—

"Your brother, you say, Sister?"

"My brother," said Sister Bridget. "Harry W. Brickey." She turned and looked the Rat Man right in the eye.

"You remember Harry, Mr. Egan. There were those who called him Two-Bits. The boy who was shot, you know, at Saint Patrick's itself, coming out of his very own wedding? He used to work for you, I believe, when he was alive."

And Thomas Egan didn't move a muscle, but I know he heard her. His smile looked painted on, all of a sudden, and his face—his nose, in particular—turned a deeper shade of purplish red, while Officer Doyle and Father Dunne sat up board-straight in their chairs, leaning in to listen, looking from Sister to me to Egan and back again.

"I'm sorry, Sister," said Dr. Bracy. His eyebrows were crinkled so deep now, they were one shaggy black line. "I'm not sure I understand. Is there a connection between the deceased—Mr. Farrell, that is to say—and this doll you mention . . . The doll I see here, I presume?" he added, indicating Harriet, safe in Betty's arms, the two of 'em smiling, same as ever.

And then the words started up again, pouring out—a whole avalanche of 'em—from every direction:

"Are you saying that your brother . . ."

"My cousin . . ."

"My nephew . . ."

"Your son . . ."

"You mean she *pawned* . . ."

"Pawned *what?*"

"But why would she . . ."

"What would he . . ."

"Surely you're not accusing me of . . ."

"Nobody's accusing . . ."

"Accusing whom? Of what?"

"He *slipped!*"

"Ah, for pity's sake . . ."

"One at a time, please! You heard the man!"

"Sit *down*, Mr. Egan. . . ."

And meanwhile Daniel frowned and smoothed his moustache, and Miss Downey looked madder and madder, and the weasel scribbled away as if his life depended on it, and everyone else seemed more and more confused, and Betty's pocket began to twitch—just a little at first and then harder and harder—and she grinned and shifted Harriet to her other knee, and took the ribbon from her own braid and began dangling it just above the lump, until a small black paw stuck *out* of the pocket and began to bat it about. And Sister Bridget saw it just as I did, and we both made stern faces, trying to get Betty's attention, but Betty wouldn't look at us anymore, and all this time Henry the Hired Boy was leaning forward, listening, with his brow knitted in knots, trying to understand the words coming out of the coroner's mouth now:

"Would you show us the doll, Miss Brickey?"

Only just at that moment, the small black lump that was Little Bear came leaping out of Betty's pocket, waving wildly at the ribbon, his fur standing right on end, and landed directly on Harriet herself, right smack in the middle of her pearls, where he proceeded to get hopelessly tangled—

"Oh dear . . ."

"Stop him, Betty!"

"Watch his paw. . . ."

"Don't pull!"

"Sweet Mary and Joseph, he's about to break . . ."

"Her lovely . . ."

POP! went the pearls, scattering in a dozen directions, while the kitten yowled and Betty laughed and tucked him under her chin, and Sister Maclovius shook her cane at the world in general, and Sister Bridget and Miss Downey and I jumped up and started chasing pearls every which way as they rolled all over the place, and even Dr. Bracy reached down for a couple that had worked their way under his shoe.

"Well now," he said, holding them up to the light, his eyebrows soaring. "My, my. What have we here?"

"It's all right, sir," I explained, holding out the handful I'd managed to gather so far. "They're only paste, that's all."

"Paste?" he repeated. "Are you sure of that, Miss Delaney? Then it's very fine paste, indeed. . . . Where did you say your brother bought this doll, Sister?"

And now Thomas Egan was sitting up straighter all of a sudden, and the Weasel Man's eyes were widening.

"Careful, ladies and gentlemen," said Dr. Bracy. "Step gently, now, easy there. . . . Paste, my eye. I saw pearls like this on a duchess once, when I sailed on the *Mauretania*. Look there, Miss Brickey—that's right—just there, by the piano. . . . Well now. Better find them all, shall we?"

Chapter 31

"Look here, girls! We're famous!" Marcella announced the next evening, grinning from ear to ear, marching into the slant-walled room after supper and waving a newspaper over her head.

DEAD MAN'S PEARLY TREASURE RECOVERED

HIDDEN IN PLAIN SIGHT FOR A DECADE

ORPHAN DAUGHTER TO BENEFIT

FOURTH WARD businessman Thomas Egan was an astonished witness yesterday to the unexpected unraveling of a ten-year-old mystery regarding the hitherto secret whereabouts of the property—said to be worth thousands—of one of his former employees, Harry W. Brickey, now deceased. Mr. Brickey, who was only seventeen years of age on March 17, 1902, was killed by an unidentified gunman as he left his own wedding that day, on the front steps of Saint Patrick's Church, which is located at the corner of Sixth and Biddle Streets, on the near North Side. The groom's sister, now Sister Bridget Brickey, a novice at the House of Mercy, in the twenty-one hundred block of Morgan Street, explained today to St. Louis County Coroner Dr. Rolla Bracy (during a related inquest) that her brother had had uncommonly good luck at the race track, shortly before his nuptials, and must have been planning to surprise his bride, Miss Maggie Meehan (also now deceased, of natural causes), with the gift of a pearl necklace. "But he never let on to any of us," said Sister Bridget. "We all thought he was giving her a china doll; that was what he had told the family. I helped him wrap it myself, right before the ceremony. It never crossed my mind that the pearls around the doll's neck might be real!"

Mr. Egan was also present yesterday at the aforementioned House of Mercy, at the request of Dr. Bracy, to give information regarding the accidental drowning death on February 21st of another Egan associate, Edward "Eddie" O'Farrell, who along with his employer was attempting to rescue Miss Julia C. Delaney, age eleven, during the recent blizzard. Miss Delaney, an orphan, resides at the House of Mercy along with Mary Elizabeth Brickey, age nine, who is the daughter and only living heir of the murdered man and his bride. According to witnesses, Miss Delaney, who was in possession of the younger girl's doll at the time, had run away from the orphanage and was crossing the frozen Mississippi on foot when the ice gave way, and Mr. Farrell, in his effort to reach her (several feet ahead of Mr. Egan), was swept beneath it, into the river. No trace of him has yet been found. It was in the course of the various witnesses' accounts of the tragic accident that the pearls—a single strand wrapped double, still adorning the china doll's neck—came to the attention of Dr. Bracy himself, who immediately recognized their worth, to the amazement of all present.

When asked what she planned to do with her unexpected inheritance, Miss Brickey declined to comment, but smiled enigmatically. Sister Bridget, however, called the discovery "nothing short of a miracle," and said that great care would be taken to safeguard the child's good fortune. Pressed as to the safety of the neighborhood and how she would respond if a thief were to attempt to abscond with the long-lost treasure, Sister's answer was, "I'd like to see him try."

Thomas Egan, meanwhile, though uncharacteristically sober in his demeanor at the conclusion of the inquest, no doubt due to the ongoing shock of his esteemed cohort's heroic demise, did rouse himself to acknowledge the many personal tributes he himself has received, in the past weeks, in recognition of his own best efforts on the ice, and has pledged his continuing assistance to all concerned, in every way possible.

"I'll *bet* he has!" said Marcella, laughing till the tears ran down her cheeks, once she'd finished reading aloud to us. And the other girls laughed along with her, whether they really understood or not.

So I tried to smile too.

"But it's not enough," I muttered, before we blew out the light. "It ain't the whole story. He ought to be under the ice with Eddie."

"Ah, sure," said Marcella. "Of course he should. But it's better than nothing—no, *listen* to me, Your Majesty: He *lost*, don't you see? And he *knows* he lost; that's the best part. He'll go to his grave remembering that a two-bit nobody who used to push a broom for him had the last laugh, in the end—got away with a piece of his precious pie that was never really his in the first place. And there's not a bloomin' thing he can do about it! That's *worse* than drowning for a feller like that. And the whole world knows it, too—the whole Patch, anyhow. They'll be hootin' behind his back till the day he dies."

"Do you promise?" I asked.

"Promise," said Marcella. "I know *I* will, anyhow." She wiped her eyes. "Oh, my, ain't it rich?"

Still, I couldn't stop thinking about it. Even after the others were all snoring in their beds beside me, the pictures kept coming back—Eddie on the ice again, reaching and reaching—and voices, too, a thousand voices, deep into the night. When I'd halfway drift off, they'd start their eternal jabbering:

Oh! Fair Thomas Egan, too bad you're going to hang,
Though no one but your mother dear . . .

Your father was there, you know. Marched 'em in at the start, playing "Haste to the Wedding," and out at the end . . .

. . . out at the end . . .

. . . things I never told you. . . .

. . . Hidden in Plain . . .

"What things?" I mumbled, sitting up straight. And no sooner had I said it than I saw it. I knew the answer. There it was, just as clear as day. I must have known it all along, without knowing I knew; I'd never *wanted* to know it, but now—*ah, sure, ah, sure*—I was wide-awake and on the linoleum and running again, just like before, but with Mary's letter tight in my fist this time; I was out of the slant-walled room and down the stairs and all the way to the cellar, to the laundry girls' alcove, where I saw a low light burning and found Sister Bridget sitting up in her own bed, reading a fat brown book—*The Comedies of Mr. William Shakespeare*, it said on the cover, though she wasn't laughing; she was half-asleep, and I almost didn't recognize her, without her veil. Her hair was cropped short all over her head—as red as Bill's, and twice as curly.

"Papa saw, didn't he, Sister?"

I tried to say it as soft as I could, but she all but jumped out of her skin anyhow.

"Ah, great gobs, Julia! What now? Saw what?"

"My papa—he must have seen. When the Rats killed your brother—at the wedding, when he marched 'em out—you said they were friends—"

"Shh, child, hush—"

"And then he sang the song at the Fair—the hanging song—and they thought he would tell, he wanted to tell, so they killed him, too, didn't they? That night at the bridge—"

"Slow down, slow down, Julia—"

"And Bill knew and Mary knew—the whole world knew—but they never said a word. Nobody ever tells me anything. Mary says I was too young but I'm old enough now, ain't I, Sister? I'm a million years old; somebody ought to tell me *something*. . . ."

"Shh, shh, well of course they should, of course they should, but we can't talk here, Julia; we'll wake the girls. Just a minute now, come with me. . . ."

And then she was up and pulling a nun wrapper around her shoulders and taking me back up the stairs to the kitchen, where she sat me down at Sister Genevieve's worktable and bustled about, lighting the stove and getting out the tea things, and putting the kettle on. And once she had it all ready to go, just waiting for the water to boil, she sat down with me and took a deep breath.

"All right, then," she said, letting it out slowly. "Ask away."

So I did. But not so fast, this time . . .

"Did he see?" I said again. "My father—that day at the church—"

"He might have," said Sister. "I was too far back to tell; I wasn't out the door yet. But he might have. He might have. I always wondered if he did. Though he wouldn't have been the only one, in any case. There were plenty of others around that morning. Passersby on the sidewalk, traffic in the street—"

"And no one ever told? Not any of 'em?"

Sister shook her head. "You know the Patch. It would have been too dangerous. Not just for the talkers, but their families—wives and children—no one could risk it. Oh, there were whispers, of course, like there always are. It wasn't even much of a mystery:

Egan gave the order; Eddie fired the shots. But no one ever said it out loud."

"Till my papa sang the song . . ."

"Till your papa sang the song."

I sat there for a minute, cold as ice.

Sister Bridget hunted up a piece of bread and buttered it.

"Well, *I'll* say it," I said. "*I'll* tell the police. I ain't afraid of Thomas Egan!"

"Well of course you're not. Of course not." Sister smiled at the butter knife. "I wish you were on the force. But it's not your job, Julia. The police know as much as you and I do; they hear the whispers just like the rest of us."

"Then why don't they do anything about it? Why's a Rat like that still walking around smiling at people, acting like he's a hero?"

"Because there's no proof—no evidence, no witnesses, remember? Not a soul left alive who'll tell it now. Not even Eddie Farrell. It's just hearsay, after all this time; that's what the judge would call it. Nothing that would stand up in a court of law."

"But it ain't fair," I muttered. "It ain't *fair*, Sister!"

A muscle tightened in the half-a-nun's jaw. "You're right. It ain't fair. It's an outrage, that's what it is. An abomination. This world's not a fair place, Julia." She put down the knife and squeezed my fist, hard. "But you never know, do you? Egan's luck might be running out. Did you see his face when the pearls broke? And my Uncle Tim—Officer Doyle—he's been after him for years. He'll get him one day, if he can be got. If there's a man on earth can do it."

"And if there's not . . . ?"

"If there's not—"

The teakettle started whistling.

Sister stood up to get it. She straightened her back. I swear, she was ten feet tall now. "Then we'll have to leave Thomas Egan to the real Judge. The true Judge. Nobody ever gets past *him*."

April

Chapter 32

It was Wednesday again. The last before Easter: Wednesday in Holy Week and all hell breaking loose at the House of Mercy, where Sister Maclovius had just declared all-out war on winter—or the soggy mess that was left of it—the minute she got her voice back.

"Spring-Cleaning Day!" she announced at breakfast with the smile we all dreaded—the one that always made Hannah tremble, and Winnie burst into tears. The whole *world* needed cleaning up, and warming up, too.

Except for that little fake spring right around Saint Pat's Day, the mercury in the back-porch thermometer had scarcely climbed above forty the entire month of March. And it had snowed three times just last week—the slushy, mushy, gray-in-an-eyeblink kind of snow that melted almost faster'n it fell and then went pouring into the rivers with the ice-melt and had 'em all on the rise. *All* the rivers had broke loose now. It wasn't just our old man Mississippi that was waking up for real, but all the rivers that emptied into it, above and below us, including the Missouri up by Boonville, the paper said—would Bill be sloshing around in the wet? I wondered; I hadn't heard a word from Jimmy—and all along the Ohio, too, and every little podunk stream that fed any of 'em. The whole *country* was full to overflowing this year—the bottom half of it, anyway—waterlogged from the waist down. The *Post-Dispatch* was full of floods and flooding. We weren't at the danger mark yet in St. Louis, it said, but the people down in Cairo were working night and day, hauling sandbags to *their* levee, and I was sick to death of all of it. If I never heard another word about another narrow escape from the icy waters, it would be too soon.

So it was almost a relief when Sister Maclovius started handing out scrubbing assignments for the clean-up crews. Never mind the nip in the air, with the wind snapping the sheets on the clotheslines out back and blustering all around the House. The calendar said spring, so it must be spring, Sister insisted, with Easter coming up this weekend and not a minute to lose. And at least we had the day off from lessons, so Spring-Cleaning Day wasn't a total loss.

"The highlight of my year," said Marcella, waving a feather duster over her head. "Come on, Your Majesty, follow me. I'll show you the safe spots. You don't want to go near the rug beaters or the stair polishers, believe me."

Which is why so many of the rest of us were sweeping and dusting away in the parlor that blustery April morning, as if our lives depended on it, with the windows thrown open to the pale yellow sunshine, and the wind flapping the curtains all around us, when Mr. Hanratty-Maguire's fine new Cadillac motorcar came sputtering and lurching and kicking and bucking and backfiring up a storm, all the way down Morgan Street, like a one-car revolution.

We heard it before we saw it.

"Oh dear," said Sister Gabriel, looking up from her knees by the radiator grate, where she was scrubbing the black away—or trying to, anyhow. She was smudged all over her face with it; she could have passed for a chimney sweep, except for the wimple.

"He's brought Miss Downey for her lessons, hasn't he? Did we forget to tell her she had the day off?"

But before anyone could answer her, the raised voices coming in from the curbside made all of us stop . . . and lift our eyebrows at one another . . . and go running to the windows to peek out at the fight.

"And why shouldn't I?" Miss Downey was saying. "Why couldn't we?"

"Because it's nonsense, Cora; you know I'd never agree to such a thing. She'd eat us both alive!"

"She would not! You don't know her—"

"And you do, I suppose?"

"I do."

"You don't. It's you I'm thinking of, sweetheart. We'll have children of our own one day; we have to consider them, too. She bites, remember? Her brother's in the reformatory. If she's to be placed, it ought to be with a family of—of a more similar background—"

"Background? *Background?* Oh, balderdash, Daniel! I'm a farm girl from Parkersburg, Iowa, for heaven's sake. Who do you think I am, Queen Victoria?"

"Who're they talking about?" Winnie whispered.

"Three guesses," Hazel hissed, and my face was burning hot as a skillet on the fire itself but I couldn't budge. I couldn't move a muscle. Sister Gabriel was on her feet and standing beside us now, trying to tug us all away, but it was no use. I'd turned to stone again. And now Miss Downey was getting out of the car and slamming the door shut and starting up the sidewalk, and Mr. Hanratty-Maguire was out, too, and coming after her, stopping her, taking her by the arm.

"Don't do this, Cora. You misunderstand me. I'm not talking about *that* sort of background. . . ."

She shook her head. "It's you who's misunderstanding, Daniel. I know you're not doing it on purpose, but . . . but you don't know how it felt, that's all, seeing her out there on the ice, hanging on to that old doll—her *friend's* doll, don't you see? She was trying to help her friend! If you'd only seen what I saw . . ."

"I'm sure she has her—her good points. If you say so. I'd never wish her ill. I'll do everything in my power to see that she's fed and clothed and treated kindly, here with the Sisters. But I'll not be adopting her. I will not. That's my final word on the subject. And if you insist on persisting with this madness . . . well, I guess it's your choice then, isn't it? You have to choose, Cora."

There was only a hairsbreadth of a pause.

Winnie squeezed my arm.

"Then I choose the child, Daniel. I choose this child."

Another pause. Winnie's grip got tighter. I thought

my heart would bust right out of my chest. Then—

"You don't know what you're saying, my dear. You're upset, that's all; you're not yourself—"

"I know exactly what I'm saying. And I've never been more myself. You're a fine man, Daniel. Any girl in her right mind would be proud to marry you. But—"

Daniel gave a hard little laugh. "But you're *not* in your right mind? She's bewitched you, is that it?"

"And what if she has? I've spent my whole life being so . . . so careful, don't you see? Always looking before I—" Miss Downey broke off there and lifted her eyes. It was me she was looking at now, in the window. Me she saw, looking back at her. "Sometimes you just have to go ahead and leap," she finished.

"Go ahead and *what*?" said Mr. Hanratty-Maguire, not understanding.

"Leap," I whispered.

He couldn't have heard me. I hardly heard myself. But he looked where she was looking, then, and saw me—saw all of us—watching him: three windows full of saucer-eyed orphans and nuns—not just Sister Gabriel but Sister Bridget and Sister Maclovius now too. When had *they* joined us? I wondered. And the poor man colored clear up to his carefully trimmed sideburns, and made two stiff little bows—first to Miss Downey, then to the rest of us—and turned and walked back to his fine car, opened the door and got in, and got it started, finally (on the fourth try), and drove off down Morgan Street, sputtering and lurching and bucking and backfiring, with his head held high.

And Miss Downey watched him go.

Then she turned back around again and started walking up the walk to the House.

And the nuns, seeing her coming, looked at one another and raised their eyebrows, and then hustled all the other girls away (though it wasn't so easy, with some of 'em; they had to practically drag Hazel down the hall), and left me there, waiting for her, with my heart thudding.

I opened the door.

"Hello," said Cora Downey.

"You're a farm girl from Parkersburg, Iowa?"

"I am," she said.

"Did you . . . have chickens?"

"I did."

I took a deep breath. "And—and cows?"

Miss Downey smiled. "Oh my, yes. Cows aplenty. It was a dairy farm, first. May I come in, Julia?"

I nodded, but I couldn't move. We were both still

standing in the doorway. I held on tight to the knob, to keep from falling over.

"So why did you come to St. Louis?"

"To visit my aunt—my favorite aunt—Aunt Lizzie? I think I mentioned her to you once. But she died last fall. And I would have gone home, but I had met Daniel by that time—at the club, you see; Aunt Lizzie was a member. And then he asked me—that is, we became engaged—but that's off now, of course."

"Because of *me*? Ah, Miss, you can't just—you shouldn't—"

"No, no, no, Julia. It's for the best; really it is. It's not because of you. . . . Not *only* because of you . . ." She had her arm around my shoulders now, and was leading me back to the parlor.

"Then why?" I asked as she sat us both down.

She sighed. "It's hard to explain. It's no one thing. It's true, what I told him; he's a good man, Julia. And loyal as a dog. And he loves me, and I know I've hurt him. And I'm sorry for that, I'm truly sorry, because he doesn't deserve it." Miss Downey's eyes filled up all of a sudden. "But—"

"But what?"

"Well . . . he's a bit of a stuffed-shirt, I'm afraid."

"A *bit*?"

"Just a bit. And he tells me I laugh too loud. And he never gets a joke unless I explain it, and then it's not funny anymore. So then I get cross, and he gets cross, and round and round we go. And have you ever in all your life seen such a *terrible* driver?" She wiped her eyes. "Oh, it never would have worked! So you see—"

"I see."

"It wasn't just you."

I nodded.

We sat there for a minute.

And then I cleared my throat. "Do you ever . . . would you ever . . . think of going back to the farm?"

"The farm?" she repeated. "In Iowa, you mean?"

"Yes'm," I said, trying to keep my voice from trembling. "I was just—well, you know. Just wondering."

Miss Downey shook her head. "I don't think so. To visit, of course, but not to live. Not anymore. Not since my parents died. It belongs to my brothers now, you see—three of them—and their wives and children. Quite a houseful. They don't need me underfoot all day, every day. Or sitting in some corner, knitting."

"Do you knit?" I asked, trying not to look disappointed.

"Not really," said Miss Downey.

"Me neither."

In my mind's eye, a whole herd of mournful-looking milk cows trotted away, mooing softly.

Now Miss Downey cleared *her* throat. "But a farm—well, *somewhere*—wouldn't be entirely out of the question. Because of Aunt Lizzie."

"Aunt Lizzie?"

"She left me a bit of a legacy, God bless her. Not millions, of course; she wasn't a Rockefeller or anything. But enough to—well, to tide us over for a bit. Make a fresh start somewhere. Though there's no rush about deciding, of course. . . . You'll need some time to think it over. . . ."

I was having trouble breathing. "Could Bill come too? And Mary?"

"Well, I . . . I'm not sure about that, Julia. About all the—well, the legal ramifications and so forth."

"Oh," I said, nodding, trying to look like I understood. "Ramifi—fi—what? Ficay—"

"Fications. But they'd be welcome to visit us, of course. They could come anytime and stay as long as they like. Your family and friends would always be welcome."

My heart gave a leap. "But—but where? Welcome where?"

"In our home."

Our home . . .

Was I dreaming? I must be dreaming. *Don't wake up, Julia. . . .*

But Miss Downey was smiling at me again, and getting to her feet, and offering me a hand. "Tell you what," she said. "Do you think the Sisters can spare you for a bit? We'll take the trolley. There's someone I'd like you to hear."

Chapter 33

And there he stands in the Grand Hall at the Union Station, under the great arch with the ladies holding their lamps up: the Razzle-Dazzle Man himself, making his pitch for the day, just as dapper as you please. Sparkling, is what he's doing, though he ain't wearing diamonds or rubies or naught like that. It's in his eyes mostly, this sparkle—black as two shiny black buttons—but the shine is all around him, too, shooting out of him somehow from every which way. Lord in heaven, can't you feel the heat? His shoes shine and his eyes shine and the little silver moons in his cuff links shine and his black hair shines when he takes off his hat and bows to the crowd—the whole crowd, sure, but the ladies in particular—and waves his hands and talks and talks:

"Montana, ma'am, that's the state of the future! Montana with a capital *M* for magnificent! Mountains reaching straight to heaven and rivers running with the purest water on earth, all of it spilling down on farmland so rich it defies description. Montana! Oh my, yes. The New Eden, that's what no less a man than Mr. James J. Hill has christened it. That's what the great Mr. Hill himself has sent me here to tell you today. And he isn't the sort of feller given to exaggeration, no sir, though I wouldn't blame you for suspecting otherwise. I didn't believe it myself till I saw it with my own eyes. That's virgin land, ma'am—begging your pardon if I seem to speak indelicately—untouched till now, the last of its kind in the country. And what might you grow in this paradise, you ask, sir? Why, anything you please! You just drop a seed in that pristine prairie soil, it'll sprout so tall, so fast, you'll be thinking you dreamed it. You'll be looking for giants humming 'Fee-Fi-Fo-Fum'!"

And it's the ladies in particular who smile back this fine spring morning, smoothing a curl in place or touching their faces, as if they suddenly feel the need to assure themselves they're still all there—eyes, noses, mouths, chins—as if in the heat of so much blinding razzle-dazzle, they might have somehow melted clean away.

The *other* ladies, that is. Miss Downey was her usual self the second he shut up, and busy with practical questions: How much and how far and the name of a good builder and "Would it be possible to take a piano?" she wondered. Though I never did hear—I missed the exact moment—when she signed on the dotted line. Once the lady decided to leap, she didn't fool around.

"Montana?" Marcella said when I gave her the news. "You're going to *Montana*?"

"Why?" said Hannah.

"Where's Montana?" said Winnie.

"Is it even a *state*?" said Hazel.

"Wasn't that where Custer had his Last Stand?" said Geraldine Mulroney.

I knew they were all just jealous. Any one of 'em would give her eyeteeth to be going to Montana with Miss Cora Downey.

"Some people have all the luck," Agnes said with a sigh.

But I knew it was more than luck.

I choose this child. . . .

I knew a miracle when I saw one.

The days all swam together after that. Lent was over and Easter was over and the floods were still flooding. Everything was speeding up, breaking loose, rushing-roiling-tumbling forward, spilling out of its banks and changing all the time, turning into something different. Something more. Nothing was the same; nobody was who I thought they were. Miss Downey wasn't a millionaire and Betty was an heiress. The poor old unsinkable *Titanic* was at the bottom of the sea. And then, one Saturday morning—

"There's someone here to see you," said Sister Gabriel, looking fit to bust with her news.

"Someone to see *me*?" I said, following her to the parlor, and there was Miss Downey, sitting across from Mary, who was on the couch next to Henry the Hired Boy, who'd brought her in the Lenahans' trap to see me and meet the lady. He was holding his cap again and his ears were as red as ever, but he stood up when I came in, as if I was somebody, so I liked him again. And Mary! She stood up, too, and I swear, she was four inches taller than before. She looked—why, all grown up and lady-fied herself, that's what. "Hello, Julia," she said. She sounded the same anyhow, and she was smiling like her old self, so I stopped being shy and near knocked her over, hugging her.

"Did they tell you? Did you meet Miss Downey? Are you coming to Montana with us?"

"Well, not—not right away," she said, and now *she* was the one looking shy.

"Well, why not, for Pete's sake? It'll be grand, Mary! You'll love it!"

But her cheeks went scarlet then and Henry's ears got even redder, though he didn't say a word himself—I couldn't recall him *ever* saying a word, now that I thought about it—and after a good deal of stammering and blushing, Mary managed to say that he'd asked her to the May Day Dance at the Parish Hall.

And *then* I understood.

"Ah, for heaven's sake, Mary," I whispered to her, when Henry was watering the horse before they left. "Fat Eddie's cousin? You *like* Fat Eddie's cousin? You ain't planning on *marrying* him, are you?" And even her nose turned cherry-red then, so I knew it had crossed her mind, no matter how hard she tried to pretend it hadn't.

"He's a nice boy, Julia. You can't judge people by their relatives."

"But it's *Montana*, Mary! It's *perfect*! Just wait'll you hear. . . ."

And Miss Downey talked then, and explained it all (she'd thought the whole thing through by this time, and made it sound wonderful—and sensible, too), and you could see that Mary approved of her. She was glad for me anyhow, and she promised to come visit, when Miss Downey invited her. But she didn't know any more about Bill than I did. She'd had no letters, no messages; she'd written him once, but she didn't know if he'd gotten it.

So I wrote him, too, telling him where he could find me out West, and I gave it to Sister Bridget to mail, and she promised she'd do it.

Goodbye, goodbye, goodbye, goodbye . . .

And then there was the judge and the doctor and the dentist to see, and shopping to do for boots and clothes and such. Miss Downey took me to Tyroler's Department Store itself and fitted me out with everything I'd be needing—she said I'd been getting so tall lately that the old things wouldn't do now—and a grand new suitcase to put 'em all in.

And then before I knew it, it was Leaving Day, with the whole House gathered in the hallway, just before Sister Bridget and Hyacinth—good old Hyacinth—took me to the station.

Miss Downey wasn't with us. She'd gone ahead three weeks before me to make the arrangements about the house and the land and all.

"We wish you Godspeed, Julia Delaney," said Sister Maclovius, "in hopes that the memory of our time together will warm your heart in the years to come, as it certainly will ours." And she gave me a gift—my own personal copy of the New Testament, with a holy card to mark my place: a picture of Saint Prudentiana, lying on a bed of coals.

And then it was time to go and everyone was shaking hands and saying goodbye—"Look out for rustlers," said Marcella, cocking an eyebrow at me—and Sister Sebastian was running out with *Gypsy Breynton* (my very own now, she said), and Sister Genevieve was stuffing my pockets full of biscuits (only slightly burnt), and Sister Gabriel was hugging me hard, and wiping away tears, and slipping a rosary in my pocket.

Goodbye, goodbye, goodbye, goodbye . . .

"Bon voyage!" called Sister Sebastian.

But I didn't see Betty. I couldn't find her anywhere. I couldn't leave without telling Betty goodbye; it made my whole chest ache, but no one could find her and the train wouldn't wait.

"I'll give her your love," said Sister Bridget, as she hauled my suitcase to the buggy.

But when were halfway down Morgan Street, I turned around for one last look, and there she was running after us, just like the last time.

"Stop! Oh, stop, Sister!" I cried, and she did it; she

pulled Hyacinth up short right there in the middle of the street and Betty came trotting up, grinning her old lopsided grin and hiding something behind her back.

"Oh, now Betty, what's that you've got there?" said Sister Bridget. "Oh dear, it's not one of your—"

"L.B.!" I cried, as she thrust the kitten into my hands—not such a Little Bear now, but half grown and fatter than ever. "Oh, Betty, I can't take your cat—not this one, not your favorite!" But she wouldn't stop grinning and she wouldn't take him back, so that was that; there wasn't a thing I could do about it, though the ache was worse than ever now. "Well, all right," I said, "but I'll just keep him for you till you come see us, do you hear? Miss Downey—I mean, Aunt Cora"—we'd decided that's what I'd call her, though I wasn't used to it yet—"Aunt Cora says you can all come visit."

And then I had a thought. I got my moonstone out of my undershirt pocket, and gave her that.

And she popped it right in her mouth.

"Oh no! No, Betty!" I said—just in time, before she swallowed it—and she popped it right out again and laughed out loud (I think she'd known what it was all along). And then she put it in her own pocket, and stood there, waving and laughing, till we were out of sight.

Oh Lord. The great gray station with the mile-high clock tower hove into sight before us, and Sister parked Hyacinth and the buggy right out front, and I gave the old boy a last rub behind the ears, and leaned into his patchy old neck, and whispered, "Thank you, sir." And then a big man came to help us with my suitcase, and my heart was pounding so loud, I was sure he could hear it, but he only tipped his cap at us and smiled, and didn't seem to notice. And I held on tight to L.B. and walked like a sleepwalker through the crowd—crowds everywhere; I couldn't imagine where they were all going—and Sister Bridget kept up a comforting stream of patter-talk all the way:

"That's it, right through here, dear. . . . Great gobs, is the circus in town? Stay close, now. . . . Look, there—I think that's the one. . . . Excuse me, young man," she said to another tall feller in another cap, who was standing beside the track where the big black engine was hissing. "Could you tell us if this is the westbound train through Hannibal?"

"Yes, Sister, this is the one," said the young man, turning toward us—

And it was Bill.

It was Bill.

And my heart—oh, my heart—

"Bill!" I cried, and I went running, and then he had me, cat and all; he was lifting me right off my feet and twirling me around and around, and I could hardly breathe; I thought I'd die of happiness. "But how? How'd you get away? Are you all right? Is your arm all right? Are you coming with me? Are you coming to Montana? Oh, Bill!"

"Easy there, J. . . . Everything's all right; don't cry! Ah, come on now, what are you crying for? I'm just fine! We're all okay. . . . Look, here's Mick and your old pal Jimmy, see there? Tell her, Jim; you tell it better than I do."

And there they were, sure enough, the pair of 'em, waiting off in the shadows a bit, keeping out of the way and looking half-shy for a change. Even Jimmy. And then Sister Bridget was hugging her cousin Mick and smiling from ear to ear, and everybody was talking all at once, but it was Jimmy talking the loudest and fastest now, of course, telling me all about their amazing adventures—well, the older boys' amazing adventures, anyhow; he hadn't exactly *been* there, he admitted. But they'd told him the whole story: how Mick had cut a hole in the fence at Boonville in the dead of night and found Bill and snuck him out of town in the boat he'd been saving up for, till it leaked like a sieve and sank like a stone, and the two of 'em had barely made it, swimming to shore—half a mile, at least, according to Jimmy. ("Maybe twenty yards," said Bill.) They'd had to bum rides on farm wagons all the rest of the way. Another narrow escape from the icy waters, God help us, but I didn't mind hearing about this one. I didn't mind anything, now that Bill was here.

"All aboard!" called the conductor.

"Are you coming?" I asked. "You're coming, ain't you?"

But Bill shook his head. He couldn't, he said. He'd be coming later, why, sure he would; he'd always wanted to see Montana. But right now—well, he and Mick were reporting for duty next week, you see. . . .

"Reporting for *what*?"

"For duty," he repeated. "We joined the Army."

"The *Army*? But you can't! You're only fifteen!"

"But *they* don't know that. And I'll be sixteen next month; they'd take me in a year anyhow. . . . Now, J, don't look like that. It's the best way; I swear it is! It was Father Dunne's idea. They worked it out with the judge—him and Mick's dad. We'll see a bit of the world, that's all, and *then* I'll come to Montana."

"Promise?" I said, still hanging on tight.

He took my right hand and put it on his heart.

"Promise," said Bill Delaney.

. . . *And Then*

The train pulls out of the Union Station, and I sit by the window, with the cat in my lap, and I try not to think, because it hurts too much. Better just to sit and listen to the cat purring and the whistle wailing and the sound of the wheels on the rails below, clicking and clacking. . . .

Goodbye, goodbye, goodbye, goodbye . . .

And the train turns east, then north along the levee, and there it is—the mighty river itself shining in the late-day sun, and the Eads Bridge looming on my right now, and the Kerry Patch, on my left, and a little girl and her sister standing by the tracks there, waving at me. And I wave back, still not thinking.

Goodbye, goodbye, goodbye, goodbye . . .

Past the bridge now, and the graveyard, where Mama and the twins and Gran are buried, and stranger after stranger with 'em. All the bones are here, all the dusty old bones. . . .

Goodbye, goodbye, goodbye, goodbye . . .

But I don't think about it. I'm leaving it all behind now. I'm carrying my own bones far, far away, a thousand miles, and the cat in my lap is fast asleep, and the train rocks beneath us as it turns toward the sun, straight into the prairie sea. . . .

Montana, Montana, Montana, Montana . . .

And my eyelids won't stay up and I'm sleeping now, too, I guess. I don't know for how long. . . . The days and the hours are all melting into one another and there's wind all around me, blowing in through the window; my lids are too heavy to lift, but I can see right through 'em—and there's my hat blowing away! It flies off my head and out the window and now I'm flying, too, chasing after it, flying right out of the train itself, and I don't know how, but it's lovely, so lovely up here, riding the wind. And there's a sound in it like music—like fiddle music—like the wind and the sun and the prairie grass are singing to me, above me and below me and all around. And I can hear it with *both* my ears for once in my life, so I guess I'm only dreaming; I must be dreaming, but I can see it all, anyhow, and look there! Oh, look there—I'm not alone, am I? I was never alone. A hundred others, a thousand others are dancing with me, reeling to the wind music, hand over hand—Papa and

Mama and Mary and Bill and Gran and the twins and all the rest—look at you there, laughing, Betty! You were all there all along but now I can *see* you, see? And you all know the steps—we all know the steps—it's a fine, fierce dance, though I don't remember learning it. . . . I can't remember learning. . . . No one ever taught us, did they?

Or maybe they did. . . .

Maybe they did. . . .

It's so hard to keep remembering. . . .

I try so hard that I wake myself up. It's a thousand miles later and I'm out of the train for real now and riding the camel-colored waves in a flatbed wagon, when it bumps and stops, and the wagon driver cusses a little:

"Confounded gophers! Just a minute here now, missy. I won't be but a minute. We're almost there. It's up just ahead, do you see?"

And I do. I see it off across the grass, with the clouds casting shadows like ships, sailing toward it: a little square house, just going up, still raw around the edges. And the cat sees it when I do, but he's quicker than I am; he jumps out of the wagon and runs straight for it and I'm right behind him, I'm running, too, and it's not a dream. This is no dream. I'm running and running,

I'm fast as a fox. . . . And the wind bends the grass and blows all around me as I reach the house and the door—just a frame—where a bright face turns toward me, and two arms open wide. . . .

And Aunt Cora says, "Oh, Julia . . . *there* you are!"

Julia Delaney
A Reel
(With words for Kitty, from Cyril)
Oh come with me, my love – Come a-way, come afar — We'll
sing the moon down from the sky and sail the morning star, and when we
reach bright heaven's gate, why, we're only begun — We'll
build a boat with angel's wings, and then we'll sail the sun!

Author's Note

This book is a work of fiction, with a true story at its heart.

Not long after the turn of the last century, a little blue-eyed girl named Julia was born in St. Louis, Missouri, not far from the great Eads Bridge, in the rough-and-tumble, mostly Irish neighborhood known as the Kerry Patch. The youngest of five children (her brother Bill—later one of Father Dunne's newsboys—was the eldest), Julia was orphaned at an early age, lived for a time with her grandmother, and was eventually taken in, along with her sister Mary, by the Sisters of Mercy, who operated an Industrial School and Girls' Home in the twenty-one hundred block of what was then Morgan Street (now Delmar Boulevard). The Sisters, struggling to make ends meet, put Mary to work in their laundry and sometimes took little Julia with them on what she later called their "begging missions" to the well-to-do of the day.

She hated the begging.

More than fifty years later, when I first met Julia (I was about to marry her youngest son, Kevin), she didn't like talking about that part of her life. She had an abiding love for the Sisters—most of them—and was forever grateful to them for coming to her aid when she and Mary were in desperate need of their help, but she would skip over that time when asked about it, and go straight to the happy miracle of meeting a "maiden lady piano teacher" by the name of Cora Downey—a farmer's daughter from Parkersburg, Iowa—who was to become her guardian, and who would take young Julia with her when she decided to try her hand at homesteading in Montana. "That's where God put his finger in my life," Julia always said.

I've wanted to tell their story ever since.

I began doing research for it in 1983, when Julia's daughter, Sheila Cooney Tybor, first sat down with me at our kitchen table one unforgettable afternoon, and kept me spellbound with bits and pieces of old memories her mother had passed along to her. By 1992, I had finally begun work on the first of many drafts of the manuscript. But the story kept eluding me until 2007, when I had the good fortune to come across Daniel Waugh's *Egan's Rats*, a fascinating work of nonfiction that had just been published by Cumberland House in Nashville, Tennessee, in the spring of that year. It was a treasure trove of information about the Kerry Patch, largely drawn from newspaper articles of the time, including accounts of a gang war that was raging in the fall and winter of 1911–1912 between the so-called "Rats" (bossed by Thomas Egan, an infamous tough guy and saloon keeper) and their enemies, in particular the Nixie Fighters, who were attempting to claim the dangerous southwest side of the Patch, known back then as the Bad Lands.

Most chilling of all were the mentions of two gang-related murders, never officially solved: one at a party given by Thomas Egan for his men on Christmas Day 1911, at the O'Fallon Pleasure Club; the other in the Bad Lands on Halloween night of that year, "in an alley near Twenty-second and Morgan streets"—*Julia's* Morgan Street—just spittin' distance from the actual address where she and Mary had lived with the Sisters. And for the first time I began to see the House of Mercy as a kind of embattled island in a dangerous sea, with the nuns standing guard over their young charges, come hell or high water.

The building itself isn't there anymore. Kevin and I walked what was left of the neighborhood, looking for it, just before New Year's Day 2005, and found no trace—only parking lots and warehouses—though we did find the old brick building at the corner of Washington Boulevard and Garrison Avenue that for many years was Father Dunne's News Boys Home. It's a Salvation Army Harbor Light Center now, still helping those in need, while Father Dunne's successors are still going strong as well, having merged with others to become Good Shepherd Children & Family Services.

Gone, too, is the old Sportsman's Park, where the St. Louis Browns used to play (they later shared the stadium with the Cardinals), and where Julia's real brother Bill used to go to games, sneaking out of the newsboys' chapel services and hopping rides on the trolley. The game between the Browns and the Detroit Tigers really did take place, exactly as described in this book, on October 7, 1911.

Father Peter Dunne and the Sisters of Mercy themselves were completely real, entirely human heroes of old St. Louis, whose work continues to this day. I didn't know Father Dunne or the Sisters of that time, of course, and wouldn't presume to pretend I did. The nuns in this book all have fictitious names, though I have the census page listing their real ones, tracked down for me years ago by my resourceful sisters-in-law, Sheila Cooney Tybor (again!) and Peggy Healy Cooney (who also told me the piercing story that Julia had told her years before, about the nuns having to peel her fingers off the lamp pole when they came to take her to the orphanage). But since I had no way of knowing which nuns were which, or what they were really like, I changed their names to keep from being unintentionally unfair to anybody . . . or possibly struck by lightning.

Speaking of weather: The temperature in St. Louis really was fourteen degrees below zero on January 7, 1912, during one of the coldest winters on record in Missouri and throughout much of the United States. It was not uncommon for the Mississippi River to freeze over in those days. A record-breaking blizzard did indeed hit St. Louis on February 20–21. (Five people died in the storm.) And the combination of so much snow melting and the breaking of ice gorges in rivers all over the country made the spring of 1912 one of the worst seasons of flooding in American history.

As for the Great Here-After, it was one of the most popular attractions on the Ten-Million-Dollar Pike at the 1904 World's Fair.

There truly is an Irish reel called "Julia Delaney," though it never had words, till Papa sang them in my head. And there's an old Irish song called "Fair Thomas Egan" (*Tomás Bán Mac Aogáin*), with lyrics very close to those he translates at the Fair—with just a bit of a twist.

But the Thomas Egan of old St. Louis notoriety died of natural causes on April 20, 1919, at the age of forty-four, and was buried in Calvary Cemetery, just seven years after the day Julia would have passed that way on the train leaving town—far beyond the Bad Lands—traveling east out of Union Station first, then north along the Mississippi, all the way to Hannibal, Missouri, where she turned west for good and all.

And as for that blue-eyed girl herself, once alone in this world, she lived to the age of eighty and was the beloved mother of six, grandmother of twenty-one, great-grandmother of forty-two, and great-great-grandmother of eight, at last count.

One last true fact that Julia—who became a lifelong reader and lover of books—always smiled about: Though it isn't told in this version of the story, it was actually Aunt Cora's older sister, Mary Downey Pfeiffer, whose charity work in St. Louis first introduced Cora to the Sisters of Mercy Industrial School and Girls' Home. Mrs. Pfeiffer was the mother of Pauline, who later married into quite an interesting family herself. Which made our Julia—eventually—Ernest Hemingway's cousin-in-law.

As her old friend Marcella might say, "Now, ain't that rich?"

. . . *And Acknowledgments*

I owe so much to so many whose help and humor, wisdom and love, saw me through the writing of this book—more than I can ever begin to repay, in too many ways to count. But I thank you all; I love you all:

David Andrew Doty
Lucy Frank
Virginia Walter
Mrs. Ernie Nortap
Carlin Glynn and Peter Masterson
William Goldman and Susan Burden
Linda Crew
Anne Steinman Montalbano
Catherine Kinsel Collins
Amy Kellman

The BWFFG

Peter and Clare Fields Flood

Charles and Chesley Krohn

Will and Patsy Mackenzie

Judie Angell and Phil Gaberman

Cynthia Burke

Richard Bradford and Millie Perkins

Kerry Madden

Ross McMahon

William and Susan Shofner Hardy

Mary Goetz Sculley

Sam and Gretchen Havens

Sheilah Wilson Serfaty

Bob and Marietta Marich

Becky Ann, Dylan, and Willa Baker

Charles and Florence Bernstein

The guys and dolls in the green room (Theatre Under The Stars, Houston, Texas, 2011)

The good old UST think tank and peanut gallery: Mark and Elaine Stevens, Bill and Suzanne Greene, and Dr. Charles Zeis

Karl Hofheinz and his sister Nancy, our kind guides to St. Louis

My dear Cooney sisters- and brothers-in-law: Sheila and Art Tybor, David and Peggy Cooney, Joe Cooney and Karl Dutt, Bill and Geneva Cooney, Linda Langdon Cooney, Mary Cooney Domingue, Tommy and Dotty Domingue

Anne Tybor Hoover, loving caretaker of Julia's Gypsy Breynton books

Julia Cooney Batdorf, true believer

Mary Katherine Downey Breckel

Cousin Bill Koch, who told me about Uncle Bill's red hair

Anne Mead, whose taped interview with Julia (at age seventy-eight) was a godsend

Joe and Lynn Muscanere (the lady who loves horses)

Tom and Annie Edmonston Hunter (Nana and Pops)

Aunt Mary Louise Terry

Aunt Marjorie Peterson Minton

Uncle Keith Hunter

Uncle Harbert Hunter

Aunt Frances Heyck

The world's best brothers, sisters, and All-Texas Pep Squad: David and Terri Nelson, Frances and Tim Arnoult, Hunter and Betsy Nelson, Mary Pat and Marty Gross, Carroll and Jeff Patrizi, Annie and Wayne Kansas, Jane and Joe Bob Kinsel, James and Cindy Nelson, John Henry Nelson, William Joseph Nelson

David and Theresa Patricia Cullen Nelson (our Gran, his darling girl)

Sister Mary Davidica Nelson, O.P. (Aunt Mary)

Father James A. Nelson (Uncle Jim)

Aunt Jane Nelson White

Aunt Patricia Phelan Milam

Father John Regis Stacer, S.J. (Cousin Johnny)

Elizabeth Cullen Nelson, fearless left-hand turner

Cousin Janice White Ondrusek, champion family chronicler

My extraordinary teachers: Sister Emily Bordages, Sister Francis Clare (Clare Mead Rosen), and Sister JoAnn Neihaus, O.P.

Mitali Perkins

Sid Fleischman

Christoper Paul Curtis

Phyllis Reynolds Naylor, the great-hearted, and everyone at PEN/America, whose Working Writer Fellowship came as such a tremendous encouragement when it was most needed

Jillian Hartke, Todd Christine, Seth Smith, Jason Stratman, and all the wonderfully helpful people at the State Historical Society of Missouri

Bonnie J. Morgan at the Montana Historical Society, and Carole Richards at the Powder River County

Courthouse, Broadus, Montana, who helped us locate Miss Cora Downey's homestead

Sean McGlade, who so kindly solved the mystery of the Irish-Gaelic lyrics

Legions of librarians—my heroes—in particular those at the Beverly Hills Public Library and the Los Angeles Public Library (downtown and at the Sherman Oaks, Studio City, and Fairfax branches)

Douglas E. Abrams, for his book *A Very Special Place in Life: The History of Juvenile Justice in Missouri*, The Missouri Juvenile Justice Association, OJJDP, 2003

James Neal Primm, for *Lion of the Valley: St. Louis, Missouri, 1765–1980*, 3rd edition, St. Louis, Missouri Historical Society Press, distributed by the University of Missouri Press, 1998

Robert Kinsey Howard, for *Montana: High, Wide and Handsome*, Yale University, 1944

Robert Hunt, for his gorgeous jacket painting

Sonia Chaghatzbanian, for her graceful book design

Ariel Colletti, Jessica Sit, Kaitlin Severini, Clare McGlade, and the whole terrific team at Atheneum and Simon & Schuster

And thanks most of all, forever and always:

To my favorite dancers and storytellers—the finest

and funniest, bravest and best—my parents, Carroll and David Nelson of Beaumont, Texas

To Kevin, my rock, and our children and grandchildren: Michael Christopher, Brian David, Errol Andrew (who helped me with Julia's music) and Erin Elizabeth Cooney; Mick, Stella Carroll, Everett Walter, and Cullen Michael

And to Richard Jackson, that dear, stubborn man, my incomparable editor and friend, who refused to stop believing that Julia would make it to Montana—once again—against all odds.